TODAY'S TO
INVESTIGATE
MURDER AND MAYHEM

"SHAGGY DOG" by Margaret Maron
Desperate days come upon an affluent couple
who face losing "Emily," the family pet, to
her former owner unless they take truly
desperate—and dotty—measures.

"WAKE UP, LITTLE SUZIE" by Ed Gorman
A body in the trunk of an Edsel kicks off a
smoothly told tale of vintage detection set
in the 1950s and laced with satire.

**"BODY IN THE POTTY"
by Marlys Millhiser**
A sudden death in the tiny toilet of a 727
flight to Vegas becomes the ultimate in
locked-room murders.

"HEAVENLY BODIES" by Simon Brett
A murdered man cannot give up his quest to
find his killer even from the other side of
the pearly gates . . . but he's having a devil
of a time solving the case.

AND MANY MORE CRIME STORIES
WITH A TWIST OF WIT

FUNNY BONES

15 NEW TALES OF MURDER AND MAYHEM

EDITED BY

Joan Hess

A SIGNET BOOK

SIGNET
Published by the Penguin Group Penguin Books USA Inc., 375 Hudson Street, New York, New York 10014, U.S.A.
Penguin Books Ltd, 27 Wrights Lane, London W8 5TZ, England Penguin Books Australia Ltd, Ringwood, Victoria, Australia
Penguin Books Canada Ltd, 10 Alcorn Avenue, Toronto, Ontario, Canada M4V 3B2
Penguin Books (N.Z.) Ltd, 182–190 Wairau Road, Auckland 10, New Zealand

Penguin Books Ltd, Registered Offices:
Harmondsworth, Middlesex, England

First published by Signet, an imprint of Dutton Signet,
a division of Penguin Books USA Inc.

First Printing, July, 1997
10 9 8 7 6 5 4 3 2 1

REGISTERED TRADEMARK—MARCA REGISTRADA

Contents

Introduction

Edgar Allan Poe wasn't funny. There, I've said it, and what's more, I will defend it to his death. Sir Arthur Conan Doyle wasn't much in the way of hilarity, nor was Raymond Chandler, Dorothy L. Sayers, or Georges Simenon (except unintentionally). These people were writing about evil, after all, and the tattered fabric of declining social mores. Their vehicles were the creaking staircase, the wind rustling the branches, the light on the moor, the footsteps in the dark alley, the glint of the upraised dagger, and, of course, murder most foul.

Murder isn't funny for the victim, the grieving relatives, the suspicious associates, the frustrated investigators, the sweaty-palmed perp, or—in the case of the American PIs—landlords. Murder is messy, splattering blood every which way and doing irreparable harm to the carpet and upholstery. Murder often takes place under cover of darkness, which means all of the above players have to get out of bed and go galloping about without a proper breakfast and a chance to read the morning newspaper. Murder is serious business.

The problem, however, is that people are funny, even in the direst of situations. I'm not saying there's a giggler at every funeral and a comedian in every courtroom. As the airplane plunges toward ground zero, the pilot may not tell a joke. On the other hand, most of us can remember blurting out something totally inappropriate in a moment of acute anxiety. It's part of human nature, I think, to try to at least take a shot at breaking the tension.

But as I said, murder is serious business, and it was treated as such in fiction until the advent of Mary Roberts Rinehart's *The Circular Staircase* (1908), a brilliant combination of comic terror and detection. Agatha Christie followed suit in 1922 with the introduction of Tommy and Tuppence Beresford in *The Secret Adversary*, Dashiell Hammett in 1934 with Nick and Nora Charles in *The Thin Man*, and Richard and Frances Lockridge in 1940 with Pam and Jerry North in *The Norths Meet Murder*. In 1931 Phoebe Atwood Taylor began the Asey Mayo series, with its droll New England humor, and writing as Alice Tilton, the series featuring schoolteacher Leonidas "Bill Shakespeare" Witherall in 1937. Beginning in 1939, Craig Rice produced eighteen screwball mystery novels under her own name, as well as two for her good friend Gypsy Rose Lee.

None of these writers was banned from polite society or excommunicated, which led others to dip into comedic mystery fiction. To name a few off the top of my head: From the United Kingdom, we are blessed with the fiction of such acerbic wits as Sarah Caudwell, Marian Babson, Peter Lovesey, Robert Barnard, Mike Ripley, M. C. Beaton, and Caroline Graham. From the United States, we have Elizabeth Peters, Kinky Friedman, K. K. Beck, Sarah Shankman, Donald Westlake, Carl Hiaasen, and Joe Gores.

And we have the contributors to this collection, all of them renowned for their less-than-reverent approach to crime. It would be impossible (okay, too much trouble) to count the number of awards reflected in this lineup of perpetrators. Some of them may surprise you. I hope all of their stories, from the blackest satire to the most lighthearted whimsy, will delight you.

—*Joan Hess*

Lady Finch-Waller Regrets

Nancy Pickard

Lady Thaddeus Finch-Waller laid down her pen upon her desk and said to her secretary, Mary Pink, "That reminds me. Mary! Has everyone responded to the invitations for our house party?"

As Mary Pink and Her Ladyship had only just then been discussing the gelding of the spring foals by His Lordship, Mary was hard pressed to comprehend what exactly it was in their prior conversation that had inspired Lady Thaddeus to broach the subject of the forthcoming house party.

Nevertheless, and feeling it not her place to question the connections between the cars on the train of thought of her employer, Mary limited herself to replying—though brightly and with alacrity, she thought, considering the span of moments that had elapsed between the closing of Her Ladyship's lips on the final consonant of her query and the opening of Mary's own mouth in preparation for the uttering of the first syllable of her response—"Yes'm."

"And?" inquired her employer, in much the same tone, Mary reflected, in which His Lordship was wont to shout "Giddyup!" to his favorite horse when they were out for one of their jolly rollicking morning rides and the horse had a mind to return to its oats in the warm barn and the master had a mind to trot in a forward-moving direction. In truth, Mary was well acquainted with His Lordship's predilection both for early-morning jolly rollicking rides and for shouting "Giddyup!" at the odd opportune moment.

But then, Mary supposed, when a couple had been wed for as many years as the Lord and his Lady had resided together in the manor house, the blissful conjugal pair were bound to share in common the odd vocal inflection.

Suddenly, into Mary's ruminations broke the startling awareness that her employer's shoulders seemed to have moved up to the vicinity of Her Ladyship's ears and that her head, indeed the entire top half of Her Ladyship's body, appeared to be thrust forward in her chair, giving Mary's employer rather the unhappy aspect of one of the gargoyles that adorned the roof of the very building in which she and Mary were seated. Mary could not help but hope for Her Ladyship's sake that no one in the manor house took it into his or her head to walk into the library at that very moment with a mirror.

Suddenly—to Mary, "suddenly" occurred with astonishing frequency, so that she sometimes felt as if her brain were a tree and the thoughts that struck it were lightning—Mary recalled that a query of some sort had been on the tip of her own tongue only moments before. Feeling it might have been important, and intuiting that it might have some relationship to the gargoylish look of frozen suspense on Her Ladyship's purpling face, Mary set herself to the stern and disciplined task of hauling the query back up from the ill-lit cave of her unconsciousness to the dappled sunlight of her awareness.

Eventually, after valiant struggle, Mary proffered the recalled query happily to her employer, as a proud, fat snake might roll out from his bulging mouth the gift of an ostrich egg to his mate.

"Wot'm?"

"Are they all coming, Mary?"

Lady Thaddeus took up her writing implement in her hand once more, though Mary Pink thought it impossible to imagine how Her Ladyship could actually employ the pen to write with, seeing as how she was grasping it like a dagger. Her Ladyship's knuckles, Mary felt proud to notice observantly, were white around the pen.

Perhaps Her Ladyship was ill, though Mary hoped not, as that would necessitate communicating yet again with every guest on the list for the forthcoming house party, including the retired Army Colonel who had served in both India and Burma, which was odd, considering how far apart those two places were, although perhaps he hadn't served in both at the same *time*—and the Spanish sports car driver who never drove but always took the train, and the famous London actress who Mary knew for a fact had emptied an entire decanter of pricey brandy the last time she was invited anywhere, and the crass American industrialist who wanted to buy the manor house that had been in His Lordship's family for more generations than Mary had either toes or fingers to count, even if she included her nose and those funny little knobs on the sides of both her wrists—whatever *they* were for, she couldn't imagine, although she could always ask the Doctor, who was also one of the invited guests, along with the Vicar, of course, and Her Lord and Ladyship's beautiful young adopted ward who was going to meet at the party for the first time the Finch-Wallers' only son, their heir, who had been off at boarding school in Africa since he was six—

Mary Pink, who had been trained by the crackerjack staff of teachers at Mrs. Parson's School for Secretaries to be observant of the tiniest details, noticed that Lady Thaddeus had upon her face an expression very nearly identical to one that Mary's brother, John, had worn on the day when he was waiting to hear if he had been sentenced to life in prison or death by hanging.

"I wonder why," Mary thought, pensively, an act of cogitation that turned her mind down a nostalgic lane, to her training at Mrs. Parson's School for Secretaries. At that esteemed institution the young ladies had been taught to follow every telling observation of the eyes with a pithy thought of the mind. The classic example, in Mary's view, had been the unforgettable and somewhat embarrassing day when dear Mrs. Parson herself had first observed how Mary Pink's eyes had a "quite dull glaze to them" (in Mrs. Parson's memorable turn of phrase) and then expressed the pithy following thought "which makes sense, seeing as how our Mary has the intellect of a ceramic bowl." Mary Pink had felt quite embarrassed at the time for her sister trainees who hadn't the good fortune, or the fortunate parentage, to be compared to smart china.

For a mere instant, Mary experienced difficulty in remembering at which station she had alighted from the car of her own train of thought. Oh, yes! If Her Ladyship were ill, that was it, which was looking to be a distinct, if sad, possibility, given the now unmistakable resemblance of Lady Thaddeus's face to that of Mary's own brother at the moment just after he had regurgitated his pitifully meager jail luncheon and only an instant before the verdict was read to the court.

Well, Mary thought pithily, having first observed.

If it were unfortunately the case that they had to cancel the house party, Mary deduced that she might have to inform not only all the guests but also Lord Finch-Waller himself, although perhaps Her Ladyship would prefer to inform His Lordship personally, herself, as it were, rather than to dictate a note to Mary that Mary would then need to carry down to the village, where she would post it along with all of the other notes, and which might well take days to wend its way back to the manor house to be delivered to Lord Finch-Waller. No, Mary suspected that would not—

"Mary!"

(Sounding so much, thought Mary, like Mary's own dear suffering mother in the courtroom when she had finally in anguish cried out to the judge, *"Gorblimey! Ha' mercy on t' poor bloody sod!"*)

Promptly, yet sympathetically, Mary articulated, " 'm?"

Lady Finch-Waller picked up her letter opener from her desk.

Some thirty minutes later, His Lordship poked his head into the parlour room where his wife sat on a cushioned seat staring out a window with what he intelligently apprehended was a happy look on her face.

"M'dear," he called to her, "can you spare a mo'?"

Squinting in at her, Lord Finch-Waller couldn't recall ever having seen his wife's countenance appear so relaxed, contented, and hopeful, except in that happy and n'er-to-be-forgot instant when he had first laid goo-goo orbs on her at the Fitzwilliam-Jameses' party, just before the future Lady Finch-Waller had turned to meet her fated hubby's admiring gaze. Since then, unhapp'ly, and until this fortuitous moment, a certain tension had laid hold the sinews and corpuscles of her face, n'doubt due to—His Lordship understandingly surmised—the mysterious burdens of womanly maturity, which was something toward which even the most loving husband could, being unsuited by nature, offer no manly assistance.

"I say! M'dear?"

When, again, his wife did not respond, His Lordship could not help but worry that she had been struck unaccountably deaf since last they met, which had been as recently as breakfast. What could have happened to her hearing in those few hours? he wondered with husbandly concern. A loud clap of a Chinese gong to which she was standing in too close proximity? A thunder of drumming from those Afric'n or Ind'n chaps who seemed to like to dance nearly naked in front of circles of admiring women? But what would his dear and proper lady-wife have been doing at aboriginal festivities such as those without the correct native attire—which, to his fairly certain knowledge, she did not possess? Or might she have stepped, all innocent and unaware, onto an explosive land mine left over from the war? But if so, wouldn't she have been more likely to have lost a lower limb rather than her hearing?

His Lordship felt quite stumped, for how was one to get the attention of someone deaf who was also far across a room? Stamping one's foot wouldn't do the trick, nor would clearing one's throat, that was plain. Should one jump up and down and wave one's arms about, hoping that the aforementioned deaf person might not also have been struck recently and tragically blind and so might happen to notice a peripheral movement out of the so-to-speak corner of her eye, and thereby be attracted to turn her head toward one? If only he could ask his wife what to do!

"Damn and bloody blast!" expostulated His Lordship.

To his great relief, she turned her head.

"What did you say, dear?"

"Oh, thank G'd, you're not deaf!"

A sensitive man, Lord Finch-Waller nearly wept with relief.

Becoming aware of how uncomfortable it feels to thrust one's head into a room ahead of one's body and to leave it hanging out there alone for any great period of time, His Lordship bestirred himself to call his wife's attention more forcefully to his manly presence.

"I've come to tell you something. Now what was it? Oh! Of course! How stupid of me! I thought you'd like to know: Your secretary's dead."

Her Ladyship looked over and smiled at her husband dreamily.

At once, he sympathetically recognized the signs of shock.

"Is she, Thaddy?"

"Quite, quite. Not only dead, but murdered, by the looks of her, although I suppose a top-notch detective sifting through all possible scenarios might at least briefly consider the notion that she fell backward onto your pointed letter opener and then rolled over onto her stomach in her final death agonies." His Lordship paused, thoughtfully, to allow his feet to do the work of bringing the rest of his body into line with his head. "I am sorry. Bit of a bother, I know, ads in the paper, applications from hundreds of unsuitable young lovelies, er, ladies, all running in and out of our door in states of pretty feminine pulchritude and dishabille."

His Lordship's countenance positively beamed with sympathy, and then he brightened even more. "I do have good news, however. It seems she left a note. Well trained, I must say! Here, I shall read it to you." He dug—futilely, it began to seem—in the variety of pockets in his sporting jacket, but then triumphantly fished out and held up to his wife's view a white piece of paper with black scrawls and red streaks on it.

" 'Luckily, I have a twin sister,' " he read.

Lady Thaddeus grabbed the edge of the cushioned window bench upon which she sat.

"It goes on," said her husband, glancing up.

"It would," she replied, in an oddly strangled tone of voice.

Observant husband that he was, Lord Finch-Waller couldn't help but notice that his dear lady-wife's countenance had altered considerably in appearance in the last few moments. It occurred to him that until this instant he had never realized how very much his wife's complexion resembled that of a poached haddock. Surprising, he thought, not to have noticed that before. The comparison was, he felt, amply validated by the appearance of her bug-eyes and loosely flapping mouth, also so like the aforementioned poached sea beast. All she lacked was scales. And, perhaps, a nice sauce and a vegetable.

Lord Finch-Waller knew his wife would be fascinated by this astute and surprising observation of his, as his lady-wife was always interested in everything her lordly spouse opined, and he determined right then and there to tell her at the earliest opportune moment, which was not, perhaps, precisely *this* moment while she was making those odd flapping motions with her fin. Er, hand, he tactfully corrected himself. He ceased inspecting his wife's face, which was changing before his eyes from an evenly and nicely poached haddock white to a rather mottled and alarming anemone purple, and re-commenced inspecting the note.

Lord Finch-Waller read aloud: " 'My beloved twin sister, who is identical to me in every way save for the mole I have on the left side of my chin while hers is located on the right side (of her chin, not mine! Ha, ha!) and also save for her rather darker hair at the crown of her—' "

"Could you skip a bit?" his wife suggested, whilst making rapidly-revolving-wheel-like movements with the hand that wasn't still grasping the edge of the bench. Or, to be even more precise, with the hand that had been previously flopping about as a fish's would, if a fish had hands, as Lord Finch-Waller was quick to parenthesize to himself.

"Certainly, m'dear." His Lordship scanned the rest of the note and then pronounced: "Nothing much here, really." He read bits and pieces, summarizing efficiently as he went: "Twin sister also trained as secretary. On her way here from penal colony in Australia. Will arrive any moment, expecting employment, it seems. Alike to our deceased secretary down to nearly every detail, including appearance and personality." His Lordship paused momentarily, after reading that revelation, and a happy smile attached itself to his reading lips and eyes. "We'll hardly notice the difference, blab, blab, blab. So forth and so forth. Smooth transition between them, etc., etc. Oh, and she says you stabbed her. Well!"

Disgusted, His Lordship hardly noticed the doorbell's ring.

"This last obviously casts doubt on the veracity of the whole epistle." Ever quick and efficient, His Lordship tore the bloodstained missive into little bits and pieces, which he quickly and efficiently thrust into the fire burning in the grate. "I think the poor girl is merely ill, comatose and hallucinating, not dead in the least, and you ought to have her removed to her room until she recovers!"

"All right, dear," said his wife, with becoming meekness.

At that moment their butler appeared in the doorway with a young woman hovering behind him. "Madam, Sir, your secretary is here, claiming to be her identical twin sister, recently arrived from Australia."

Husband and wife both stared at the young woman.

"Damned tasteless idea of a joke if you ask me," Lord Finch-Waller huffed on his way out of the room, though he forgave the young woman enough to allow her a private pinch on her bottom. (However had she managed that business with the moles? he wondered. Then he recalled that with theatrical makeup unprincipled persons could work miracles of deception. Just look at how dead this same young woman had appeared to his own sagacious eyes not half an hour before!)

Lord Finch-Waller quit the house in order to go pet his dogs.

The butler returned to his post near the kitchen.

Lady Thaddeus stared at the young woman, who stood just inside the doorway, and felt a sharp and piercing regret that she had left her letter opener in such an inconvenient place.

Heavenly Bodies

Simon Brett

1952

"I was murdered."

"Oh, dear," said Saint Peter. "Bad luck. Never mind, though." He chuckled and favoured the new arrival with a bland, professional smile. "Doesn't matter by what route you got here, you are still faced with the prospect of Perpetual Bliss."

Christopher Dickson looked dubious and scratched his chin with his right hand. As he did so, he was aware that his face felt like new. The lividity caused by the convulsions of asphyxiation had been eased away. His jaw was no longer locked in a rictus of agony. His skin felt as soft and smooth as a baby's.

The movement of his arm made him aware of the robe in which he was dressed. It was white, made of an airy, seamless fabric with a slight sheen of satin. Long-sleeved, it spread down to the ground, covering his feet.

At the same time, Dickson realised he was carrying something in his left hand and looked down to see that it was a golden harp, strung with parallel strings of gold.

Next he sensed something unfamiliar above him

and peered upwards to see a palely glowing, translucent ring of light suspended overhead. A halo.

Saint Peter was still smiling patiently. "Don't worry, you'll soon acclimatise," he said cheerfully. "I'll just lock up here and then introduce you to someone who'll show you round."

The venerable saint, white beard trailing down below his waist, turned to close the tall, cloud-mounted gates. Ethereal light glinted on the rainbow sheen of their bars. Yes, they actually were pearly.

"Good Heavens," thought Christopher Dickson, "this is what Heaven's really like. All those religious fantasists and artists actually got it right."

"Doesn't do to bear resentment," said one of his new friends soothingly. "This is Heaven, you're up here for Eternity, and if you let little details niggle away at you, then that's going to feel like a very long time."

"It is not a little detail," Christopher Dickson objected. "I was murdered. My life was cut short at the age of twenty-six. I hardly regard that as a little detail."

They were sitting in Saint Raphael's Bar, one of the many watering holes in which the Blessed could while away the Infinity of Time that lay before them. The new friends with whom Christopher Dickson sat were called Morton Peabody and Aethelfrith. Peabody had been a cotton mill owner in the early nineteenth century, but his enlightened care of his staff and substantial contributions to church funds had ensured an easy passage to Heaven when he died in 1857.

Aethelfrith's admission had been even smoother.

An ascetic hermit who had survived on roots, worms, and prayer in a Wessex cave, he was so holy by the time of his death in 673 that he had hardly noticed the change of venue to Heaven.

Both of Christopher Dickson's new friends wore shiny white robes like his own. Above each of their heads a halo wobbled, a substantial doughnut of light on Morton Peabody and a thinner annulus over Aethelfrith's narrow cranium.

Saint Raphael's Bar was cosy, though a little shabby. Stuffing spilled from some of the cloud sofas; the display of Last Trumps on the walls could have done with a touch of polish; and the marble tabletops were disfigured by intersecting rings of stickiness. (There was a downside to the Management's well-intentioned policy that all cups in Heaven should overflow.) The wings of Saint Raphael himself, who slouched pensively against the bar wiping a grubby goblet on a scrap of gossamer, were greasy and could have done with a little fluffing up.

"But look at it my way," Morton Peabody persisted. "You've achieved Perpetual Bliss earlier than you had any right to expect it. You're in Heaven now. Getting to Heaven has been the ambition of all civilisations since records began. There's nothing on Earth you need worry about."

"If you were unable to achieve such unworldliness while you were alive," said Aethelfrith in his rather prissy voice, "now that you're up here for all Eternity, you should definitely forget about the things of Earth."

"I can't. There are still things of Earth I care about. I've got a wife called Adele, for instance, whom I adore. I'm desperate to see her again."

Aethelfrith let out a pitying sigh at such materialism, but Morton Peabody was eager to jolly Christopher along. "You will, you will. Adele'll come up here eventually. I mean—" a fruity chuckle. "—that is, assuming she doesn't blot her copybook too seriously and get sent to the Other Place. . . . She'll be along here in no time at all."

"How long?" Christopher Dickson asked truculently.

"Can't say exactly, but it won't *feel* long. Time's elastic up here. Remember, 'a thousand ages in His sight are like an evening gone.' Oh, yes, you'll soon have your wife up in Heaven with you."

"But as an old woman. I want Adele like she is now. We have—had—a wonderful physical relationship. I want her—want to continue to make love to her."

Aethelfrith winced again, but if Morton Peabody had ever had any Victorian inhibitions about the discussion of sex, a century in Heaven had clearly eroded them. "Oh, it can probably be arranged," he said breezily. "Most things can be arranged up here, you know, if you ask the right people, fill in the right forms."

"You mean, there *is* sex in Heaven?"

"Of course. Wouldn't be Heaven otherwise, would it?" There was a reflective silence. "Mind you, not many people take advantage of it after a while . . ."

"Why not?"

"I don't know, do I? I suppose it's like most things up here—so perfect that you begin to get tired of it after a bit. Certainly, when my wife came up and joined me in 1884, I had . . . certain expectations, but I soon lost interest."

"Are you sure that's the explanation?"

Morton shrugged. "What else could it be?"

"You don't think . . ." Christopher Dickson's eyes narrowed. ". . . that it's something they put in the Nectar, do you?"

"Really, old fellow." Morton Peabody gave him a jovial slap on the shoulder. "You see conspiracies everywhere. Tell you what your trouble is—you're still in postmortem shock. Does happen with some of the chaps up here, particularly those who've come to a violent end. And I gather yours was a touch on the violent side?"

"I'll say!" Christopher Dickson's halo wobbled like a candle flame in the wind as an involuntary shudder ran through his body. "Did I actually tell you what happened?"

"No," said Aethelfrith in a tone of deterrence. 'It's not thought very good form up here to talk about the circumstances of your death."

Morton Peabody diplomatically rose halfway to his feet and reached out toward their Nectar cups. "Same again, will you both—?"

But he wasn't quick enough. Christopher Dickson fixed both his new friends with a glittering eye, and Morton Peabody sank defeated back onto his cloud sofa as the narrative of murder unwound.

"I married Adele in March of last year. She was only nineteen. It was a love match. I adored her, she adored me. We were comfortably off—I'd come into quite a lot of money when I was twenty-one, and I joined the family stockbroking business. Well, as you know, that kind of work's not too onerous—have a few client lunches to deal with, otherwise just sit back and let the money accumulate. Adele and I had this splendid big house in Surrey—horses, tennis court, you know the kind of thing—and everything was set fair for us to have a wonderfully happy marriage—children, money, success, the lot.

"We had plenty of good friends, too. Mixed on the fringes of the aristocracy, actually. Adele loved that. She was quite childlike in some respects, very giggly, kept saying things like, 'Fancy someone like me actually knowing people who've got titles!' "

A tear came to Christopher Dickson's eye at the recollection. Morton Peabody again reached forward for the Nectar cups, but again wasn't quick enough.

"One of our best friends, actually," the narrative continued, "was a chap called Lord Greveleigh. Ralph Greveleigh. Very good chum. Partner in the stockbroking business. 'Round thirty. Lovely wife called Veronica. She hadn't actually been born to that kind of lifestyle, but you'd never have known it. I did know, because by chance her parents had owned a grocer's shop in a town near where I was brought up, but Veronica had quickly become assimilated into the aristocracy, and most people took her for the genuine article.

"Well, the Greveleighs really took us under their wings, introduced us a bit in society. Devoted to Adele, both of them—loved her uncomplicated appreciation of the finer things of existence. No, as I say, our life was really set fair . . ."

There was another tiny silence, but Morton Peabody didn't even make a token move. He and Aethelfrith had already exchanged looks of resignation. Both knew they wouldn't get away until the story had run its course.

". . . if it hadn't been," Christopher Dickson continued, "for a little rat called Bernard Fisher." He allowed a dramatic pause this time, confident of his listeners' attention. "Bernard Fisher was not our class at all, a common little grammar school oik. No breeding, no background. Sold insurance, of all things . . . which is how he came to be involved in our lives—and, as it turned out, in my death.

"The fact was, after we married, Adele thought we ought to review our financial arrangements. Obviously, the insurance provisions a single man might make would not be suitable for a married man with a wife and potential children to consider. My instinct was to make the new arrangements through the insurance broker my family had always used, but Adele, who, in spite of her youth, had a very shrewd business brain, thought we could get a better deal by shopping around.

"It was as a result of her 'shopping around' that she introduced into our lives the odious Bernard Fisher—a circumstance whose fatal consequences explain my appearance here with you today.

"To cut a long story short . . ." Neither Morton Peabody nor Aethelfrith could repress a sigh of relief at these words, but Christopher Dickson ignored their censure and pressed on. "Bernard Fisher had the nerve to fall in love with my wife. I've only pieced all this together since my death, but it all makes sense now. I only wish I'd realised sooner. Perhaps I could have saved myself.

"Anyway, being the kind of common little bounder he was, Bernard Fisher was unaware of how entirely inappropriate his romantic aspirations were, and must actually have begun to fantasize that, if I were 'out of the way,' Adele might succumb to his minimal charms and marry him.

"The whole idea was, of course, laughable. Had Adele been aware of the thoughts that were fermenting in Fisher's grubby little mind, she could very quickly have put him right about his chances. But he kept his aspirations to himself and began to plan what he thought would ease his passage to fulfilment—in other words, my murder.

"In his planning he was helped by the nature of his work. The endless questionnaires Adele and I had had to fill in to secure our insurance policies had given Fisher a very detailed knowledge of our medical histories. In particular, he had discovered that I suffered from an allergy to peanuts. At a stroke, the murderer was presented with his method.

"I don't want to dwell on the precise details of what happened." Again an exchange of looks between Morton Peabody and Aethelfrith confirmed how much they endorsed this sentiment. "Suffice to say that one evening, when Lord Greveleigh and his wife, Veronica, were round for dinner, the odious Bernard Fisher insinuated himself into the house. He made some excuse for his presence having to do with the need for us to append our final signatures to the insurance policies he had arranged, though no one with any breeding would have contemplated turning up unannounced at someone's house in the evening.

"Fisher's arrival when we had guests was, of course, deeply inconvenient, and Adele bustled him off into the kitchen till a suitable moment arose for us to join him and sign the relevant documents. It must have been while he was waiting in the kitchen that he doctored the food, sprinkling ground peanuts over the chicken casserole that was simmering on top of the stove.

"Adele and I had signed the papers and the villain had left our home before his wicked plan came to fruition. As soon as I took a mouthful of the casserole, my allergic reaction started. In seconds, to the horror of my wife and guests, I was gasping for breath, and within three minutes, I was on my way up here."

There was a finality about his last words, so Morton Peabody once again bent to the cups with a cheery "Dear, oh, dear. Same again is it, everyone?"

But once again he was immobilised by the glare of Christopher Dickson's eye. "If I ever see Bernard Fisher again," the murder victim murmured ferociously, "I'll have my revenge on him."

"Well, you are never likely to see him again," Aethelfrith pronounced with some satisfaction. "If he's guilty as you say, then he won't be coming up here. He'll be off to the Other Place."

Christopher Dickson looked despondent. "That's a thought."

"Anyway," said Morton Peabody heartily, "you'll soon forget about the idea of revenge. It's not actually thought of as quite the thing up here to talk about that kind of subject. Not on, really. I'd put it out of your mind if I were you."

"But I can't! I'm still so furious about what happened! And furious that I don't know what happened afterward." Dickson looked appealingly at his two new friends. "Is there any way of finding out about what's happened on Earth after you've gone?"

The two halos wobbled as the heads beneath them shook decisively.

"We can't look down?"

"No. Can't see a thing, anyway. Too much cloud."

"So I'll never know?"

"The only way to get any information," Aethelfrith replied judiciously, "is to ask new arrivals at the Pearly Gates."

Morton Peabody shook his head. "But the chances of meeting anyone who knows anything relevant to your case are pretty slender."

At last he picked up the Nectar cups and started toward Saint Raphael at the bar. After a couple of steps he turned back to Christopher Dickson. "Also, it is thought to be pretty bad form—you know, like a criticism of the Management—to show too much interest in what's going on on Earth. We are in a state of Perpetual Bliss up here, you know. Doesn't do to look a gift horse in the mouth."

The new arrival nodded, as if taking this advice to heart. But beneath his halo, Christopher Dickson's mind still seethed. He was determined to find out what had happened back on Earth after his untimely demise.

1953

"Let go of me! Let me get my hands on the bastard!"

There was an unseemly commotion in the Perpetuity Lounge. Halos bobbled around like soap bubbles while white-robed figures tried to restrain one of their number from attacking a newcomer to their ranks. Harps twanged as they banged against incorruptible flesh. Behind the bar Saint Emilion phoned through for a couple of Guardian Angels to come and sort out the fracas.

"Let go of me! I'm going to throttle him!"

In the intervening year of His Eternal Reward,

Christopher Dickson certainly hadn't forgotten the
things of Earth. Despite the celestial distractions of
his environment, despite copious drafts of Nectar, resentment still burned in his hallowed breast. In the
face of unctuous disapproval from fellow Blessed
Souls, he remained a regular hanger-on at the Pearly
Gates, accosting each newcomer with the same desperate plea for information about his sweet child
bride.

His obsession was generally felt to be rather embarrassing; it let down the tone of the place. In a
more adversarial environment than Heaven, action
might have been taken against the misfit. But the
Management took the long view. It was early days
yet. Christopher Dickson had only tasted one year of
Perpetual Bliss; sooner or later, Eternity would sort
him out.

But the possibility that two of the Saved actually
were coming to blows in the Perpetuity Lounge was
something else again. Even though the incorporeal
nature of their bodies meant that no damage could
be done to either Soul, such a confrontation was very
much against the ethos of Heaven. Under the circumstances, the Management felt obliged to intervene.

The two culprits—or rather the attacker and his
bemused victim—were discreetly hustled out, and an
extra ration of Ambrosia was handed round to restore the equanimity of the regulars in the Perpetuity Lounge.

Christopher Dickson and the newcomer, meanwhile, were taken off to one of the Mediation Mansions. (There was plenty of such accommodation in
Heaven. As the Boss's son put it: "In my Father's
house are many mansions.") There the disputants

were put in charge of two judges, one an appointee of the Spanish Inquisition, who had died after a life of virtuous torturing in 1411, and the other a Scottish lawyer, dead of consumption one grey Edinburgh afternoon in 1774.

"Well, now," catechised the Inquisitor, "what is the cause of your dissension?"

"This man . . ." Christopher Dickson's finger pointed straight at the newcomer's pale and saintly face. "This man murdered me!"

The Soul of Bernard Fisher—for that indeed is who it was—looked aghast and was momentarily incapable of speech.

"This would be on Earth, would it?" asked the Scottish lawyer in a voice of small nitpicking. "On Earth that he murdered you?"

"Yes, of course it'd be on Earth!" Christopher Dickson replied testily. "When did you last have a murder in Heaven, for Heaven's sake?"

"I just wanted to be certain of the facts," said the Scottish lawyer demurely.

The Inquisitor stroked his chin. "The charge of murder is a very serious one. What have you, the accused, to say in your defense?"

"I have to say I've had just about enough of it!" Bernard Fisher's voice had a whining, suburban petulance.

"Just about enough of what?"

"All this talk of murder. I've heard nothing else for the last year. First they arrested me for murder . . ."

"For murdering me?" asked Christopher Dickson.

"Yes. Then they tried me for murder. Then they had the nerve to find me guilty of murder. And, finally, indignity of indignities!—oh, that it should ever have happened to a member of the Fisher family!—only this morning I was hanged for murder."

"There!" Christopher Dickson raised a triumphant finger. "I was right. The majesty of British justice is not mocked. You murdered me!"

"But I didn't!"

"Nonsense. If you were found guilty in a court of law, you must've done."

"It was a miscarriage of justice!"

"That's been said by every guilty man since time began."

"But in this case it's true!"

"Could we have a little calm in these proceedings, please?" the Scottish lawyer requested urbanely. "What was the evidence brought against you, Mr. Fisher, that formed the basis for your conviction?"

"Well, it was all circumstantial. For a start, a half-empty packet of peanuts was found in the pocket of my suit."

"Aha!" said Christopher Dickson.

"But I always carry peanuts in my pocket. I spend so much time on the road trying to sell insurance that I don't often get the time for proper meals. I find nibbling the odd peanut stops my stomach from rumbling."

"A likely story!"

"It's true, Mr. Dickson, it's true!"

"What other evidence did they find against you?" asked the Scottish lawyer drily.

"Oh, they fabricated some nonsensical story about my being in love with Mr. Dickson's wife."

"See!" said the aggrieved husband.

"But it's not true. It's ridiculous. I'm very happily married to my Dierdre—well, that is, I was. As you can imagine, all this has been very upsetting for her as well as for me. And her ordeal's still going on. She and the kids can hardly hold their heads up when they go out shopping in Orpington."

"But did they have any evidence of your attachment to Mrs. Dickson?" the Scottish lawyer persisted.

"They found some letters in my briefcase."

"From whom to whom?"

"Well, they were supposed to be from Mrs. Dickson to me. But she denied ever writing them, and I know I never received them. They were forgeries."

"So how did they come to be in your briefcase?"

"I don't know that, do I? If I'd been able to give a proper answer to that question, I wouldn't have had to go through all that unpleasantness in the prison this morning. I wouldn't be here now, would I?"

The Inquisitor looked thoughtful. "While such evidence would have been quite sufficient to convince in my day—indeed, I've had many men disembowelled on much less—I understood that judges in the twentieth century had got rather more . . . picky about such things. I'm surprised that a contemporary jury convicted you on such tenuous grounds."

Bernard Fisher grimaced awkwardly. "Well . . . you see . . . there was something else as well."

"What?" The Inquisitor's eyes fixed on the insurance salesman's like the red-hot pincers he'd had such fun with during his lifetime.

Bernard Fisher squirmed. "There was an eyewitness."

"What!" said Christopher Dickson.

"That's what really ruined the case for my defence. Someone claimed they'd seen me in the Dicksons' kitchen, grinding up the peanuts and sprinkling them over the casserole."

"Under oath they said this, did they?" asked the Scottish lawyer.

The insurance salesman nodded wretchedly. "Yes. But it wasn't true!"

"Well, you would say that, wouldn't you?"

"It wasn't! It really wasn't! I think the witness was lying to incriminate me. It was a plot. I think it was the witness who put the peanuts in the casserole and then forged the letters, and planted them in my briefcase."

"But wasn't the witness cross-examined in court?" demanded the Scottish lawyer.

"Of course."

"And they stuck to their story under cross-examination?"

"Yes."

The Inquisitor's eyes misted over. "Nobody ever used to stick to their story under *my* cross-examinations," he recalled wistfully.

The Scottish lawyer looked with scepticism at Bernard Fisher. "It sounds to me as if you didn't have a very strong case."

"I did! I was a victim of class prejudice, that's all. Just because I didn't go to public school and university, the jury thought I must be guilty. It was my word against his, and they believed his."

"Whose?" asked Christopher Dickson, suddenly quiet.

"Lord Greveleigh."

"It was Lord Greveleigh who said he'd seen you poisoning my dinner?"

"Yes, of course it was."

"Oh, well, then . . ." The murder victim shrugged. "There's no question about it. You did kill me."

"I didn't!"

"Ralph Greveleigh," Christopher Dickson explained patiently, "was at Eton and Oxford, and subsequently in the Guards. Such men do not lie."

Bernard Fisher opened out his white-robed arms in helpless appeal to the two judges. "You see what I was up against? What chance does someone of my background stand in the snob-ridden society of the nineteen-fifties?"

"Stop whining!" snapped Christopher Dickson. "You revolting, deceitful little swine! You murdered me, and nothing will ever persuade me otherwise."

"Oh, no?" A small gleam of triumph came into the insurance salesman's beady eye. "Even when I tell you I have absolute, total proof that I didn't do it?"

"And what proof might that be?" demanded the Inquisitor.

"Where I am," Bernard Fisher replied calmly.

All three Souls looked at him in puzzlement.

"Look where I am," he continued. "I'm in Heaven, aren't I? Nobody who'd committed a murder would be allowed up here, would they?"

"Ah." The Scottish lawyer rubbed his chin reflectively. "Now you may have a point there."

1955

Christopher Dickson did feel a certain amount of guilt about Bernard Fisher. Anyone was bound to feel guilty toward someone they'd unjustly accused of murdering them, particularly if the wronged one had then been hanged for the crime.

So maybe, in the early days of Bernard's Perpetual

Bliss, Christopher Dickson did overcompensate by being particularly affable to the insurance salesman. He assuaged his guilt by showing the newcomer around the various delights and watering holes of Heaven and by introducing him to other Souls.

But, as time went by, Christopher Dickson's sensations of guilt were replaced by irritation. Bernard Fisher had become very clinging. He regarded his former client as his "best friend," and he seemed always to be around. It was as if he thought that their connection through the crime of murder provided some bond, like having been at school together.

Christopher Dickson's upbringing meant that he would always think of Bernard as a common little man, but it didn't do to say such things in Heaven— particularly after the awkward confrontation in the Perpetuity Lounge. No, the murder victim was stuck with the cross of Bernard Fisher; he would just have to grin and bear it.

The trouble was that Souls without any burden of guilt towards the insurance salesman felt no compunction about avoiding his company, leaving Christopher Dickson ever more isolated in endless, circuitous conversations, all of which ran more or less along the following lines:

BERNARD: Tell me, Chris, old man, have you given much thought to the future up here?

CHRISTOPHER: The future?

BERNARD: I'm speaking to you as a friend, of course, but I wouldn't like to think of you wandering around up here in Heaven without sufficient insurance.

CHRISTOPHER: What?

BERNARD: Well, I mean—Heaven forbid—but if anything were to happen to you . . .

CHRISTOPHER: What do you mean—"if anything were to happen to me"? Everything that could happen bloody has happened. I'm bloody dead, aren't I? What on earth do I need insurance for?

BERNARD: Ah, well, you have to be ready for the unexpected. I mean, everything seems fine at the moment, but it may not last forever.

CHRISTOPHER: Of course it'll bloody last forever! That's what Heaven's about—Perpetual bloody Bliss!

BERNARD: Oh, yes, that's what it says in the prospectus, but prospectuses have been known to lie, you know. And, as a friend, I would not feel I was being fair to you if I let you go around with insufficient insurance cover. Now, I do have a new policy that I think could be just the thing for . . .

And so on, and so on. The prospect of spending Eternity in the company of Bernard Fisher made it look to Christopher Dickson like a very long time indeed.

The constant presence of his new companion did, however, have another effect. It made Dickson even more determined to find out the true circumstances of his own death. Perpetual Bliss did not produce in him the fading of interest in the things of Earth that had been promised; rather, the urgency to get at the truth increased with every celestial minute.

Whenever he could wean Bernard Fisher off the subject of insurance, the murder victim would go through with him again the precise sequence of events on that fateful evening in the Dicksons' house. The insurance salesman could provide no more details than he had before, but with each rehearsal of what had happened, Dickson's suspicions as to his murderer's identity hardened into conviction.

The obvious suspect remained Lord Greveleigh, but Christopher Dickson was not seduced by the obvious. His business colleague was a gentleman. Ralph wouldn't lie . . . unless there was some overriding reason for him to do so.

And for a man of Ralph Greveleigh's upbringing, the only reason strong enough to justify perjury would be the protection of the honour of a lady.

Veronica.

Veronica boasted considerable charm and beauty, but she'd never been quite the thing. Parents in trade, for a start. She came from the kind of background that might engender all kinds of inappropriate behaviour.

Finding a motive for Veronica's actions proved only a minor obstacle. Of all the Greveleighs' friends, Christopher Dickson was the only one who knew the true circumstances of Lady Greveleigh's upbringing. Suffering from the appalling insecurity that so bedevils the British lower middle class, Veronica had let this knowledge fester inside her until it became an obsession. The higher she moved up the social ladder, the greater to her tormented mind became the danger of exposure. Only one person in Lady Greveleigh's current circle had the power to unmask her as a mere grocer's daughter. That risk had to be eliminated. Christopher Dickson had to die.

Once this idea was fixed in his mind, the murder

victim had no problem in supplying the concomitant scenario. In the comings and goings of that fateful evening both Greveleighs had had opportunities to visit the kitchen. Christopher Dickson could see Veronica sprinkling the ground peanuts into the casserole, could imagine Ralph Greveleigh witnessing his wife's actions and asking what she was doing. "Nothing, darling,' she'd probably replied. "Just spicing up the dinner a little."

And her trusting husband would have accepted that explanation . . . until the moment when his host began to gag and, within moments, expired.

The situation must have posed an appalling dilemma for a man of Ralph Greveleigh's honourable character. Though undoubtedly appalled by his wife's actions, it would never have occurred to him to betray her to the police.

No doubt perjuring himself to get Bernard Fisher convicted for the crime had caused Lord Greveleigh considerable heart-searching, but ultimately he had recognised that to be his only possible course of action. To have a Greveleigh—even a Greveleigh only by marriage—accused of murder was unthinkable. The sacrifice of an insurance salesman from Orpington was a small, but necessary, price to pay for the maintenance of the aristocratic status quo.

So convinced had Christopher Dickson become by his new reading of the situation that he was entirely taken aback when one afternoon (it is always afternoon in Heaven) he saw a face that he recognised in the Immemorial Suite (which tends to be first port of call for new arrivals).

She stood there, blinking with the slightly bewildered expression of the newly dead, a cup of Nectar in one hand, an unfamiliar harp in the other, like a guest who didn't know anyone else at a cocktail party.

Christopher Dickson had instinctively rushed forward and placed a bloodless kiss on her bloodless cheek before he remembered that he was confronting the woman he believed to be his murderess.

"Veronica! Lovely to see!" Incongruous though they were in the circumstances, his words were also instinctive.

He found a secluded cloud sofa in a corner of the Immemorial Suite and sat Veronica down. Already his conviction about her guilt was trickling away. By the same logic that had exonerated Bernard Fisher, Veronica's very presence in Heaven made her unlikely casting for the role of murderess.

Christopher Dickson was by now sufficiently *au fait* with the etiquette of Heaven to know it would be bad form to start talking immediately about either his own or Veronica's death, so his first enquiries concerned Adele.

Yes, it turned out, his widow was physically in good health. She was coping bravely with bereavement and trying to find positive attitudes toward her new role as a single woman. Yes, Ralph and Veronica had continued to see a lot of Adele. They had been as supportive as they knew how and . . .

The awkwardness with which Lady Greveleigh's words dried up indicated that something was amiss, and it took only a minimum of probing from Christopher Dickson for her to confess the truth. Veronica was still in what Morton Peabody had described as "postmortem shock." The proximity of Perpetual Bliss had not yet made her lose her memory for "The things of Earth." In fact, she was still entirely obsessed with "the things of Earth"—particularly with the circumstances of her own recent death.

"I'm afraid something rather terrible's happened, Christopher," Veronica confessed. "I'm afraid Ralph's fallen in love with Adele."

"What!"

"Oh, don't think badly of her—please! Adele hasn't given him a word of encouragement, I promise. It's just . . . well, you know Ralph's a very strongwilled man. When he wants something, generally speaking he just goes out and gets it. When he wanted me, he didn't really ask what I thought about the situation. And now he wants Adele . . ."

"Are you telling me that, down on Earth, my wife is having an affair with your husband?" Christopher Dickson blustered.

"No, no! As I say, no blame is attached to Adele, none at all. She's behaved wonderfully about the whole thing. I overheard them discussing the subject only last week."

"Overheard them discussing having an affair?"

"Overheard Ralph trying to persuade Adele to go to bed with him."

Christopher Dickson's halo wobbled with the strong emotion that ran through his body.

"You mustn't blame her, Christopher. Adele behaved impeccably. She was staying down with us for the weekend at Greveleigh Towers. They thought I'd gone to bed, but I came downstairs to get a glass of water and overheard them through the hatch between the kitchen and the sitting room. Ralph was telling Adele how much he would pamper her if she became his mistress, and she replied that, with the insurance money she'd received after your death, she was quite capable of pampering herself, thank you very much.

"She then lashed into him for even raising the suggestion that she might become anyone's mistress. She had her standards, she said. She believed in the sanctity of marriage, and she would never sleep with anyone outside its confines—least of all with someone else's husband."

"Oh, bless her!" Christopher Dickson's eyes glittered with emotion. "That's my precious darling!"

"Yes . . ." For a moment Veronica was pensively silent. "Sadly, though, I fear it may have been Adele's words that signed my death warrant."

"What?"

"As I said, Ralph's a very determined man. And he was absolutely besotted with Adele. She'd said—unaware of the possible consequences of her words—that he stood no chance with her outside marriage. So, to Ralph's obsessed mind, the logical thing to do was to get himself unmarried. With me off the scene, he must have reasoned, he would be able to approach Adele as a grieving widower and maybe then stand a chance of winning her."

"The swine! To think how much I trusted him!" Christopher Dickson muttered. Then, with proper heavenly reticence, he went on, "I hope you don't mind my asking, but, er . . . what actually happened?"

"It was . . . goodness, only last night . . . only a few hours ago. The three of us had been out for dinner locally. A good dinner, with a lot of wine, and maybe—I can't be sure, but I think Ralph may have put something in my drink as well. Certainly, I fell very deeply asleep in the car on the way back to Greveleigh Towers.

"Then I remember waking up. I was still in the car, alone. The car was in the garage and the engine was running. I was vaguely aware of a tube coming in through the passenger window . . . and of a typewritten note on the seat beside me . . . and I knew I had to get out . . . but I couldn't breathe . . . I was choking . . . I felt the . . . I felt the . . ."

She cleared her throat.

"And the next thing I knew, Saint Peter was opening the Pearly Gates for me. I'd been murdered."

"Oh, Veronica," said Christopher Dickson inadequately, "I am most frightfully sorry."

1990

The next thirty-five years were a bit quiet but, then, Heaven was meant to be quiet. The Management brought in a few minor changes, but the only one that caused much stir was the instigation of regular cocktail parties at which the recipients of organ transplants were introduced to their donors.

Otherwise, the eternal afternoons of Nectar and Ambrosia continued as before, and Bernard Fisher spent thirty-five years trying to convince Christopher Dickson that he had insufficient insurance.

Dickson didn't see much of Veronica after her first day. The sexes tended to segregate themselves in Heaven. Once the element of sexual tension had been removed from their relationships, they didn't have much interest in each other.

But Christopher Dickson did not forget about Adele. He still ached for her; he still longed to know what had happened between her and Lord Greveleigh; he still, in the face of general disapproval, spent a lot of time down in the Immemorial Suite near the Pearly Gates, questioning new arrivals.

But he got no helpful information. Lots of details of wars and famines, of man's incompetence and inhumanity, but no news of his innocent child bride.

Until one day in 1990, Saint Peter ushered through the Pearly Gates a white-robed and haloed figure with a familiar face.

"Ralph! You bastard!" Christopher Dickson shouted. "What the hell are you doing up here?"

The newcomer gaped, incapable of speech, as Christopher Dickson rounded on the white-bearded saint. "There's been some mistake! This bounder's been sent to the wrong place!"

Saint Peter looked down at the scroll in his hand. "No problem on the paperwork. This docket says he's definitely due up here." His frail finger pointed to the relevant words written in flame on the parchment: "Ralph, Lord Greveleigh—Fast Track Admission."

Christopher Dickson swallowed his anger. He didn't want to get involved in another session in a Mediation Mansion. Throwing a bonhomous arm around his friend's incorporeal shoulder, he said, "Sorry, old man, my mistake. I'll give him the guided tour if you like, Saint Peter. Looks as if you've got a crowd at the gates."

The saint looked back to the mob beyond the pearly bars and shook his head wearily. "Oh, yes, it's another of those suicide bombs. I'll leave him in your capable hands, then."

In a quiet corner of the Perpetuity Lounge, Christopher Dickson gently pumped Ralph Greveleigh for the details of his life since Veronica's death. The interrogator managed to subdue his feelings and allow no hint of censure to be voiced until the picture was complete.

Yes, Adele had become the second Lady Greveleigh. She had been unwilling at first, still in shock, still mourning her friend, but eventually Ralph had persuaded her. She had been a dutiful wife, though she always gave her second husband the unspoken but distinct impression that he was a poor substitute for her first. (Christopher Dickson had felt a little inward glow at this information.)

The couple had not in fact spent a great deal of time together, Ralph living mostly in London, and Adele, when she was not in the Caribbean, the Seychelles, or Gstaad, spending most of her time at their country seat, Greveleigh Towers. It had been a workable marriage, though Adele had proved unwilling to provide Ralph with the heir that the Greveleigh family so much needed. He had a feeling that this too might have been because she felt to have children would be a betrayal of her first husband. (This news gave Christopher Dickson another warm glow.)

He tentatively brought up the subject of Ralph's death. What had been the precise circumstances?

"Stupidest thing," his friend replied. "Only blew my head off with a shotgun, didn't I?"

"Deliberately?"

"Good heavens, no! Not my speed at all, suicide. No, I was cleaning one of the Purdies down at Greveleigh Towers. Always like to do it myself, don't trust any of the staff quite honestly, and the strangest thing . . . I'd have sworn both barrels were empty and I'd put the safety catch on, but, damn me, if when I was peering down it, bloody thing didn't go off. Must've made a hell of a mess of my study. Don't envy whoever had to clear that lot up." He brought his hand gingerly up to feel his smooth baby face. "Must say, they do a damned good repair job up here, don't they?"

Christopher Dickson went to the bar to recharge their cups with Nectar. He was pensive. There was no doubt that Lord Greveleigh's presence in Heaven had dealt another blow to his investigative logic.

2013

They now met as a regular group in Saint Raphael's. The bar had become seedier with the passage of celestial years. Even Brightness Ineffable can only last so long, after all, and the whole place could have done with a good spring clean. The cloud sofas were grubby and marked now, like cotton wool that had been used to remove makeup.

And it had been a long time since anyone had seen Saint Raphael. Due to staff downsizing, the counter was now unattended and an "Honour Bar" system operated. Souls helped themselves to Nectar and filled in details of what they'd taken on endless scrolls. Since the drinks were free, this all seemed a bit pointless, but the Management's latest report (prepared by a firm of outside consultants) had insisted on the paperwork being kept in order.

The group of regulars who gathered in Saint Raphael's Bar through the endless afternoons of Heaven comprised Christopher Dickson, Ralph Greveleigh, Bernard Fisher (whom neither of them had managed to shake off), and a relative newcomer called Dermot Hood.

He was a successful businessman who'd died of

cancer in 1999. Ever one to cover all options, he had made copious donations to most of the world's major religions and been somewhat surprised on arrival to find himself at the Pearly Gates, about to enter the traditional Heaven of Christian mythology. He'd half expected to find himself in a Nordic Valhalla or reincarnated as a dung beetle.

Another option Dermot Hood had covered was cryogenics. His head was expensively frozen in a drum in Santa Monica, waiting for medical science to advance sufficiently to cure his illness and clone the rest of his body. He constantly referred to Heaven as a transitory experience—"I'm not stopping, you know."

But as the Immeasurable Ages rolled on, and his summons back to Earth failed to materialise, Dermot Hood became reconciled to sitting with the others in Saint Raphael's Bar, moaning about how much Heaven had gone downhill.

"It's not what I'd hoped for," he would frequently say. "I thought Heaven was meant to be a state of Perpetual Bliss."

"Ah, that was before it got privatised," Bernard Fisher would explain. "Nowadays the best you can hope for is a kind of Intermittent Bliss."

Their conversation didn't change a lot. For example, one afternoon—any afternoon, they were indistinguishable—Christopher Dickson launched into a winge about the admissions policy. "I mean, it's so erratic these days. In the old days, whenever anyone died, rain or shine, whatever the time of day or night, they always used to be greeted by Saint Peter at the Pearly Gates. But now you get contract staff. No, I mean, if you were to come through often, you'd see a different face on the gates every day."

"Yes. Of course, though . . ." Bernard Fisher interposed judiciously, "nobody does come through that often, do they?"

"I wouldn't be so sure," said Dermot Hood, who could always be relied on to bring more up-to-date knowledge of life on Earth. "These days there's such a vogue for 'near-death experiences,' people'll soon be shuttling in and out of Heaven like a government's hand in the taxpayer's pocket."

"Saint Peter's presumably bunked off with all the other angels." As he spoke, Christopher Dickson shook his head with disapproval. "I mean, ask yourself, when did you last see an angel up here?"

"When indeed?" Dermot Hood agreed gloomily. "They're all down on Earth manifesting themselves to the gullible and doing book-signing tours."

Lord Greveleigh looked pessimistically down into his cup. "I swear the portions of Nectar are getting smaller," he groused.

Bernard Fisher added his contribution to the communal gloom. "And the Management's just chaotic these days. I met someone yesterday in the Immemorial Suite who'd got sent to the Other Place by mistake and only just escaped."

"Computer error?" asked Christopher Dickson.

The insurance salesman nodded. "Hmm. Maybe it would be possible to devise a policy so that people could ensure against getting sent to the Other Place by mistake," he mused with mounting enthusiasm.

"What did the chap you met say about . . . Down There?" asked Lord Greveleigh. "Was it as terrible as it's always been cracked up to be?"

"Apparently not."

"Still a bit hot, though, isn't it?"

"Pleasantly mild, I hear." Bernard Fisher answered Lord Greveleigh's quizzical look. "Economies on the fuel, the bloke said. And the punishment regime's getting very lax, too, I hear. Soon you won't be able to distinguish their place from ours."

"Isn't that bloody typical?" Christopher Dickson grumbled into his Nectar. "All that good work we put in on Earth, and in the end it counts for nothing."

He hadn't forgotten about Adele. No, the things of Earth remained very much with him. Every celestial day he still went down to the now-somewhat-tarnished Pearly Gates to inspect the new arrivals.

And every day he was disappointed.

The second Lady Greveleigh did die eventually, in 2013, of a surfeit of champagne and oysters. Or possibly from the overvigorous sexual attentions of her nineteen-year-old swimming pool attendant (the seven hundred and fortieth lover she'd had since she married Lord Greveleigh, the nine hundred and seventy-fourth since her first wedding day). She died an extraordinarily rich woman, having cleaned up on the insurance policy her first husband signed just before his death and inherited huge estates from her second.

But Adele never made it to the Pearly Gates and an encounter with the contract staff who'd replaced Saint Peter. Hardly surprising, really. With her track record, having murdered two husbands (food adulterated by peanuts, a sabotaged shotgun)—and one of their former wives (staged suicide with exhaust fumes)—as well as deliberately sending an innocent man to the gallows, she was always destined to go straight to the Other Place.

Where, incidentally, amongst like-minded Souls, she continued to have a wonderful time.

The Cremains of the Day

Joan Hess

Eloise Bainbury realized it was far too early in the day for sherry, much less gin, but there she was, composed but a bit teary, wringing her hands and staring numbly at the Louis XVI armoir that had been refitted as a liquor cabinet. Her hands shook, but somehow she managed to fill the glass without splattering her wool skirt. How foolishly she was behaving, she thought with a sigh. This was not the first time he'd stayed out all night, prowling the streets and eventually sauntering home as if he'd spent the night in a church waxing the pews. She knew better.

She was standing at the kitchen window when her attorney, Milton Carruthers, called with the bad news. It came in installments, as always, and never in the trite good news–bad news format.

"I'm sorry about this, Eloise," he began nervously. "The accountant's gone over all the tax returns. He said there were some questionable deductions but nothing we can use in court. I warned you that it would be a waste of money."

"So instead of facing his responsibility to me, Justin will go on with his sumptuous lifestyle while I try to find a job in a department store or fast-food establishment? I'm fifty-seven, Milt—not twenty-seven like that tramp he intends to marry as soon as the divorce is final." Eloise took an unladylike gulp of gin, shuddered, and continued in a slightly raspier voice. "You know as well as I that Justin has stashed money in other accounts across the country. Can't you just make him tell you? What about the judge?"

"Oh, Eloise," Milt said in such a tortured voice that she could easily imagine his face screwing up like a dried apricot, "we've been over this time and again. As long as Justin denies the accounts exist and we can't prove that they do, our hands are tied. His attorney dropped off another proposal for the property settlement. It's closer to what we asked for initially, although hardly a capitulation. Why don't you schedule an appointment with my secretary for this afternoon and we'll review it?"

"I suppose so," she said without enthusiasm.

"There's something else I have to tell you. The judge signed a restraining order this morning. If you continue to harass Justin at his house or place of business, you'll be subject to contempt charges. I promise you that the amenities at the jail are not up to your standards."

Eloise sniffed. "I have no idea what you're talking about. I have never harassed Justin at any place or time since he moved out three months ago. Why, even when he was staying at the tramp's apartment, I never so much as made a crank call."

Despite her frigid tone, she was smiling at what she imagined Milt's expression to be as he floundered for a tactful response. Men, she thought, were like agitated guppies when it came to civilized discourse. "Don't you believe me?" she added.

"You had all of the girl's mail forwarded to Azerbaijan."

"Don't be absurd. I have no idea how to spell it."

Milt cleared his throat. "You sprayed Super Glue in the locks of his car doors. You put him down as a new subscriber to one hundred and fifty-three periodicals. In his name you pledged ten thousand dollars to a televangelist whose organization is infamous for its tenacity, and the next week used his calling card number to spend seventy-six hours talking to a psychic friend."

"Nonsense," Eloise said firmly.

"Justin and his attorney were the only two people in the courtroom not sniggering, but the judge signed the order and you have to comply with it. Please, Eloise, no more jokes."

"I am the maligned party, and I deeply resent these accusations, Milton. I do hope it won't be necessary to have a word with your father."

"Only if you have a Ouija board, Eloise. He died twenty years ago." Milt made a small noise that to others might have been interpreted as frustration. Since Eloise would not condone such a reaction, she could only assume he was experiencing allergy problems. It seemed likely, since most of his conversations these days were interspersed with snuffles and grunts. They were actually rather dear, as if Milt were a beloved asthmatic hound that had won the honored position on the hearth.

Eloise did approve of loyalty. "Yes, dear. No, dear. I'll make the appointment and I won't continue doing these things I never did to begin with. We will bargain in good faith and settle this once and for all. You'll receive your very hefty fee, Justin will honeymoon with the tramp, and I will live out my days in a trailer park. Will you and Maggie miss me at the country club?"

"That's the other thing," Milt said, now sounding as if he wished he were in the outlying suburbs of Baku, which everyone knows is the capital of Azerbaijan. "Justin and Kelli were there last night. Maggie was not the only woman who had her claws out as if she were a peregrine falcon. The consensus was that he should have waited until the divorce was final, but there he was . . . with her. Trust me, Eloise, not one person in the room knew what to do except mumble and nod."

"We do what we must," murmured Eloise, wondering how next to sabotage Justin's mail now that the magazines and other periodicals had been halted. Of course, one hundred fifty-three did not begin to cover the available subscriptions when one chanced upon coupons that requested only a circle and an address. Perhaps it would be better to concentrate on other venues. After all, she'd never seriously considered the possibility of having his car reported as stolen or calling in a tip to the television show *America's Most Wanted*.

Shivers of gleeful expectancy ran down her spine as she replaced the receiver, but they subsided as she realized he still had not returned. She went to the window and pulled back the drapes. The front lawn was populated only by a robin on the impeccable grass and a mockingbird at the feeder.

He was usually home by dawn, demanding to be let in despite his ill-defined transgressions. More often than not, Eloise was obliged to daub his wounds with peroxide and judiciously apply Band-

Aids to whatever bits of anatomy were oozing blood. All this solicitude was accepted without emotion, without gratitude, as if he felt it was nothing more than his just desserts for bothering to return home at all.

Puddy, Eloise thought with a flicker of irritation, could be a very naughty cat at times. But he was all she had left to keep her company. She and Justin had not been able to have children. They'd looked into adoption, but she'd always suspected he was much too self-centered to truly want a potential disruption in his life. They'd turned their energies elsewhere, he to his automobile dealership (Lincoln-Mercury) and golf game (single-digit handicap), and she to her clubs (garden and book) and charitable endeavors (historical society, hospital auxiliary, symphony guild).

And Puddy, of course. He'd arrived one rainy night, a sodden little creature, emaciated, wide-eyed with panic but desperate for food and warmth. The following morning Justin had suggested she take the kitten to the animal shelter, but Eloise was already enchanted with her foundling.

It had been seven years since Puddy had arrived—and nearly twelve hours since he'd swaggered out into the backyard and disappeared. He was wearing his collar with an engraved tag bearing her telephone number, so it did not seem likely he was lapping milk in someone else's kitchen, or even yowling in a cage at the animal shelter.

To distract herself, Eloise called Milt's secretary and arranged an appointment later in the day, then looked up the number of the local newspaper and asked to be connected to the classified advertising department.

"Here's what I want in the ad," she said to the young woman who answered. " 'Must sacrifice entire collection of Elvis memorabilia, including complete record set, home movies filmed inside Graceland, and an authenticated love letter, handwritten and signed, to Priscilla from Germany. Can be viewed anytime day or night. All offers will be considered, no matter how low.' " She gave Justin's address, then asked the woman to read it back to make sure she'd phrased it properly.

"Don't you want to give a name and a telephone number?" the woman said. "Most people do."

Eloise coughed delicately. "Our phone has been disconnected due to a financial crisis. I'm calling from a neighbor's house. Please send the bill to the address I gave you."

After she replaced the receiver, she went outside and circled the house in hopes Puddy was sleeping off his night's depravities under a hydrangea. The garden was especially magnificent this year, the envy of the entire garden club membership. A local television station had used footage of it during a tribute to springtime.

The idea of being forced to move into an apartment was more painful than Justin's announcement that he was leaving her for an uneducated, ill-bred secretary at his dealership. She'd been shocked, of course, and hurt. Her women friends had rallied around her at first, including her in luncheons and theater parties, but their collective concern was waning. Eloise knew that Justin and his tramp were being entertained on some of the same patios she had once frequented.

When she went back into the kitchen, she noticed that the red light on the coffeepot was no longer lit. The control panel of the microwave no longer showed the time. The light on the ceiling failed to blink on, as did lights in the hall and living room.

Eloise called the electric company and reported that her power was out. A weary-sounding woman asked for her address, then came back onto the line and said, "Yeah, it was cut off this morning as per customer's request. We're going to need a forwarding address for the final bill, ma'am."

"I did not make any request."

"I got your account on the screen, and it says you did last week, says you're moving as of today. Like I said, we're going to need your new address."

It took Eloise more than an hour to convince the various strata of the electric company that she had no intention of moving—or of living by candlelight. Once she'd been given a promise that her power would be restored before evening, she poured herself a second glass of gin and sat down to make posters telling of Puddy's disappearance and offering an unspecified reward.

She left the house in time to tape the posters onto telephone poles around the neighborhood, then drove to Milt's office.

Thirty minutes later she threw down the proposal. "Absolutely not!" she said, her face flushed and her jaw quivering with outrage. "I don't care about his mother's silver service and his precious antique golf clubs, but I refuse to allow the house to be sold. I've spent countless hours in the garden over the years.

Furthermore, I cannot believe Justin earns less than fifty thousand dollars a year, Milt, and can get away with offering me alimony of one thousand dollars a month. He used to complain that he sold so many cars he could barely keep a minimal inventory. He won a company-sponsored vacation every single year, and he has enough gold plaques to pave the Yellow Brick Road."

"I know that as well as you," Milt said patiently, "but we're stuck with the figure. The accountant discovered that the vast majority of Justin's living expenses are listed as corporate expenditures. Club memberships and expensive restaurants to entertain clients. Travel to explore the feasibility of satellite dealerships. The corporation is currently paying for his house, telephones, car and health insurance—"

"Oh, stop." Eloise took a tissue from her purse and began to shred it as if it were made of Justin's flesh. When the last fragment fluttered to the floor, she picked up the proposal between her fingertips and dropped it in the trash basket beside the desk. "I refuse to sign any property settlement that deprives me of my home and fails to provide for me in the fashion to which I am accustomed. I may not be able to prevent the divorce from taking place, but I intend to delay it as long as possible. File something to that effect."

"Eloise," Milt whimpered, but it was too late. She sailed out of the office, then drove home as quickly as she dared, hoping beyond hope to find Puddy complaining in the kitchen about his litter box (which, for the record, was pristine, but Puddy could be unreasonable).

She was unable to do more than play with a bowl of soup that evening, torn as she was between Puddy's disappearance and Justin's transparent attempt at chicanery. Did thirty years of marriage mean nothing more in the eyes of the court than a cold-blooded division of whatever property Justin opted to put on the chopping block? What about her career, cut short during college? The children she'd been denied. The so-called golden years?

If only Puddy would come home, she thought as she unsuccessfully battled back tears, if only a warm, purring body were curled in her lap, offering unconditional love in exchange for the meager emotions she herself had to offer after a lifetime with Justin.

Puddy was nowhere to be found in the morning. Eloise called the animal shelter, but as she'd anticipated, no twenty-pound male cats had been nabbed on the street. Puddy would have required a battalion to take him captive. Then where was he?

For the second morning in a row, Eloise scorned tea for gin. And why not? Her lawyer disliked her, her soon-to-be ex husband was making a pathetic attempt to coerce her into a menial existence of poverty and servitude, her friends had deserted her, and her only source of uncritical devotion had chosen to abandon her.

She passed the morning clad in plastic gloves, writing graphic death threats to various political figures, signing them with an arrogantly scrawled X, and using Justin's return address on the envelopes. She was in the middle of clipping letters from magazines that would eventually create a message that a bomb would be found in one of the local elementary schools if Kelli Kennison was not rehired as a substitute when the doorbell rang.

No one was visible when she opened the door. On the welcome mat was an envelope with no address. Doubting that Justin had discovered the technology for so thin a bomb, Eloise opened the envelope and read: "I have the cat. You know what you need to do."

Her initial reaction was instinctive but futile. Justin's driveway and, indeed, the entire street for several blocks in both directions were jammed with pickup trucks, station wagons, and peculiar-looking people on foot, clad in sequined jackets. Many held garish guitars and were grouping to sing, as if this were a street festival.

Eloise watched them for a long while, marveling at their hair, then drove to Milt's office, barged through the reception room, and found him in conversation with a white-haired man who may or may not have been a senior partner. Eloise did not care. She slammed down the cryptic note and said, "Call the district attorney! This is nothing more than blackmail!"

The white-haired man who may or may not have seen a senior partner grabbed his briefcase and scurried out of the room. Milton Carruthers, who'd just seen his best shot at a promotion evaporate, picked up the paper and read it with only a faint wuffle.

"Eloise," he said, "this isn't blackmail. It could be a message from your paperboy."

"And I could be Lisa Marie Presley Jackson," she retorted as she poked him in the chest. "I can tolerate only so much, Milt. I stayed calm when Justin dumped me for an ignorant, flat-bellied little tramp. I said nothing when you and Maggie invited them into your home last—"

"Oh, Eloise," Milt said, clutching her hand, "I'd hoped you would understand that was business. Our firm has always had a policy of—"

"Can it. Justin can hawk my soul, trash my remaining years, hold me up to ridicule in the community, even drive me into poverty and obscurity—but he will not steal Puddy! Do you understand, Milt? He will not take away the only thing I have left on this miserable planet! He will not!" She lunged at him, her hands curled and her expression distorted with anguish. "I must have Puddy!"

Milt's secretary opened the door, then hastily closed it as Eloise sank back into the sofa that was conveniently situated to prevent clients overwhelmed with legal realities from flinging themselves out the window. A three-story dive was rarely fatal, but the firm of Guzman, Kirkpatrick, and Kirkpatrick preferred swoons to accusations of negligence.

"Do something," Eloise said in a somewhat calmer voice, although her demeanor remained suspect.

"What can I do? We can't be sure this is from Justin. It sounds as though it is, that he has the cat and is willing to use it as a bargaining ploy—but we can't prove it." Milt pushed a button on his intercom. "Marsha, please bring a cup of tea for Mrs. Bainbury."

Eloise sat up and found her purse. "I have no need of tea, Milton. I had hoped that you could do something, but I see that you can't. I shall go home now and wait for a further message."

She sailed out of his office, not so much calm as determined to do what was necessary to liberate Puddy from the evil clutches of a man she'd once respected and now loathed as if he were an emissary from hell. He and his tramp, she thought, as she drove home without regard for her personal safety or that of small children chasing balls into the street. Up until now, the pranks had been somewhat . . . well, if not harmless . . . well, not exactly heinous. She'd done nothing that wasn't deserved. After all, it had been her life that was snatched from under her feet like a frayed area rug, sending her head over heels, depriving her of the essence of her existence.

Eloise was exhausted the next morning, having been unable to sleep for even the briefest amount of time. The house was too quiet without Puddy's repertoire of yowls and rumbles of contentment. No accusatory eyes watched her as she came into the kitchen, filled the kettle, then set it down and continued toward the liquor cabinet. She knew she must look hideous, like a disheveled old crone out of a Brothers Grimm story.

Which meant Justin was winning, she realized with a scowl. He was bulldozing her to the abyss of madness, where she would sign whatever he wanted and then slink away, grateful for the few crumbs he'd given her. She couldn't even be sure she'd get Puddy back if she complied with his demands. He had been ruthless in his business affairs, and he'd never once had a kind word for Puddy. Her poor Puddy's body might be in a garbage bag at the curb in front of Justin's house, soon to be interred in the city dump.

Eloise banged down the glass. "I will not allow him to win," she said, spitting out each word with such anger that a haze of venom seemed to fill the room. She called her beauty shop, demanded an immediate appointment, and then carefully dressed, combed her hair, and applied lipstick and a faint dusting of blusher to disguise her pallor.

As she drove toward the center of town, she became increasingly bewildered by the expressions of pedestrians, as well as those in other vehicles. Women stared at her in horror, while men mouthed vulgarities and made unseemly gestures. A teenaged girl clapped her hand to mouth and sank to her knees on the sidewalk. A small child pointed at Eloise's car and screamed.

Eloise knew she'd been exaggerating when she described herself as a disheveled old crone, but she was beginning to wonder if she looked much worse than the image she'd seen in her mirror. Was there some sort of invisible stigma attached to a middle-aged woman who'd been discarded by her husband? Before leaving her house, she'd checked the car for any sort of vandalism, from a swastika spray-painted on the passenger side to obscene bumper stickers. Experience had taught her caution in such matters.

She could think of nothing to do but continue on her way, despite the revulsion she was leaving in her wake. She'd just turned the corner when she saw blue lights flashing in the rearview mirror and heard the momentary burp of a siren. She pulled over obediently and forced herself to assume a demeanor of expectancy and the slightest trace of self-righteousness as she watched the police officer emerge from his car.

To her surprise, he squatted down behind her car for a long moment. When he arose and came to her window, his expression was stony.

"You think that's funny, lady?" he said. "Well, you're the sickest damn practical joker I've had the displeasure to deal with. Driver's license and registration."

"I don't understand," Eloise said with as much civility as she could muster. "I was not exceeding the speed limit, and I am always careful about coming to a full stop at stop signs. I've never had a traffic ticket in my life, except for the odd parking ticket."

"Yeah, right. I'm gonna have to radio in and find out what the violation is. License and registration— now."

Eloise handed over the pertinent documentation, adding her proof of insurance to emphasize her willingness to cooperate, then sank back as the officer returned to his car. Why was she being treated with this unmistakable contempt?

She was startled out of her reverie when a woman pushing a stroller glared at her and said, "You make me want to puke."

Eloise got out of the car and blinked at the woman, who mutely pointed at the back of the car. There on the asphalt, attached by a rope tied under the bumper, lay a bedraggled stuffed toy sprinkled with red paint. At a distance, Eloise realized, as her stomach knotted with disgust, it looked very much like a dead cat.

"Oh, my God," she said, fighting for breath and oblivious to the tears streaming down her cheeks. "I didn't know it was there. What must everyone have thought of me? I would never harm a cat! You must believe me! I'm not—not like that."

She sat down in the car and dully waited for the officer to return. When he finally did, she explained rather inarticulately that this was a cruel joke played upon her by her estranged husband and then, regaining control of herself, made sure the officer wrote down Justin's name and that of the Lincoln-Mercury dealership.

The officer nodded solemnly. "We get some pretty strange calls when people are divorcing, but this is the nastiest trick I've heard of. You want me to untie the rope?"

She did, of course, and when the evidence had been put in her trunk, she turned around and drove home. After a glass of gin took the knots out of her stomach, she donned gloves and wrote anonymous letters to the homeowners in Justin's new neighborhood, warning them that he was a convicted child molester. Then, feeling steadier, she called all the cemeteries in town and made evening appointments for Kelli so that she and Justin could explore the possibility of spending eternity in adjoining slots. Inspiration struck, and she called all the funeral homes and arranged for representatives to drop by and assist the lovebirds in preplanning their funerals.

Although the activity was satisfying, it did little to erase the dreadful image of the stained toy cat with the rope around its neck. It was obviously a threat against Puddy, held captive and no doubt being abused and neglected. Would she find him at the end of the next rope?

Again she found it impossible to sleep, and by the next morning she was so exhausted that she could barely focus on her surroundings. The furniture seemed unfamiliar, the walls bulging, the windows presenting a surreal picture of her yard. The telephone rang several times during the day, but Eloise could only stare at it.

By nine o'clock that night the gin bottle was empty,

as were the sherry, scotch, and vermouth bottles. Eloise was trying to coax the last olive out of the jar when the doorbell chimed. She sat where she was, paralyzed at the possibility that she might find herself confronting Milt or even one of her treacherous friends. Then she remembered the posters she had put up offering a reward for Puddy's return and stumbled to her feet.

No one was waiting on the porch, nor was there a second envelope on the doormat. What she did see was a box, six inches square, with printing on its side. She gingerly picked it up and read the swirling words: Memorial Funeral Home and Crematorium.

She looked wildly at the empty sidewalk, then stepped back inside and locked the door. Her hands trembled violently as she forced open the box. Inside was a small brass urn with decorative etching and inlaid mother-of-pearl flowers. Biting her lip, she opened the lid and gazed at the soft gray ashes.

At that point, automatic pilot took over. She placed the urn on the coffee table, picked up her purse, and went out to the garage to find the three-gallon gas can left by the yardmen. She drove to the gas station and managed to fill the can at the pump, then continued to Justin's house in the posh neighborhood on the top of the hill.

There were no lights shining from the downstairs floor, but a glow came through drawn drapes in a second-floor room and she could hear what she thought was a television show.

She soaked the porch with gasoline, then went around to the deck at the back of the house and did the same. She dropped a lit match, returned to the front of the house and did the same, and watched until flames began to leap like devilish ballerinas.

Her task completed, Eloise drove home. She had no delusions that she would not be apprehended and charged with arson. She could only hope that first-degree murder would be added once the ruins had been sifted.

She was seated in the living room, cradling the urn and reminiscing about Puddy's days as a mischievous kitten, when the doorbell chimed. So soon, she thought as she set the urn on the mantel and prepared herself to face the consequences of her actions.

A nervous woman, vaguely familiar, stood on the porch. "Mrs. Bainbury, I live down at the corner across from the park, and I want you to know how sorry I am."

"Sorry?" echoed Eloise.

"Four nights ago we got a call that my father had had a heart attack. I bundled everybody into the car and drove all night to get to the hospital. It turned out not to be all that serious, but we stayed to help my mother get through the ordeal. When we arrived home less than an hour ago, I opened the garage door and saw a large yellow cat shoot out and disappear into the shrubbery. My son recognized it as yours, and the poster on the telephone pole confirmed it. I suppose he must have been locked in the garage all this time. I'm really, really sorry."

"These things do happen, don't they?" murmured Eloise. She was going to offer a word or two of sympathy for the woman's father when she saw a police car coming down the street. "If you'll excuse me," she said, "I need to make sure Puddy finds fresh kibble and water on his return. Thank you so much for coming by, dear."

When the police car pulled into her driveway, Eloise was in the yard, sprinkling ashes on the rose bed. Ashes added important nutrients to the soil, she thought with a smile. The roses would be glorious by the end of the summer.

Accidents Happen

Carolyn Hart

Jimmy Kramer specialized in charm. And he was careful to tailor his attitude to the customer. Businessmen liked fast, unobtrusive service and, if they were from out of town, maybe some tips on the good clubs with friendly ladies. Older women liked deference—"Yes, ma'am." "No, ma'am." But he was best with middle-aged women, especially lonely middle-aged women. They liked his Nordic blond hair, diffident smile, and muscular surfer's body. Just a suggestion of sexual attraction, that was the best.

Jimmy raked in high-dollar tips.

That's all he was thinking about in the beginning with Opal Morrison.

He knew who she was. It was a small coastal town. Excellent surf. That was the attraction, that and the fact it was several hundred miles north of Long Beach and the pregnant girl he'd walked out on.

But he quickly picked up on the locals. Opal was a successful realtor, had her own agency. Around fifty, she was just a little chunky in her fashionable suits, and her red hair had dark roots. She worked eighty-hour weeks, but she spent more and more evenings at the Casbah. Sappy name, but the owner was a pretty good guy, not hard to work for.

Pretty soon Opal came in for dinner every night, and she always picked Jimmy's corner. Pretty soon she was leaving 20 percent tips.

One evening his hand touched hers, and he gave a little squeeze. When she left, giving him a gigged-fish look, he knew he could make a move.

But Jimmy liked to be sure. He spent an afternoon in the library looking at old issues of the local paper. Interesting what you could pick up by skimming. OPAL MORRISON, REALTOR OF THE YEAR. OPAL MORRISON, FIFTH YEAR TO SELL OVER FIVE MILLION DOLLARS. Opal Morrison, owner of a $450,000 Spanish mission house.

Opal—rich, single. And lonely.

It didn't take him long. He started working out at her health club. Pretty soon they were ending up in the hot tub there after he got off work. Then she invited him to her house. And her hot tub. And so, yeah, she was fifteen years older than he, but she was pretty sexy. Not great, but okay.

They got married on a Valentine's weekend.

They'd been back from their honeymoon at Prince-ville for a week when she told him briskly that he would work at the agency. After all, he certainly didn't have to be a waiter anymore.

The other realtors were nice to his face, but he could feel their disdain. What the hell, it didn't bother him.

He missed surfing every day. Opal expected him at the office. But he could still surf on the weekends. Most of the time. Except when Opal planned for him to do something else.

This had been a pretty lousy weekend.

Opal was driving. She always drove.

Jimmy slouched in the passenger seat. The sleek red Mercedes hummed along in the slow lane. What a waste of horsepower.

Jimmy could feel his face tightening until a pain began to pulse in his temple.

". . . and I certainly do think you could try a little harder, Jimmy. It isn't asking much for you to be nice to my niece."

He forced a mild answer. "I tried to be helpful." And God knows, he had. His back ached like hell from spading up that flower bed at Gina's house. And he'd damn near fallen off the roof when he re-screened that ventilator opening that the squirrel had broken into.

"Jimmy, would you sort this stuff for the recycling bin. . . . Jimmy, would you mind trimming that mimosa. . . . Jimmy, maybe next week you could reseal the deck . . ."

Opal's hair streamed in the wind.

Sounded sexy, right?

Actually, she looked like an old witch. In the unforgiving afternoon sunlight, he could see the faint pink lines below her ears from her face-lift.

"Jimmy, get my sunglasses out of the pocket."

No *please*. No *thank you* as he handed her the designer sunglasses.

"Did you find the Willet file?"

Did she think he'd managed to retrieve the missing file by ESP? Hell, he hadn't been out of her sight the entire weekend. Opal knew he hadn't found it.

"Not yet." He grabbed the newspaper.

"Maybe you could run down to the office when we get home. Take another look."

"Yeah." Jimmy kept the paper raised. He skimmed

the stories. The San Andreas fault was moving, according to earthquake experts. Deaths from car wrecks had risen sharply following the increase in the speed limit. The body of a hiker had been found in the ocean near Carmel.

"Jimmy." There was the same foreboding tone his mother had used when he tracked mud across the kitchen floor.

"Yes." He managed not to hiss. Opal didn't like it when he said yeah. She said it didn't set a good tone at the office.

"Oh, good grief! It looks like a semi's jackknifed. I wonder if I can get off at the next freeway . . ." Opal muttered to herself.

*Jimmy read a two-paragraph story:

> The body of a woman hiker washed ashore at Carmel today. Esmeralda Winslow of San Francisco fell from a cliffside trail Friday.
>
> Sheriff Dan Colby said the accident was reported by Winslow's husband, Mack.

"Jimmy. Jimmy!"

He lowered the newspaper, looked at Opal.

The afternoon sun was harsh on her raddled skin. She looked every one of her fifty years.

"Jimmy, you could at least answer me when I speak!"

"Sorry, Opal. I just noticed a story about a rise in house prices for beach properties."

. . . body . . . washed ashore . . .

Opal sniffed. "Honestly, Jimmy, that was in the realtor roundup last month. Didn't you read that material I put in your in-box?"

His in-box was stuffed with notebooks, pamphlets, and rental magazines. Nobody could have waded through all of it.

"I read it."

"Then you should have known prices were going up."

He almost blew up. What difference would it make if he did know? Opal never let him close a deal. She kept him on a very short leash. Yes, he got to drive prospects around, but when it came time to sign on the dotted line, the money went to Opal. Not to Jimmy.

Opal had all the money. Of course, she was generous. He had a nifty Porsche. But she expected him to be as crazy about her business as she was. She'd insisted that he study for the realtors exam. When he passed the damn thing, she would expect him to work as hard as she did.

It wasn't exactly what he'd had in mind. And now, more often than not, there was a sharp edge to her voice when she spoke to him. Opal never quite jumped on him. But she was always pushing, prodding, encouraging, demanding.

He wasn't willing to do battle, but he was quite adept at delaying, skirting, and ignoring.

That night, as he walked the elderly, whiny Pekinese around the back garden, he kept seeing that small story.

. . . body . . . washed ashore . . .

He waited while Peky sprayed a pottery frog.

He could get a divorce.

Actually, he didn't even have to do that. He would just walk out, never come back. Go down to L.A. Wait tables. There are always those kinds of jobs.

There would be no more cashmere sweaters. No Porsche. No silk sheets.

He would have to start over with nothing. He knew Opal well enough to be sure he'd better not take his car or take much cash out of the bank. So it wasn't his car. Or his cash.

... body ... washed ashore ...

But if something happened to Opal ...

Jimmy didn't write anything down. He didn't keep that paper. But he started thinking.

It would have to be a good accident, look like a real accident.

The next morning over breakfast, he said casually, "Opal, I think you're working too hard. You know how the doctor said you need to walk more. How about if we go out and do some hiking on weekends?"

It got to be a regular thing. Every Sunday they went up or down the coast and tramped around on the cliffs for an hour or so. Of course, on Saturdays he was still Mr. Handyman at her niece's. But he even suggested improvements. Everybody thought he was just grand. Gina took him aside one afternoon to say she'd never seen her aunt happier.

Jimmy buckled down at the office too. He worked out a new computer program for their listings. It took him several months to put it together and a lot of tedious copying.

Nora, who'd been there for six years, raised an eyebrow. "Trying for Realtor of the Month, Jimmy?"

For a moment, he shook with genuine mirth. "Nope, Nora. Just having fun."

"Oh, my," she murmured. "Being married to Opal must be the next best thing to a lobotomy."

And that was when he started bringing odd gifts

and little bouquets to Opal. Just a little something every few weeks. They got to know him well at the florist. And at the nearby jeweler. Nothing terribly expensive. Just little remembrances, a ceramic hedgehog for Groundhog Day, a silver deed with her initials.

Opal blossomed, and she carped only occasionally.

Sometimes Jimmy almost forgot his objective. But he was tired of trying so hard. And he missed surfing. And he was bored with hurrying through breakfast to get to the office and update the computer program. Opal loved the damn computer program.

"Jimmy, it gives us a boost ahead of every other realtor in the county." Her eyes gleamed.

"Yeah—Yes." He automatically corrected himself now.

And on Sundays they hiked, up and down the coast. But Jimmy drove. He insisted on taking his car and driving for these outings. "More of a holiday for you, Opal."

She smiled at that and leaned back against the headrest.

This Sunday he was heading for a particular path, narrow and twisting, high above heavy surf crashing against black boulders. Just outside Carmel, actually.

Opal was attractive in a cream blouse and green linen walking shorts that made her look slimmer than she was.

When he pulled off the road, Opal held up her hand. "My God, Jimmy, be careful. It's a long way down."

"Hey, we've got good brakes," and his voice was exuberant.

. . . body . . . washed ashore . . .

It was more than a year ago that he'd seen the little article.

He handed Opal her backpack, slipped into his own. As he followed Opal—she went first, of course—the sun glistened on her hair. But Jimmy was concentrating on the path. A few more steps and they were out of sight of the road.

He looked past Opal, his eyes sweeping the bay. It was a small curve in the coastline. No sailboats. And no surfers here. The water was too rough, huge waves that slammed against towering rocks.

He tensed his knees, lifted his hands. He drew in a ragged gulp of breath, deep in his lungs, then slammed his palms against Opal's backpack.

Opal hurtled off the trail, plunging down toward the rocks. Her scream began deep and guttural, then exploded like a banshee's wail.

Jimmy shuddered, long quivers shaking his body. That scream . . . Finally it was quiet. Nothing could be heard but the rumble of the surf and the rustle of the cypress.

Jimmy turned and began to run back up the path.

Opal was gone. Dead and gone.

. . . body . . . washed ashore . . .

He reached the road and looked both ways.

No cars.

He looked up and saw a windswept redwood house on top of the ridge. It seemed to hang between the earth and the sky.

Jimmy ran toward it. "An accident!" he shouted. "An accident! Please, help me, my wife's had an accident!"

He was winded by the time he reached the house. His chest heaved. He pounded on the wooden door.

When the door opened, he couldn't speak.

"What's happened? My God, what's wrong?"

Jimmy had seen a person like this only in classy fashion ads. Or in the movies. Sleek golden hair framed a fascinating face, thin, elegant, fine-boned, intelligent, aristocratic.

The slender woman's green eyes widened in concern. She wore a golden silk blouse open at the throat and black slacks.

"My wife." His voice shook, cracked. "The cliff. It gave way."

Jimmy read the certainty of Opal's death in the sudden sharp intake of the woman's breath.

"Oh, God. Come in. I'll call. Come in." She reached out a thin, graceful hand that clasped his, drew him inside.

Jimmy had never felt smoother skin.

She ran to the phone, dialed 911. "This is Joanna Clements. There's been an accident . . ."

Jimmy didn't listen to her words. He was repeating her name in his mind. Joanna Clements, Joanna Clements, Joanna Clements . . .

She came down to the road with him, waited with him until the sheriff's car and a county rescue motorboat arrived.

Jimmy wished they'd turn off the whirling light atop the sheriff's car.

Flash. Flash. Flash.

A helicopter maneuvered just above the roaring surf.

Jimmy's head hurt.

Joanna Clements stood with her hands deep in her pockets. "I wish I could help. I know this is so hard on you, Jimmy."

They were already Jimmy and Joanna.

An occasional shout rose from the beach.

Jimmy shivered.

Joanna said immediately, "You're cold. I'll be right back," and she hurried up the steep drive.

His eyes followed her. He'd never met anyone who attracted him the way she did. He loved the way she moved, her body lithe and athletic, and he was exhilarated by the brightness in her eyes. And her voice rang in his mind, husky, with a timbre that was fascinating and unique.

"Mr. Kramer."

Jimmy jerked around.

Sheriff Dan Colby was a big man with blunt features and cold light-brown eyes. He wore his round-crowned hat jammed down over his big ears, but he didn't look clownish. He looked ominous. The strap from his hat had worn a sore spot on one cheek.

Jimmy felt suddenly breathless. Afraid.

"You known Mrs. Clements long?"

"No." Jimmy wished his voice had come out stronger. He tried again, and the word was almost a bark. "No." He cleared his throat. "I'd never seen her until today. But she's been so nice, so—" He broke off. Even he could hear the too-warm sound in his voice.

The sheriff's eyes had a funny, sardonic look. He nodded slowly. "Hold out your arms."

Jimmy stared at the big man blankly.

"Your arms."

Jimmy lifted his arms. He looked, too. The sun glistened on the blond hairs along his forearms. He had good arms, strong, muscular.

The sheriff nodded and turned away.

Jimmy still stood there, puzzled, his arms out-thrust. Why the hell did the sheriff want to look at his arms?

It was like a kick in the chest. Jesus, the man was looking for scratches. Jesus!

It was an accident, Jimmy wanted to yell after him, an accident!

Shouts rose from the beach.

Jimmy wrapped his arms tight across his chest.

The sheriff's walkie-talkie buzzed. He lifted it, held it close.

They all heard the metallic voice. "The chopper's spotted the body, Dan."

The sheriff flicked it off, looked at Jimmy.

"Opal." Jimmy buried his face in his hands. Should he break down? No. Not with that fish-eyed bastard watching him like a hawk. Maybe he should act mad. He jerked his head up. "Listen, maybe she's okay. Why can't you get her, help her?"

"Mister, nobody could survive a fall from that cliff. Not onto those rocks."

Joanna ran lightly to them, thrust a parka toward him. "Here, put this on."

The touch of her hand—Jimmy looked at her in wonder, then his eyes jerked back to the sheriff. He grabbed the parka, shrugged into it.

The sheriff stared hard at Jimmy. "Okay, Mr. Kramer, tell me how it happened."

"I've told you."

"I'd like to hear it again."

It helped to have Joanna's sympathetic face there. "We hike—hiked—every Sunday. And this was like any Sunday. We'd started out. Opal was in front of me. And all of a sudden she was falling. I think maybe the path crumbled. Right under her feet." He tried hard to look straight at the sheriff, but finally his eyes slid away.

They let him go at last. Joanna walked him to his car, told him to call her if there was anything she could do, anything at all.

Everybody was great to him the next few weeks. Opal's niece couldn't have been nicer. Of course, she inherited half the estate, so that probably made her cheerful. But she made a point of writing Jimmy a really nice note about what a great marriage he and Opal had had. Jimmy didn't mind sharing. It was a hell of a big estate. He was a very rich man now.

The women realtors brought casseroles.

Jimmy thanked them. And said bravely, "Accidents happen."

Two weeks later, he answered the front door to find Sheriff Colby standing there.

Jimmy simply stared at him.

"Can I come in?"

Jimmy licked his lips. Could he slam the door, tell the sheriff to go the hell away? But maybe he couldn't. And why would he, if everything was on the up and up?

"Sure." Jimmy led the way into the living room.

They sat in two overstuffed chairs near a long, low glass coffee table.

The sheriff took off his round-crowned hat, held it in his lap.

"So you wanted to talk to me?" Jimmy asked.

"Yeah. I been checking around. I understand Mrs. Kramer was a lot older than you."

Jimmy felt his face flush. "What's that got to do with anything?"

"I don't know, Mr. Kramer. I'm just trying to find out all about you. And Mrs. Kramer."

"Why?" Jimmy wished his voice was stronger, firmer.

The sheriff looked around the huge room with its indirect spot lighting and luxurious rugs and crystal on side tables. "Was this Mrs. Kramer's house? When you married her?"

Jimmy swallowed. "Look, Sheriff, my wife fell off a cliff. What difference does it make whether this was her house? Or how old she was?"

"I don't know, Mr. Kramer. But I like to fill out my files real carefully. And I'm not finished looking into Mrs. Kramer's fall."

Jimmy stood up. "I don't have to talk to you. If you want to talk to me again, you call my lawyer."

The sheriff took his time getting up. He loomed over Jimmy and his eyes were sharp and cold. "I'll do that, Mr. Kramer. I'll do that."

Jimmy took sleeping pills that night. But he kept waking up, struggling to breathe. Damn the sheriff. Damn him!

Jimmy heard later that the sheriff visited a lot of people and that they'd all told the sheriff what a devoted husband he'd been and that the difference in age between Jimmy and Opal hadn't meant a thing.

Sheriff Colby checked. And checked. And checked. But three weeks after Opal Kramer fell to her death, Sheriff Colby closed the file.

Jimmy waited another two weeks, then drove down Highway 1.

Joanna Clements opened the front door. And smiled. To Jimmy it was like watching a sunrise on a lush summer day, streaks of gold and mauve and apricot blending in iridescent glory. Her pale yellow cashmere sweater molded gently against high breasts. Tan jodhpurs emphasized her slim legs. Delicate gold earrings shimmered in the sunlight.

She looked surprised and hesitant—and pleased.

Jimmy burst into awkward, hurried, desperate speech. "I'm so sorry to bother you. But I had to come back. My pastor said the only way to come to grips with what happened was to come back here and go to the cliff. Can you understand that?"

She nodded slowly, her eyes huge with sorrow. She reached out, took his hand tightly in hers. "Yes. I do understand. My husband—"

Jimmy felt frozen. Husband.

"—was killed in a scuba accident last year. I've made myself swim there. Again and again. Oh, Jimmy, I'll go down to the cliff with you."

Jimmy came to see Joanna every weekend. He was swept by feelings he'd never known, never imagined.

They fell in love, gently, then with eagerness and passion.

Jimmy couldn't believe his luck.

Joanna—dear, sweet, beautiful, magnificent Joanna. And she cared for him. Yes, she was fifteen years older than he, but it was so different from Opal. Joanna never seemed old, she simply seemed more vital and exciting and knowledgeable than anyone he'd ever known. And he knew she would never grow old to him.

She would always be his beloved Joanna.

They waited six months to marry.

There was only one shadow on his happiness. As they walked out of the chapel, he saw the sheriff's car parked nearby. The sheriff sat unmoving in the driver's seat. Mirrored sunglasses were turned toward Jimmy and his new wife. Jimmy shivered.

They honeymooned in Kauai. Climbing, hiking, and kayaking with a vibrant companion, Jimmy realized that he'd never enjoyed himself so much in all his life.

Most of all, they loved to climb.

Upon their return, he moved into Joanna's house. One of the first things he did was to pay off the mortgage. He hadn't realized that she'd been in financial straits. And it was wonderful to be able to help her, to say, "Oh, don't worry about that, I'll take care of it." It turned out that she and her husband had been in debt—their bank had gone under—and the insurance policy on his life had been just enough to pay off most of the bills, but she still had an almost insurmountable monthly payment on the house.

Joanna had been so grateful, so thrilled. "Oh, Jimmy, I love my house and I've been so afraid I would lose it. I would die if I didn't have my house."

And he realized that she did love the house. Sometimes he almost felt a tiny quiver of jealousy. But she was so happy when she found a new vase for a sunny corner or re-terraced the hillside. The house took a lot of money. But he had a lot of money.

Every day Jimmy was struck again by his good fortune.

By now he'd almost forgotten the ache in his hands when they'd struck Opal's backpack.

And life with Joanna was filled with joy. He loved her happiness, knowing the house she adored was now hers forever.

Jimmy realized he enjoyed selling houses more

than he had thought. He bought some business property in Carmel and opened his own office. And everything he did seemed to turn to gold. He made more and more money.

He'd been going to the office for several months—KRAMER REALTY was printed in gold letters on the frosted door—when he heard the main door open. He looked up eagerly.

Sheriff Colby stepped inside. He walked across the thickly carpeted floor, stood and looked down at Jimmy. Then he looked around the office. "Pretty nice."

"What do you want, Sheriff?" Jimmy hated the way his voice shook.

"Just to say hello, Mr. Kramer. Welcome you to Carmel. I suppose you know your wife is highly thought of around here."

"Joanna. I know. She's wonderful."

The sheriff nodded. "And she's a real healthy woman."

"Of course she is."

"She'd better stay that way, Mr. Kramer." And he swung on his heel and walked out.

Jimmy stared at the closing door.

He didn't tell Joanna, of course. He couldn't. And it seemed to him that he saw the sheriff just a little too often, sometimes at night, sometimes in the middle of the day.

But it didn't matter, he told himself. Sheriff Colby couldn't do anything to him.

Finally Jimmy began to relax. Time passed and he was happy, happy all the time. And so was Joanna.

The night before their first anniversary, she fixed a special dinner.

"Jimmy, I have a wonderful idea for tomorrow."

"Whatever you want. Whatever in the whole world you want, Joanna."

"I want us to go together on the path and take flowers for Opal."

Jimmy didn't want to seem reluctant. After all, they'd gone swimming several times where Joanna's husband, Roger, had drowned.

"We have to remember those we've loved," Joanna said solemnly.

"Of course we do," Jimmy agreed resolutely. "After all, accidents happen. But that was yesterday. Today belongs to us."

"But we won't forget Opal. And Roger."

The next day, their first anniversary, was perfect—the soft blue sky cloudless, the air soft and warm. Even the windswept cypress looked benign in the soft air.

Jimmy went first along the narrow path, carrying a spray of orchids. Joanna followed, with a small bouquet of violets.

The surf boomed. Glancing down at the glistening boulders and the roiling water, Jimmy felt a surge of sheer pleasure. He was living a dream come true. Nothing could ever be better—

The violent push struck him in the small of the back.

His arms flung wide, but there was nothing to grasp. As his body turned and began to plummet, he glimpsed Joanna's face, the elegant features smooth and satisfied, a tiny smile curving her lips. Always graceful, she swung her hand and the violets curved out into space.

He heard his own scream and felt himself falling faster and faster.

The scream ended abruptly.

Joanna turned and walked swiftly up the path toward her house. Her beloved house. All hers.

An Unsuitable Job
for a Mullin

Susan Dunlap

"Can't do." Mullin regretted he'd answered the phone.

"He needs you."

"I don't work anymore."

"I said, *he* needs you." The voice was unfamiliar, but the tone and cadence were always the same. They never changed, these callers. Did a night school offer "Speak Like the Godfather"?

"I'm retired."

"There's only one way you retire from this racket."

Mullin shook his head. Maybe there was another class: "Triteness Made Easy." "Look, uh . . ." But, of course, the kid hadn't given him a name. He'd probably taken a Saturday seminar in "Identity Concealment for the Ambitious Thug." "I can't—"

"You cross him, you're gonna be the one hit."

"Well, kid, we all gotta die."

"He'll get somebody else to do him—and then take care of you."

Mullin scratched his head.

But before he could come up with the next line, the kid hit him below the belt. "He knows you ain't worked in fifteen years. He knows you act like you can retire. He knows you, Mullin, and what yer gonna say. Here's what he says: He'll get someone else, someone not as good as you, someone messy. And when the mark's mooshed all over the sidewalk, he'll put out the word that you did the hit."

Mullin was offended, first, at the august *he* assuming that Mullin still cared about his professional reputation and, second, that he did. Messy meant not merely a sanitation challenge but a painful death for the victim, an angry crowd of the victim's relatives, friends, "business associates," all of them out for revenge. All of them looking to take the shine off his golden years.

Still, he couldn't . . . "I can't."

"Name's Maddis Esterbee Groom. Lives with his wife at two two seven Pacific Avenue, San Francisco." He added phone numbers. "His mug's in the society section of your paper out there today. All you gotta do is drive across town. It's an easy hit. *He's* flying in at five, your time. He don't want Groom to be around to meet him, y'understand?"

Mullin felt the walls closing in, walls two feet thick. But he couldn't do the hit. He sighed. He'd vowed never to admit the reason to anyone in the profession, much less the family back East. That was why he'd moved a continent away. But now he had no choice. "Look, I'm not kidding, I can't—"

But the kid had hung up.

He put down the receiver. Now he really had no choice. He wondered what the story on him was back East. Lost his nerve? Got religion? Or some shaking disease? Whatever they thought, it was fine with him. Just as long as they didn't dig up the truth—

the one thing in the world he could not bring himself to do ever again.

Mullin the hit man didn't drive. Not couldn't. Didn't.

Five o'clock! In his shock he hadn't dealt with that at all. Because he was focused on the driving thing, not the hit itself. It wasn't like he could have said, "I don't drive anymore." Even if he could have stood the cackles of laughter coming over the phone lines— and the prospect of cackles all over the East Coast. It wouldn't be long before *he* wondered what else would spook him and how easy it would be for the feds to turn him. *His* solution to that problem Mullin knew only too well. Mullin was so flustered by the miserable situation he hadn't thought to ask the kid about payment, or even why, after fifteen years, *he* had tracked Mullin down on this cold summer day in San Francisco. Jeez, he had been out of the business too long.

Or maybe not. "Look for the ray of sun in every cloud, Cornelius," his sainted mother had said. His ma was no meteorologist, but he took her point. He could see the yellow ray peeking out of this cloud.

Warn Groom, that's what he should do. Letting a mark go would never have crossed his mind when he was still working. He would have been insulted at the idea. A mark who escaped just upped the ante. But retirement gives a man time for reflection.

It felt good doing the right thing.

It felt wise. Virtuous.

He checked the paper. In the photo Maddis Esterbee Groom, 55, president of Groom Consulting, was a barrel-chested man with sharp features and a

wiry ruff of brown hair. His hand was on the arm
of his wife, Alice, while he talked intently with the
man beside him.

Virtue was rewarded, right? Groom could afford
to reward him. He called.

"Groom."

"Maddis Groom?"

"Right. What is this in regard to?"

A matter of life and death, Mr. Groom, he could
have said. But there are some subjects unsuitable for
the phone. This one called for a face-to-face. Pulling
up from memory one of the credos of professional
behavior—Lead with Greed—he said, "It's about the
morgue photo—" Mullin stopped. What was wrong
with him? Did he have a one-track mind? He *had*
been retired too long. "We need a better picture for
the feature we're running tomorrow. A news photo."

"What?" Groom grumbled. "You need a new De
Soto?" His voice was muted.

"Could you speak louder?"

He didn't. But he was still talking. He hadn't
stopped even for Mullin's question. His words were
covered by squeaking noises. Groom's hand, he realized, was over the phone.

Mullin let out a sigh. He had expected a certain
degree of awkwardness in this conversation. There
was no delicate way to lead into "Mr. Groom, I've
been hired to murder you by five o'clock. Clean up
your act, square with *him*, leave town, whatever."
He'd assumed by now that he would have delivered
the warning and be off the phone. But he was still
listening to squeaks.

Groom's voice boomed at him. "Excuse me, Mr.

er . . ., you were saying something about a new
quota. I really—"

"Mr. Groom, I've been hired to—"

"Right, Taffy, get that mailing ready this morning." Maddis Groom's hand was only partly over the
receiver. "Yeah, I want to see it before it goes out.
And call Burns; tell him I'll be late for lunch."

A whoosh of noise smacked Mullin's ear.

"Now about the dues quota," Groom said, "I can't
see why—"

"Mr. Groom, I've been hired to murder you."

Mullin waited for a gasp. A denial. A threat. It was
a moment before he realized Groom's hand was back
over the receiver and he was saying something
about Guaymas.

Mullin's face was red; he could tell. Sweat was
running down his brow, his neck, his back. "Groom,"
he shouted, "I'm going to murder you. Murder!
Today! You hear me?"

But Mullin, the murderer, was on hold.

In the old days Mullin had learned everything
about his marks' movements but nothing about *them*.
He didn't want to know. He didn't watch the news
of their deaths or read about their funerals. But now,
since he was sticking his neck out to let this mark
live, he was tempted. And just in case Groom didn't
understand how grateful he should be, it would be
good to know how to get to him, socially and eco-
nomically speaking.

He paged through the phone book to find the library reference desk. Sure, call them and leave his
phone number on their records? No. He'd drive
over . . .

He groaned. Driving was like smoking: no matter how long you'd been clean, in your gut you were never a non-driver. So, okay, he could *walk* to Mission Street, wait for the bus to Market Street, transfer to a streetcar . . . Or he could walk to Twenty-fourth Street and take BART and hope there were no delays underground. Or he . . .

Forget the library. It was already quarter to twelve.

He'd just go across town to Pacific Heights and deal with Groom.

Well, not just . . . If he took the bus to Market and changed . . .

Hell, he'd splurge on a cab. He hiked up to Market and Sanchez and scanned the street. No cabs. He tried around Castro and Market. One cab, grabbed by a guy with suit and briefcase. Mullin waited. He had to watch his pennies now; cabs were a luxury of the past. After all, there was no Hit Men's Benevolent League, no group medical with riders for gunshot wounds, no disability coverage for those nasty mishaps so common to careless bombers. No Old Hit Men's Home He couldn't look forward to evenings in a rocker replaying the year's greatest hits.

It wasn't as if he was going to get paid for this job that he wasn't going to do.

He paced to the corner, checking in all directions. Buses passed, trolleys passed, and streetcars, pedicabs, motorcycles, bicycles, and a lone unicycle. No taxis.

He spotted the bus to Pacific Heights on the far side of Market—getting ready to pull out. The light was against him. But the wait for the next one would be— what—half an hour? He raced into traffic, hand thrust out as if those few inches of pallid flesh would halt thousands of pounds of station wagon. He squirted between cars. A Muni bus swerved precariously. "Fucking asshole!" the driver yelled at him and suggested an alternate destination. Mullin bounded heavily across the tracks, relieved that no trolleys were near, and into the traffic. A brown truck screeched to a halt. The driver shouted an epithet understandable in any language. Ahead, the bus belched smoke and gave an uphill lurch like a fat guy's first try out of the chair. Mullin ran faster, arms waving. He clambered onto the bus and rooted through his pockets, shooting change across the floor. Thank God he'd decided not to do the hit. If he had, it wouldn't be dimes rolling under seats, it'd be bullets.

He got off at Pacific and walked three blocks. The Groom house was on the Bay side of the street, with a view to kill for.

From habit, he stood across the street to get his bearings.

The Groom garage door opened. A shiny, expensive black car oozed out. Once he'd have known if it was a Mercedes, a Jaguar, a Maserati. Now they all looked the same, archaeological artifacts of a long-dead life. Now the only way he'd be connected to one of them would be in a hit-and-run. Just the idea of being compressed behind the wheel, squeezed in by the closing door, turned his stomach sour. He shook off the thought. But there would be other ways to enjoy Mr. Groom's gratitude.

He shook off that thought, too. In less than five hours someone else would be after Maddis Groom, and *him,* and the only reward he'd get would be eternal.

He waved his arms as Maddis Groom backed out across traffic. Straight at him. He threw up his hands in warning. The car kept coming at him. He leapt to the right. The bumper skimmed his jacket. His arm was still raised. Groom waved absently.

Mullin started after the car, half running, half staggering. A car pulled up next to him. A cab, he thought in the hopeful instant before he turned his head. On a scale of one to ten the cab would have been a ten. "One," he muttered under his breath as he took in the black-and-white.

"You looking for trouble, buddy?"

Mullin forced a sticky smile. "No, sir, officer." I don't have to *look.*

He was panting by the time he got to a phone at Van Ness Avenue. The chill wind iced his face. A big reward, that's what Groom better come up with. Huge. The man could have killed him! And him still trying to help out. He dialed Groom's cell phone and stuck his head into the nook to mute the roar of traffic.

"Yes?"

"Mr. Groom, I called you this morning. I said I was calling about the news photo."

"You hung up."

"You left me on hold."

"Mr. er— I am a busy man. I'm already late for a lunch. I don't have time to discuss risotto."

"This won't take long. I just want you to know that I was hired—"

"Hang on, I've got a call through."

"—to kill you!" He would have shouted, if his quarter's worth of time hadn't run out. When he dialed back he couldn't get through. He looked at his watch: 12:30 P.M. He couldn't hang around the phone here all afternoon, watching the fog grow thicker, the wind whip faster, the chilly sands of his life run out.

Guaymas, he thought. Maybe Groom was flying out this afternoon. Then they'd both be saved, for a while at least. A miracle, his sainted mother would say. He looked down and saw another miracle: a phone book, still hanging under the phone nook. It was a moment before Mullin realized that in his miraculous awe he'd looked up Guaymas, rather than an airline.

But Guaymas was there. A restaurant!

Groom wasn't skipping the country. The man was just going to lunch. At Guaymas. In Tiburon.

Tiburon! The suburbs!

Tiburon. There was a bay between San Francisco and Tiburon. Did buses run there? Did they arrive the same day? The whole thing was impossible. Maybe he could call back the connected tough, tell him . . .

The ferry—he'd forgotten the ferry. Through the fog he spotted a cab across the street. A nun was getting in. He shoved her out of the way. "Ferry, and step on it!" he said.

The driver grinned, shot forward, whizzed right, flew left, slammed to a halt at a stop sign and shot forward again. Mullin's fingers overshot his forehead and shoulders as he tried to make the sign of the cross. Won't help, he muttered to himself, not after the nun. When the cab hung a U across four lanes and screeched to a stop an inch behind a cement truck, Mullin's feet were wedged against the front seat, his hands clinging to window and seat, his eyes stuck shut. He flipped the cabbie a ten.

"Hey! Is that all! For a Grand Prix ride . . ."

But Mullin was out of the cab and trying to get through the crowd in front of the ticket hut.

"Cheapskate!"

Mullin ignored the cabbie. He had bigger problems than pique. He'd forgotten it was summer—an easy thing to do on a typical cold, foggy July San Francisco day. But the tourists hadn't. Pairs of pale, shivering legs stuck out of Bermuda shorts, two in front of two, sometimes two beside two, in a line half a block long—enough to fill the ferry six times.

Mullin raced to the front, pulled an extra twenty out of his wallet. His hand was extended, palm still closed, when he eyed the tourists more carefully. Leather jackets, gold jewelry. A twenty wasn't going to buy their place in line.

He stepped in front of the woman. "Excuse me, ma'am. I'm sorry. Please excuse me. My wife— I just got the call. Hospital. I have to get home." He sounded upset, desperate. He *was* upset, desperate.

"Of course, of course. Go right ahead," the man said.

"Poor man," his wife added.

Mullin flushed, thrust the twenty at the ticket seller and grabbed the ticket. As he stood waiting for the change, he could see the tourist couple exchanging glances. He grabbed the bills, stuffed them into his pocket, and edged back when the man spoke. "Look, we've got friends picking us up in Tiburon. We can take you to the hospital."

"No, no." The panic in Mullin's voice was very effective. "I can manage."

"It'll be no problem," the wife insisted.

"No, really. I'll call a cab from the boat."

"We insist. *Anything we can do.*"

Corner Maddis Groom in the restaurant and make him listen to me, can you do that? "Sarcasm never helps, Cornelius," his sainted mother had said. "Use your brain to think, Cornelius." He pulled himself together and adopted his most solemn expression. "Thank you. You're too kind. Now you won't think the worse of me if I take the time on the boat to prepare myself for the ordeal—alone? I'll just ride on the upper deck."

They understood, of course. They were so sorry. They pulled their jackets tighter around them and shivered in the summer fog.

Mullin was sorry, too. If he'd used his brain to think, he would have sent them to the top level and stayed on the bottom himself where he could make a quick exit. Now he'd have to figure out how to scoot around them.

But he'd have the twenty minutes on the ferry to do that. Twenty minutes to figure his approach to Maddis Groom in the restaurant. How to get to him, cut him loose of whoever he was meeting? Mullin wasn't so shabby as to be denied service, but no one would mistake him for Groom's peer. He looked, he had to admit, like a bill collector, a skip tracer, an aging ex-hit man who got his sartorial taste when he was hanging around with hoods back East.

So how to make sure he got Groom's full attention—enough so he'd take measures, but not so much that his lunch friends would remember Mullin in the restaurant, in case he failed to convince Groom, and *he* sent in the messy guy to do him? And to do Mullin.

Mullin shivered in the wintry gust. In his mind his

sainted mother whispered, "Spot your opportunity, Cornelius. Find the ray of sun in the clouds."

Mullin stood, his back toward the tourist couple, his face drawn in worry, watching the ferry angle into the slip. The last San Francisco–bound passengers were barely off when he hurried on and bounded to the stairs.

Even in port the wind whipped his hair. The tourists would think he was crazy to be up here. No one but a loon would choose to face the icy fog when he could be in the warm saloon having a glass of Chardonnay.

Surely, no one.

But there were footsteps on the stairs.

The boat lurched away from the dock.

Mullin turned and stared into the face of the first good fortune of his day. Emerging at the top of the stairs was Maddis Groom.

It was all Mullin could do to keep from racing over and yelling, "Eureka!" Maybe his mother did have an in with the saints. Twenty minutes alone with Groom! Surreptitiously he eyed the mark. The man's news photo was a miracle in itself. The real Groom was not impressively barrel-chested, he was more like a barrel on sticks. Groom veered to the far side of the boat and rested his gut on the side rail.

Mullin waited till the ferry was out of port. Alcatraz was a foggy blur on the left, Angel Island ahead on the right, Tiburon straight on. He strolled across the deck and stood beside Groom, as if both of them were fascinated by the water passing alongside the boat. "Mr. Groom."

Groom glared. "Who are you?"

"I called you twice today, said it was about the news photo."

"Oh, the *news photo*." Groom was fingering something in his breast pocket.

Automatically Mullin moved into defense mode. He shot a glance around. No cover. And himself totally unarmed. Maybe *he* had heard about Mullin. Maybe *he'd* hired Groom to . . .

"I'm a busy man," Groom said, not even looking toward Mullin. "It's almost one o'clock. If I don't reach him by one, my lawyer's going to be gone for the weekend." His hand came out of his pocket. In it was a cell phone.

Mullin sighed deeply. It was a moment before he refocused on the real threat. He grabbed Groom's arm. "Groom," he shouted over the wind, "I've been hired—"

"You've been *fired*? Then why are you hounding me about the newspaper?" He punched in a phone number.

"I've been hired—h-i-r-e-d—hired, employed, commissioned," he screamed, "to kill—"

"I know you're grilling me!" Groom's ear was to the phone.

Mullin took a deep breath, thought of his sainted mother, and waited to see that ray of light so well hidden behind the clouds.

Groom shouted into the phone, "Yes, it's about the divorce."

The clouds opened, sunshine shot down on a grateful Mrs. Groom.

Mullin lifted up her husband's sticklike legs and tossed him into the Bay.

They Only Kill Their Asters

Deborah Adams

"Wait a minute." I stopped Maline at the back porch steps, just before we entered Freda's house. "They say the killer always returns to the scene of the crime. Maybe I should've brought along an extra glass to steady my nerves—just in case he's still in there."

"Oh, good grief, Sheila!" Maline tucked her pencil behind her ear and clutched the ever-present steno book to her scrawny bosom. "Can't you go five minutes? You've been drinking all afternoon."

"I am distraught," I reminded her.

It was just like Maline to be so insensitive to my grief. She'd probably never had a best friend, and she'd certainly never lost one at the hands of a brutal killer. I was still reeling from the trauma, having been the one to find Freda's body, right in her own backyard. The police told me she'd been coshed by a blunt object, which wasn't terribly enlightening. Any fool could have deduced that from seeing the mess her head was in.

Later we learned from the medical examiner's official report that the injury was consistent with a blow from a shovel. I knew for a solid fact that Freda had never owned such an item. What's more, I'd given the police a list as long as my arm of people who had whole collections of shovels. The officer I talked to didn't write down a word I said—not after I explained the motives that surely tied the shovel owners to Freda's death. Deep in my heart I knew the investigation would turn up nothing if the police failed to follow up on my leads. I would have to call them in a few days and offer my help again.

For the moment, though, I was absorbed by the mission at hand.

"The way that woman kept house," Maline said with disgust, "we'll never find it." Maline is obsessive-compulsive, if you ask me. Always invoking *Robert's Rules of Order* at our otherwise friendly meetings of the Brown Plant Society. She only joined because she wanted desperately to be a member of something and the Garden Club blackballed her when it was revealed that she'd forgotten to dig up her dahlia bulbs one winter.

Membership requirements for the society are considerably less stringent. We welcome anyone who professes dedication to the eradication of inherently evil, oxygen-sucking, people-enslaving plant life so prized by the likes of Denise Pemberton and Harve Landsdown, president and vice president, respectively, of the North Side Garden Club. It was poor deceased Freda who started the Brown Plant Society and who led the drive for vegetation scale-down and free-range dandelion preservation. Now my cherished friend was on her way to a relentlessly grassy plot in Everlasting Meadows. Just thinking about her covered over by zoysia sent a chill through me, but I fought it off with a warm, soothing gulp of my Jack Daniel's.

"We must remember to suggest charitable donations in lieu of flowers," I said as we climbed the porch steps. "The final irony would be lush green plant life surrounding her."

"That's really up to her family," Maline said shortly. "But as president of the BPS, I suppose I ought to—"

"Whoa!" I held up a hand to stop her right there. "Who died and—I mean, who named you president?"

"Well, I have been vice president for the past three years," she reminded me haughtily, as if this proved something.

She'd been vice president because she'd appointed herself, I could have said. What's more, Maline had been trying all along to take over, but fortunately we don't hold elections in the BPS.

"Who's to say," I began, "that Freda won't continue to lead our happy group from the Great Beyond? For that matter, why do we even need a leader? Surely we're capable of ignoring yards and neglecting shrubbery without being told how to do it." It was an eminently practical solution, I felt, but one with which Maline was sure to take exception.

"Someone has to take charge of The Project," she pointed out.

It had been Freda's most inspired idea, one that would surely have put grubs in the pants of Denise Pemberton and her nitrogen-loving groupies. "Cement!" Freda had proclaimed at our last meeting. Which, like all the others, had broken out spontaneously during an extended cocktail party. "We'll have our yards converted to giant parking lots! Concrete surfaces all through the subdivision!"

The idea had come to her about midway of the meeting, by which time I was feeling the warm, fuzzy glow of camaraderie. "You besha!" I agreed. "Concrete. A toush of big-city atmosphere in the shu-burbs!" And then I proposed a toast to Freda, which brought a modest blush to her cheeks. It was her finest hour.

Remembering brought a tear to my eye. I slugged a gulp of Jack to steady my nerves, then reached into my pocket for the door key. "Let's get this over with," I said sharply.

Maline had spent the better part of the afternoon whining about how Freda's death affected The Project. I didn't see why we couldn't go on as scheduled, but she picked, picked, picked at the details. "If you'd been half sober when we discussed it," she said, "you would remember that we're getting a spe-cial discount for the five yards. If only four of us have the cement, the price goes up and becomes pro-hibitive for some."

Of course, we could have let the cement trucks roll—it was possible, wasn't it, that Freda's heirs would be every bit as enamored of a concrete lawn as the rest of us were?—but Maline positively in-sisted that we call the cement people, explain our situation, and renegotiate the deal. And since The Project was due to begin in two days' time and Freda had been our contact person, Maline had demanded that we snoop through Freda's house, find the name of the company she'd hired, and call as soon as it opened the next morning.

Maline sneaked a look over the redwood fence as we stepped inside Freda's house. "Can you see Harve anywhere?" she whispered. "We don't want him to spot us."

"Why're you whispering?" I demanded loudly.

Maline shushed me with a finger over her skinny lips. "For all we know, he could be the one who killed Freda."

I glanced across the fence at Harve's immaculate side yard. "That's ridiculous. I know he was mad about the RoundUp incident, but he wouldn't kill because of a little dead grass."

"That man's a fanatic," Maline reminded me. "And besides, Freda took out half his yard with that one."

"It was years ago. I'm sure he's over it," I said coolly, but my confidence ran no deeper than the azalea roots Harve had lost in the same attack.

"I've always suspected him of putting those CON-DEMNED signs on our houses," she mused.

The other members of the BPS had been up in arms about that, but I'd been amused. In fact, I still had the sign tacked to my front door. I figured it could only help when the tax assessor came around.

There was something else that amused me, too, but I wasn't going to share it with Maline. I knew that Harve's anger had recently given way to admiration and respect. Not a week before, I'd dropped by Freda's place unexpectedly one night to borrow olives and found her sitting at her kitchen table in deep conversation with Harve.

Naturally I pretended there was nothing unusual about this, even though the tension in that room was so thick it could've choked kudzu. Harve made a hasty exit without so much as an excuse, and Freda dove headfirst into her cupboard, ostensibly in search of the olives I'd come for.

"You don't have to carry on so," I said noncha-lantly. "It's perfectly fine to be friendly with your neighbor. Just don't let Denise Pemberton catch you at it."

It was no secret that Denise had lusted after Harve's gardening skills for years. Rumor had it she'd used her position as president of the Garden Club to have Harve named Garden Designer of the Year. I'd meant to lighten the room with my cynical observation, but the plan backfired on me.

"Now, you know it's nothing like that," Freda said. She jumped back from the cupboard and turned to face me, but her eyes just couldn't seem to meet mine.

"Freda, you've never been much of a liar. Now tell me what's going on between you and Harve."

She fidgeted and twitched, but I stood my ground, making it clear to her that I wouldn't leave without an explanation. When the story trickled out, it was stranger than I had imagined, even bordering on the bizarre. Always a good combination, in my opinion, as life is too often predictable and dull.

"Harve is thinking of converting," she said.

"You mean he's joining us?" I sank into the nearest chair and fanned myself with Freda's plastic place mat. "Gads! Won't that twist Denise's branches? Give me a drink and tell me how you managed this!"

So Freda had related a lively tale of her secretive efforts over the past weeks. She'd started by taking Harve an icy cold drink one day when he was sweating over his thatch buildup. Another time she thoughtfully shared with him a magazine article about common but deadly plants. Slowly, deviously, she dug into his entrenched beliefs about horticulture. Finally her efforts were paying off; she was on the verge of actually deprogramming a Garden Club victim when her life was snatched away.

I pushed open the door and faced Freda's house, with its hollow, empty rooms. I knew it was only my imagination; nothing had been removed from the house. Except her spirit, I remembered, and felt a cramp in my chest.

My drink was nearly gone, so—first things first— I dug around under Freda's sink, hoping to find a few drops in the bottle she kept there. "Look on the bulletin board by the phone," I directed Maline.

"I am looking," she sniped. "There's everything except what we need."

I hadn't found anything useful under the sink either, so I polished off the liquid in my glass and joined the search. "It may not be a written estimate," I said as I rummaged through Freda's junk drawer. "Could be she jotted down the name and number on a scrap of paper. Just watch for anything that seems likely."

Maline's little huff of disapproval didn't escape me, but I was willing to let it go. Bickering would only delay us, and I wanted to complete our mission as quickly as possible so I could get home to my comfortable chair and a cool drink.

"I know," I said. "She probably called from the bedroom phone. Freda liked a plump pillow behind her when she talked. I'll see if the number's in there."

Maline's nasal twang echoed down the hall behind me. "How can anybody live like this? No system of organization, phone calls in her pajamas . . ."

Why didn't someone thwack Maline over the head, I wondered. I'd have done it myself, right then, but the sight of Freda's bedroom distracted me. She had nested in that room, bringing in a phone and a television, a dozen pillows for propping herself into the best position for whatever activity took her fancy—reading, napping, snacking. She'd even gotten one of those Clapper gizmos, so she wouldn't have to reach all the way over to the bedside table to turn off her light.

People like Maline thought that meant Freda was a lazy woman, but they couldn't have been more wrong. Freda kept busy; she just didn't waste time and energy on endless tasks like dusting and bedmaking. Instead she used every minute of her life to enjoy what she loved—like chats with friends and needlework and planning terrorist attacks on the Garden Club.

I moved to the phone, which was half buried under a pile of junk mail (reading it had been one of Freda's favorite pastimes), and, sure enough, stuck underneath was a paper towel with "Joe's Surfaces" and a phone number scribbled on it. I folded the towel into a neat square and silently promised Freda that the BPS would carry on the fight she'd begun.

Then I indulged in a moment of sweet sorrow. The crumpled bedsheets smelled like Freda's favorite cologne, and the crazy quilt was a loving reflection of her colorful personality. A basket of knitting sat on one of the pillows and beneath it was an oversize book—*Rose Diseases and Their Treatment.* A half-empty Whitman's Sampler rested atop the comforter. Freda was everywhere in that room, and in my heart.

"Did you have any luck?" Maline stuck her pointy nose into the room but was obviously reluctant to go any farther. I didn't believe for one minute she was

afraid of encountering Freda's ghost. Oh, no. Maline
was just horribly averse to clutter.

"Got it right here," I said, holding up the paper
towel. "And that's not all. Let's go talk to Harve."

Night had fallen with a thud while we were rum-
maging in Freda's house, but you'd never have noticed it from Harve's backyard. Outdoor lights
accented his night garden and fish pool and illumi-
nated half the neighborhood. His neighbor on the
other side, Denise Pemberton, took advantage of that
to spy on the subdivision after dark. Maline sputtered along behind me as we entered through the
gate on Freda's side of his property. Harve was a
nut about garden gates—he even had a freestanding
one in the middle of the yard.

He was out there on his hands and knees, mulching
an asparagus bed. He jumped to his feet and faced
me, startled and nervous. Guilty conscience, no
doubt.

"I've got your green thumb in a vise!" I shouted.

"What's this all about?" Harve wiped his hands
on his shirt, looking for all the world like a poorly
cast Lady Macbeth. "What do you want out here?"

I gave him my steeliest gaze. "You know why I'm
here, Harve. I am the spirit of vengeance. I am the
voice of justice."

"You are drunk, as usual," Maline muttered under
her breath.

I'd been about to raise my arms over my head,
hoping to suggest that the avenging sword of truth
might suddenly appear in my hands, dripping the
blood of saints.

For a moment I believed I really had invoked

something from the celestial courts, but that eerie sound turned out to be just the creaking of one of Harve's gates as Denise Pemberton opened it.

"What are you doing out here, Harve?" Denise patted her steel-wool hair into place. The scent of Aqua Net wafted through the air, overriding the night bloomers. She pretended that Maline and I weren't there, and after so many years of ignoring us, she was almost good enough at it to keep her eyes from twitching in our direction.

"Sheila's having one of her spells." Harve turned to face me, looking about as petulant as a grown man can look. "Now what was it you wanted?"

"I want your shovel, Harve. The one you used to kill poor Freda. And don't get any nasty ideas, either, because there's more of us than of you. I expect even Denise would break the feud and take our side if you try anything, although I'd feel more confident of that if you'd killed one of her precious peonies instead of my best friend in the world." My voice broke up a little there at the end, and I felt tears welling up in my eyes.

"Well, if that isn't the most ridiculous!" Denise zipped right over to Harve's side and slipped her arm through his. "You don't have to put up with this, Harve. You go on back in the house and I'll handle these crazy women!"

Harve shook himself loose and took a step toward me. "How'd you come up with that crazy notion?"

Maline, needless to say, was cowering behind me, mortally afraid that Harve might snap her up like a Venus flytrap gobbles bugs.

"Yes, how?" Denise demanded. "Why, Harve

could sue you for slander! I think he should, too!"
She was on him again, like aphids on spring leaves.

"That's just one more of Sheila's nutty ideas. Truth
is, Freda and I had gotten friendly lately." Harve
crossed his beefy arms over his chest, daring me to
deny it.

Denise meanwhile was chewing on her bottom lip
as she tried to figure out how to respond to Harve's
revelation. I enjoyed watching her artless flirtation.
Wasn't she in for a surprise when the truth came out?

"Freda told me how friendly y'all had gotten," I
said. "I know all about your plans to defect. You
were set to dump the Garden Club for a better, more
natural way of life."

Harve's eyes bugged out and Denise's mouth
dropped open. They were peas in a pod, those two.
Never could control their emotions. Guilt was as
plain as fungus on Harve's face, and Denise—well,
she was just plain confused.

"But then you chickened out, didn't you, Harve?
After Freda worked so hard to convert you, you be-
trayed her trust. She was planning her revenge,
Harve. Did you know she was studying up on rose
diseases, with a mind to spread some spores around
your floribundas? Is that why you killed her, Harve?
Or was it because you knew she would spread the
word about your near-defection and get you kicked
out of the carnation cult?"

At first I thought he was roaring with rage, and I
heard the pitter-patter of Maline's little feet as she
skittered away in terror. I hoped she'd have the good
sense to call 911, but I wasn't counting on it. I wasn't
feeling so brave myself all of a sudden—until I realized Harve wasn't roaring, but laughing. It was a

real booming laugh, too, that nearly shook the
ground beneath my feet. The sound of a man who is
solid and sturdy and knows how to have fun. Odd
that I'd never noticed that about him before.

Finally he pulled himself together and pointed
toward the back of the tool shed. "Look over there,"
he said and snorted.

"You first," I insisted.

Harve shrugged and led the way to a patch of
ground not four feet square. It was marked off with
those landscape timbers that all the Garden Club
members find so fetching, and in the middle was a
scrawny, near-leafless rosebush. It was about as ugly
and evil-looking a specimen as I'd ever seen, and it
reminded me of just why the BPS was a necessary
opponent to the rampant nurturing of insidious
green life.

"That's Freda's," Harve said. He leaned over and
pulled a brass marker out of the ground, holding it
up for my inspection. "I gave it to her just two weeks
ago. A little gift between neighbors."

In the bright yard light I could read it without
even squinting. It said FREDA'S GARDEN.

"Hmph," I said, unimpressed. "I don't believe
Freda even knew about this."

"I'm telling you, it's true. Look, Freda and I have
been getting along real well lately. Real well. She
wanted to mend the rift, try to bring peace to the
neighborhood. And this is how she planned to start."
Harve glanced sadly down at the scrawny little rose.

"Are you saying it was Freda who planned to go
over to the other side?" I didn't want to believe it,
but the story was too outlandish to be anything but

true. How could my very best friend have lied to me about something so important?

Harve nodded slowly. "That's why she was studying up on rose diseases. This little fella's got black spot. You should've seen Freda out here on her knees, plucking off the infected leaves as gently as a mother tending her babe."

I suddenly felt light-headed—probably because of dehydration—and my knees buckled under me. Fortunately Harve's reflexes were good, and he caught me before I hit the ground. I couldn't help but notice the aroma of pesticide that clung to his clothes. It was vaguely reminiscent of Hai Karate, a scent I've always found appealing.

"Sit down here and take it easy," he said, lowering me gently to the soft grass.

"Oh, don't worry about her," Denise sneered. "Just let her crawl back to that barren wasteland across the street where she can drown her sorrows."

"Now, Denise," Harve said. "This isn't the time to carry on with some silly feud. We should all be reminded of the fleeting nature of life. Surely we can find some common ground and sow the seeds of friendship."

"Harve Landsdown, don't you dare let this . . . this nematode get her suckers into you! It was bad enough when that clinging vine Freda tried to take you, but I did what I could to protect you from her. Men have to sow their wild oats. I know that, and Lord knows I have tried to be patient, but you are about to go too far. Don't you dare take Sheila's side against me."

It was the way Harve's night lights reflected in her eyes that made Denise look like a rabid animal. I know that. But I will always believe that someone or something higher—possibly even Freda's dear spirit—caused those lights to shine at just the right angle to show me the real gopher in the carrots.

"Denise," I said as I got to my feet with Harve's assistance, "maybe we'd better take a look at your shovel."

"Not without a search warrant!" I swear the woman hissed it like a snake before she ran off into the darkness.

She headed straight for her own tool shed, intent on destroying the evidence, but Harve caught up to her before she could dispose of the shovel. It was a simple matter for the police to match the blood traces and make an arrest. They hauled her downtown and interrogated her for an hour in that cold, windowless room, and at last Denise broke into tears and confessed to the murder of my oldest and dearest friend.

Right after Denise was formally charged, Harve called a joint meeting of both clubs. He was especially solicitous of me, knowing that my nerves were jangled by all that had happened. During the meeting we all agreed that, while our organizational rivalry had not been directly responsible for the terrible tragedy, it may have contributed to Denise's jealousy and hostility toward Freda. Maline took notes as we voted to form a committee to explore ways in which the Garden Club and the Brown Plant Society could develop greater tolerance for each other. I made the motion that the meeting come to a close, and Megan Blinkoff, Garden Club treasurer, seconded.

Afterward, when we were alone, Harve offered to share his gardening magazines with me, but I told him truthfully I'd rather have my own subscriptions. I spend several pleasant evenings every month tucked up in my favorite chair with a bracing drink in my hand, going through the catalogs page by page by page. With a black marker I carefully draw an X over every petal and blossom . . . and then I mail them to Denise in the state prison.

The Man Who Beat the System

Stuart M. Kaminsky

"You Fonesca?" the voice behind me said as I scooped at my regular-size chocolate-cherry Breeze at the Dairy Queen across the parking lot from my office-home. I have to stick with frozen yogurt because I have a lactose intolerance.

I felt like answering the voice that had interrupted my late breakfast with, "No, I can't Fonesca, but I can do a pretty mean tango when my life depends on it."

I didn't say anything. I was in a good mood. It was a typical summer morning in Sarasota. The sun was hot. The air was humid. The ultraviolet index, which I could never understand, was over ten, which meant that if you stepped out into it you'd probably die of skin cancer faster than you would of exposure in the middle of winter at the North Pole. I sat at one of those round white painted aluminum tables with a DQ umbrella. I had the *Sarasota Herald-Tribune* laid out in front of me.

The tourists were gone until winter, and I didn't regret having left Chicago two years earlier so that I could exchange winters for constant heat and humid-ity, afternoon thundershowers, and possible hurricanes.

I was content. I even had a bicycle, almost two hundred dollars in cash, and my combination office-living quarters—two rooms not much larger than the dressing rooms at Burdine's or Saks.

I didn't give the voice my smart-ass answer. Instead I paused, adjusted the blue Albany State College baseball cap that shaded my eyes and helped cover my rapidly balding head, and turned around.

I recognized him.

"I'm Fonesca," I said.

"Went to your office," he said, nodding toward the open seat across from me. "Note on the door said I could find you here."

I invited him to sit. After all he was a distinguished local gadfly, a member of the city council, and the only African American in the city or county government.

The Reverend Fernando Wilkens was in the newspaper and on the two local television news stations almost every day. Now that I had cable in my room—for which I was two months behind in payments—I was not only up on the international news, the national news and whether Scully and Mulder would catch the giant worm before it turned the town of Feeney, North Dakota, into a larder of zombies. I now also had the privilege of knowing almost nothing about local politics.

The Reverend Wilkens was a big man, running toward the chunky side, in tan slacks and a white pullover short-sleeve shirt with a little green alligator on the pocket. I was wearing my faded jeans and a Chicago Bulls T-shirt. He was about my age, forty-four. He had good teeth, smooth skin, an even smoother bass voice, and a winning smile, which he was not sporting at the moment.

"Breeze?" I asked.

"No, thank you," he said. "I have eaten, and my doctor says I should stay away from snacks. You recognize me?"

"I read the paper," I said, tapping at the Local section in front of me, which featured an article on the mysterious death of more manatees. Now a scientist was blaming red tide. Red tide seemed to roll in once a month and linger in the warm water and hot sun over the Gulf of Mexico, stinking up the beaches and killing fish. It gave the Local section reporters surefire stories and once in a while made the front page.

The doings of both the city council and the county board, on the other hand, made the front page only when there was a controversy so major that at least twenty citizens protested with marches and placards and complaints before the open hearings of the council or the board. Few people went to meetings on the lingering issue of the new city library location and branch location with any real hope of convincing the council or board that the new library would cut off parking downtown, cost seventeen million dollars, and have fewer books than the library that was about to be torn down and that the proposed branch would be too far from human life to make it usable. Few people, in the midst of their passion, when addressing the council for their allotted three or four minutes, even expected their elected officials to listen to them. Often members of the council in the middle of an impassioned speech by an ancient resident would pass notes on the latest College World Series scores.

All of this was on television for those who chose to watch, who were few.

"There's a council meeting tonight," the Reverend Wilkens said soft and deep as I dug deep into my breakfast while a couple of shirtless boys, with lean bodies and a desire to sacrifice themselves to the sun, ordered large Oreo-cookie Blizzards.

"I know," I said.

Reverend Wilkens nodded, taken aback only slightly that a citizen actually knew when there was to be a council meeting.

"There's going to be an open hearing about six items," he said. "The last one is where to put a new branch library."

I nodded, thinking I could see where this was going but not what I had to do with it.

"I want the new branch in or near Newtown," he said. "I want it to serve the African American community. It will be the last item on the agenda and probably won't come up till after midnight. I've got the feeling that a few of my fellow board members who have a much different site in mind will have lots to say on the earlier items, such as tearing up Clark Road again or replanting blighted trees on Palm Avenue. We'll listen to the public and then vote. The vote won't be subject to review unless there's a violation of the state or federal constitution."

I used to work for the state attorney's office in Cook County as a process server and investigator. One day I packed the little I owned in my car, called my landlord, called the office and quit over the phone, saying I'd let them know where to send my last check. I was still waiting for that check. My battered Toyota had barely got me from Chicago to Sarasota and away from the winter and an ex-wife whom I kept running into when she was with other men.

Newtown is the African American ghetto in Sarasota, running about four blocks or more in either direction north and south of Martin Luther King Jr. Street. The far south end of what could be called Newtown was within walking distance of downtown, where the new library with fewer books was going to go up. Members of the council, downtown business leaders, and community money people said the blacks could walk to the new library. The branch containing books would be out on the east side of town close to I-75, too far for any Newtown kid to walk and even six miles from my office behind the DQ. A pedal to the closest proposed branch would leave me looking like John Wayne in *Three Godfathers* when Ward Bond shoots his water bag and leaves him and his fellow robbers to wander in the desert.

I was about to say, "What's this got to do with me?" when Fernando Wilkens told me.

He leaned over and whispered,

"I've got the votes."

"The votes?"

"To get the library branch on Martin Luther King right on three-oh-one," he said. "Easy walk for my constituents. Easy drive for others."

There were five members of the city council. They took turns serving as mayor for two years, depending on seniority, the last time they served, when they were elected, and some computer math system beyond the comprehension of the Unabomber. Votes, sometimes involving contracts for millions of dollars, were decided by simple majority.

Maybe it was the way I slowly poked at the bottom of my Breeze searching for bits of chocolate clinging to the sides of the cup. Maybe my face is not as inscrutable as I like to think.

"This a privileged conversation?" he asked softly, though no one was listening. He looked around to see if we were being watched by anyone. Cars drove by, but on a day like this only out-of-work teens and the homeless wandered the streets of Sarasota.

"One question first," I said. "How did you find me?"

I'm not listed in the phone book either in the white pages or in the Yellow Pages. I don't know what I'd call myself anyway—asker of questions? researcher in obscure publications and mud that sometimes contained both animal and human snakes and gators?

"My lawyer, Fred Tyrell," he said.

I nodded. Tyrell was the token black in the downtown law firm of Cameron, Wyznicki, Forbes, and Littlefield. Tyrell's job was to take minority clients and even drum them up. Sometimes it worked. Sometimes even the most committed African American activists wanted a smart white lawyer, preferably a Jewish one. Cameron, Wyznicki, etc., had one of those too—Adam Katz. I had done work for both Katz and Tyrell. The partners had their own short list of investigators and process servers.

I nodded again, looked at my empty cup.

"You want another?" asked Wilkens.

I'm what is usually called medium height and probably seen as being on the thin side, but I pedal to the downtown Y every day, work out for at least an hour, and have grown hard in a town of white sand beaches and lazy hot days. I grew hard in my effort to stay away from my own tendency to turn into a vegetable.

"Patormi will vote with me," said Wilkens.

I nodded a third time. This was no surprise. Patormi was the closest thing we had to a liberal radical on the council. He was old and crusty, had moved down from Jersey thirty years ago, and would have gladly voted for Eugene Debs for governor if Debs had been alive and eligible. Sometimes the other council members kept certain issues to be addressed late in each session in the hope that Patormi would be too tired to protest or might even doze off. Patormi was too crafty an old Socialist to let that work. He sat with his thermos of black coffee, did crossword puzzles while he pretended to take notes, and waited for the big vote.

"Three votes," I reminded Wilkens.

The other three council members always voted in a block on money issues. They would debate furiously for hours whether they should approve an unbroken or broken yellow line down the middle of the recently widened Tuttle Avenue, and you'd never know how that one would go, but on expenditures they were closer together than the Statler Brothers.

"Zink," the Reverend Wilkens whispered, leaning even closer to me.

I thought delusions had set in on Wilkens and considered advising him to wear a hat and stay indoors.

I even considered inviting him across the parking lot to my barely air-conditioned office and living closet, but decided that whatever confidence he might have in me would evaporate with his first view of my professional headquarters.

"Zink is one of the solid three," I said.

Wilkens smiled. Nice teeth. Definitely capped.

"August Zink is dying," he said.

I was glad the prospect made him happy. He explained.

"Zink came to my office day before yesterday, told me. Said there was nothing they could do to him now and that he'd enjoy surprising the board by voting with me and Patormi. It would be a done deal."

"Still two questions," I said, pitching the empty cup toward the white-plastic-lined metal-mesh trash basket and sinking it for a solid two points. "First, what did Zink mean by saying there was nothing they could do to him now? Second, what do you need me for?"

"Zink wouldn't say much," said Wilkens, "but we were either talking past payoffs or things someone had on him for deals he might have made for his contracting business. Since Zink is up to his kneecaps in money, I'd say it was the contracting deals. We've got buildings in this town that crumble after a decade. Zink's company put up a lot of them, some of them public buildings. It doesn't cost him anything to meet his maker on the side of righteousness. Get him some good headlines and maybe a ticket to Heaven, though I think the Good Lord will look hard and long at the scales of this man's life before making a decision."

"And me?" I reminded him.

"Vote is tonight," he said tersely. "Zink is missing. I want you to find him, get him to that meeting so he can vote. If he doesn't show up, we deadlock. If

Zink dies, we have an election fast and I have no doubt that, given the constituency and the inclination of both parties, the new member will not vote with me and Patormi, who stands a good chance of being defeated in the next open election if he lives long enough to run."

"You don't risk losing?"

"I'll be the token everything with Patormi gone," said the Reverend Wilkens. "The token black, the token liberal, the token clergyman. I am the exception that supposedly proves fairness. Every hypocrite on the council and in the business community will support me."

"How do you know Zink is missing?"

"I called his office," said Wilkens. "He hasn't come in for four days. I called his home. His wife didn't want to talk, but she said Zink was out of town on a family emergency and she had no idea when he would be coming back. I called the police and they asked me what the crime was."

"You think he's in town?" I asked.

"I pray he's in town," said Wilkens, clasping his hands. "He led me to believe that he didn't have very much time and that even coming to the meeting tonight was against his doctor's recommendation."

"Let's say one hundred and twenty-five dollars plus the cost of a car rental," I said. "I'll take care of my own meals, since I live here. If I have to slip someone cash, I'll try to keep it below fifty and I'll bill you."

"That will be satisfactory," he said, holding out a large right hand.

We shook, and he immediately reached into his pocket and counted out six twenties and a five. He also handed me his card. On the back in dark ink was his home number.

"Receipt?" I asked.

"Under the circumstances, I would prefer a strictly cash business arrangement," he said, rising. "For a change, Patormi and I will stall on other issues on the agenda. Members of my congregation will also be present to speak out at the open forum. I would guess that we can keep the meeting going till at least midnight. I would also guess, if they truly don't know yet, that the solid two will want to wait for Zink, assuming he will vote with them."

"Unless they know about his illness and the fact that he is missing," I said.

"Precisely," said the Reverend Wilkens, shading his eyes and looking toward the sun almost overhead and then at his watch.

"You'd best begin," he said.

"I'd best," I agreed.

"Find him, Lewis," he said. "I'll pray for you to find him."

He got into a clean, dark green five- or six-year-old Geo Metro about a dozen yards away in the small parking lot and pulled away, waving at me.

This wasn't going to be easy, but it was a day's work and I had just pocketed one hundred and twenty-five dollars.

I went back to my office. For about five minutes, I sat at my desk thinking and watching the air conditioner in the window drip into the bucket. I listened to the ancient machine shudder and clank and do its best to keep almost reasonably cool air coming in. In the adjoining room, where I slept on a cot and had my small-screen Sony and cable, I usually turned on a fan I'd purchased at Walgreen's last winter when the prices were down.

Then I got up and changed into my usual work clothes, an old, only slightly frayed pair of navy blue slacks well ironed, a light blue short-sleeved shirt, and my black patent leather shoes with dark socks.

It took Eb Farrell less than ten minutes to get there after I called him. I was back in the chair behind my desk when, even over the clatter of the air conditioner, I heard his motor scooter come into the DQ lot and park below. I didn't hear him climb the metal stairs to the second floor or hear his footsteps approach my door. Eb Farrell was polite, seventy-three years ago born a child of polite, God-fearing Methodists in Texas, near the Oklahoma Panhandle. Eb knocked. I told him to come in.

Eb had once been close to rich and lost it all. He trailed the partner who had cheated him to Sarasota, where the partner had changed his name and grown even richer, a steel pillar of philanthropy and high society. I found Eb's partner, and the two of them, in spite of my attempts to reason or threaten them out of it, had an old-fashioned shoot-out on the beach in the park at the far south end of Lido Key. Eb was the better shot. The former partner took a bullet in the heart. Eb served eight months for having an unregistered weapon and engaging in a duel, a law that still existed in Florida. Eb's age and the evidence of what his former partner had done kept the sentence reasonably short.

Now Eb lived in Sarasota. He had a room with a bed and old record player in the back of Edwardo's Bar and TexMex Restaurant on Second Street. Eb's job was to keep the place from being broken into at night. He got the room and food but no salary. It didn't cost Eb much to live, but even though he shopped at Goodwill, the motor scooter needed gas, and once in a while a man needs a new toothbrush.

Eb came in standing tall and lean in jeans and a long-sleeved shirt. The jeans were worn white in patches but clean, and the shirt was a solid khaki that looked more than a little warm. On his head was the battered cowboy hat he had putt-putted into town with more than a year ago. Once Eb must have been close to six-six. I figured age had brought him down a few inches. Age seemed to be the only thing that could bring Eb Farrell down.

"Have a seat," I said.

Eb sat.

"How've you been?" I asked.

Eb's face was the color and texture of high-quality tan leather. His hair was clear, pure white and recently cut almost military short either by himself or one of the four-dollar old-time places still trying to compete with First Choice and the other new chains.

"Fine," said Eb.

"Got a job for you," I said.

"You said on the phone," he reminded me.

"I'm looking for August Zink, the councilman. Heard of him?"

"Heard," said Eb, taking off his hat and putting it on his lap the way his mother had taught him back when Hoover was president.

"I need to find him soon," I said. "Today. Can you ask some of your friends and see what you can come up with?"

Eb nodded.

I was sending him among the homeless, the afternoon barflies, and the other Sarasotans that tourists were usually kept away from.

Eb got up.

Eb had once been an electrical engineer. University of Texas graduate. That was a long time ago. I pulled out the cash I'd received from the Reverend Wilkens and handed Eb twenty-five dollars. He gave five back. I gave the five back to him again.

"This is a rush job," I said in explanation.

He nodded, accepted the five, and left.

A short bike ride from my place, I rented a sub-subcompact car, double-cheap, more than slightly used, from a place on Tamiami Trail where I got my usual deal. I left the bike in the closet inside the rental office, as usual.

Then I was on my way. First stop, Zink's contracting office. Downtown, high up in a fifteen-year-old, sixteen-story building that Zink had no hand in building. The receptionist was well groomed and in her forties, with a nice smile. She seemed like more than receptionist material when she deftly parried my lunging questions about Zink. I figured her for a mom who was just rejoining the workforce and starting at the bottom.

She finally agreed to talk to Mr. Zink's secretary, which she did while I listened. She handled it perfectly, saying a Mr. Fonesca wished to speak to her on a matter of some urgency regarding Mr. Zink and that Mr. Fonesca would provide no further information. There was a pause, during which I assumed Zink's secretary asked if I looked like a badly dressed 'toon or acted like a lunatic. The receptionist said, "No."

Two minutes later I was sitting in a chair next to

the desk of Mrs. Carla Free. Her desk in the gray-carpeted complex was directly outside of an office with a steel plate on the door marked AUGUST ZINK.

Mrs. Free was tall, probably a little younger than me, well groomed and blue-suited with a white blouse with a fluffy collar. She was pretty, wore glasses, and was black. Actually, she was a very light brown.

"I have to find Mr. Zink," I said.

"We haven't seen him in several days," she said, sounding like Bennington or Radcliffe, her hands folded on the desk in front of her, giving me her full attention. "Perhaps I could help you, or someone else in the office could?"

"Does he often disappear for days?" I asked.

Mrs. Free did not answer the question but said, "Can I help you, Mr. Fonesca?"

There was no one within hearing distance. Her voice sounded like all business and early dismissal for me. I decided to take a chance.

"Where do you live?" I asked.

She took off her glasses and looked at me, at first in surprise and then in anger.

"Is this love at first sight, Mr. Fonesca?" she asked.

"You don't live in Newtown," I said.

"No, I live in Idora Estates. My husband is a doctor, a pediatrician. We have a daughter in Pine View and a son who just graduated from Pine View and is going to go to Grinnell. Now, I think you should leave."

"I have reason to believe that if Mr. Zink goes to the city council meeting tonight, he will vote for a branch library in Newtown," I said.

I waited.

"Who are you working for?" she asked quietly.

"Someone who wants that branch library in Newtown," I said.

"I was born here," she said so softly that I could hardly hear her. "In Newtown. So was my husband. My mother still lives there. She won't move. I had a long bike ride to the Selby Library."

"Where is Zink?" I asked.

"Off the record, Mr. Fonesca," she said, "Mr. Zink is not well."

"Off the record, Mrs. Free," I said, "Mr. Zink is dying and you know it."

She nodded. She knew.

"You really think he'll vote for the Newtown location?" she asked.

"Good authority," I said. "A black man of the cloth."

She looked away. She understood. The sigh was long and said a lot—that she was risking her job, that she was about to give away things a secretary shouldn't give away.

"You've heard of Nils Anderson," she said.

"I've heard," I said.

"He has a large estate on Casey Key," she said. "High walls, a high iron gate. I believe strongly that Mr. Zink is there. Being 'tended to' in his illness by a close friend who happens to also own two large pieces of land near I-75, large pieces of land where the branch library site is proposed."

"He owns both possible sites?" I said.

"You can check it out in the tax office right down the street," she said. "Which would be more than the local media have done."

"Thanks," I said, getting up.

"No need," she said, doing the same and accompanying me down the hall. "I've told you nothing."

"Nothing," I agreed.

When we stood in front of the receptionist's desk, she shook my hand and she said, "I'm sorry I couldn't help you, Mr. Fonesca, but I will give Mr. Zink your name and number as soon as he returns."

This was hard and easy at the same time. I probably knew where Zink was, but getting him out might be a bit tough. I was not a wall climber, a particularly fast talker, or a good threatener. My skill was in getting people to talk and listening to them.

I drove to Zink's house. It was big, new, not on a Key, and facing the bay. I rang the doorbell and waited. In about a minute, the door opened and I found myself facing the elusive Mrs. Zink. Mr. Zink had done his best to make excuses for the absence of his wife at social and public functions over the years. She was ill or she was touring Europe or visiting one of her brothers or sisters in Alaska, Montana, California, or Vermont. The Zinks had no children.

Mrs. Zink was hefty, in her sixties, dressed in a black silver-studded skirt and vest over a blue denim shirt. She wore boots and looked as if she were on her way to do some line dancing. She was a barrel of a woman, with too much makeup, large earrings, and the distinctly vacant look of the heavy drinker. Even through the heavy perfume, there was a smell of scotch, probably good scotch. I understood that she was known to hold her alcohol well, but once in a while there was a scotch overdose and the well-rounded Mrs. Zink turned honest and foul-mouthed.

"Who're you?" she asked.

"Lew Fonesca," I said. "I need to find your husband."

"I don't know where Gus is," she said.

"I do," I answered.

She looked me up and down.

"I know where he is and I know a lot more," I said. "I'd like to keep it all quiet."

"Blackmail, Fonesca?" she said.

"No," I answered. "I've got a client. I'm poor but honest."

"No crap," she said. "No self-respectin' black-mailer'd be caught parboiled in that sorry-ass pair of pants and cracked leather shoes that should have been retired three seasons back. Come on in and have a drink."

I stepped in and she shut the door. The floors were smooth, expensive tile. The place was furnished ersatz Western.

"How you like it, Fonesca?" she asked, leading me to a living room with a view of the back and furniture that looked as if it belonged on the set of a Clint Eastwood Western. Wood, old brown leather, a rough-hewn table made from a thick slice of redwood, and animal skins for rugs. Two paintings on the wall looked like (and probably were) authentic Remingtons—galloping cowboys, Indians riding bareback.

"Western," I said.

"I mean your drink," said Mrs. Zink.

"Beer would be fine, Mrs. Zink," I said.

"That's not a drink," she said. "You can call me Flo. If you're stayin', you're drinkin'."

"I'm drinking," I said.

"That's better," she said. "I'm a flush lush and I

don't like being cooped up and I don't like drinkin' alone."

She mixed drinks. I don't know what was in them. When she handed me mine, I sipped at it. It burned going down and tasted like molten plastic. She downed hers in two quick gulps and a satisfied smile.

She poured herself another, and I showed her that mine was barely touched. She shrugged and pointed to a leather chair with arms made from the antlers of something from the far north. She sat opposite me and went slowly on the second drink.

"Flo," I began, "I've got to find your husband."

"Out of town, business. Urgent," she said, working at her drink and glancing at mine.

"He told you he had to go out of town?" I said. "In person?"

"No," she said. "The usual way. On the answering machine from wherever he was."

"Didn't give you a number or address?" I asked.

"Hell, I don't even know what country he's in," she said. "Hey, didn't you say you know where he is and a lot more?"

"Do you know Nils Anderson?" I asked.

She paused in mid-sip, lowered her glass, and looked at me with her head bird-tilted.

"What's this got to do with that crooked piss-head?" she asked.

"I've got good reason to believe that your husband is at Anderson's house."

"What the hell for? He and Anderson are . . . Why would Gus go to Anderson's when . . ."

"When he's sick?" I asked.

Her eyes were moist now. She blinked them, blew out air, and took another drink.

"You know?" she asked.

"Your husband is very sick," I said.

"Shit, he's a dead rider on a dead horse," she said. "We've been up and down and had some good rides and made lots of money till we moved here and he wanted respectability. Wanted to be king of the city, meet movie stars who have houses on the Keys, and have his picture in the papers. I wouldn't change. Zink's wife's a lush and a little loony, with a foul mouth to go with it. Bunch of assholes and hypocrites. But you know what hurts, Fonsca?"

"Fonesca," I corrected.

"He never cheated on me that I know," she went on, talking to a spot somewhere a dozen yards from me where an overstuffed chair sat high and heavy with the indentation of a human behind. "He gave me what he thought I wanted and left me out as much because I wanted to be left out as he wanted me to be. I love Gus and, I'll be goddamned, the old fart loves me, always has."

"And so?" I prompted when she went silent.

"Gus is too sick to take business trips, and I'm for damn sure he'd want to spend his last days with me," she said. "He told me."

"Flo," I said, "I think we can help each other. I want your husband to be at the city council meeting tonight. There's an important vote and . . ."

"You're one of them," she said with a sigh.

"One of . . . No, your husband promised someone very reliable that he was going to vote to put the branch library in Newtown."

"Gus?" she said.

"Yes," I said.

"Gonna buy his way into heaven with a last good deed," she said. "He thinks God is one of those num-nutz he's been conning for half a century. What you want me to do?"

"Call Anderson. Ask to speak to your husband. Tell him you want to come with a friend and get him."

She nodded, pursed her lips, and reached for the portable phone on the table. She opened a black phone and address book and dialed.

"Mitzi," she said amiably, "how are you? . . . That's good. Nils? . . . Pleased to hear it. Now let's cut the crap and put Gus on the phone . . . Bullshit. He's there."

Long pause and then, "Anderson, you son of a bitch, I want to talk to Gus, now."

Flo looked at me, burning red and ready to explode, while she listened to what Anderson was saying.

"We'll see what the police say," she said and hung up.

She looked at me and said, "If I smoked, I'd be smoking now."

Instead, she got up, topped off her drink, and said, "He's there. That gas-station-toilet-bowl Anderson says Gus doesn't want to talk to me or see me, that he wants to convalesce away from my vulgarity and drinking. Lew, Gus likes me vulgar. He respects me and he knows I love him. He's not convalescing. He's dying."

"The police won't help," I said. "Anderson's probably got a doctor with a big check who'll confirm that your husband can't be seen today and if they let you see him, they'll be sure he's asleep and will promise to have him call you tomorrow. Tomorrow is too late."

I reached for the phone and dialed one of the few numbers I knew in Sarasota. I called Edwardo's.

"Eddie? Lew Fonesca. You seen Eb? He is? Thanks. Eb?"

"He's at the house of a fella named Anderson," Eb said.

"I know. What I need is someone who knows how to get into a house, a big house with walls and maybe dogs and a guard or two."

"Wait," said Eb and put the phone down.

Flo stood looking down at me, her hands clasped tight. Eb came back in about two minutes.

"Got a fella right here—Snickers. Got one of them sweet teeth. Says he broke into the Anderson place two years back, doesn't want to talk about it. Says he'll get you in and out if the price is right."

I put my hand over the speaker and asked Flo Zink what she'd pay to have Gus back.

"Name a price," she said.

"Five thousand," I said.

"Hell, I've got that and a hell of a lot more in our safe," she said.

"Five hundred," I told Eb.

Eb left again and a nervous voice came on the phone.

"A cash thousand," Snickers said.

"Deal," I said. "Meet me across the street from Anderson's gate at eleven tonight. Don't be late. Cash comes half when you get there, half when we get out."

"Fair," Snickers said and hung up.

"What about the five thousand?" Flo asked.

"I've been dealing with the world of Snickers for a long time," I said. "He'd smell a big deal if we offered him five. He'd ask for ten. We give him ten and he feels he has to brag to his friends over whatever they put into their bodies. One of his friends tells . . ."

"I get it," she said.

She looked around and went for another drink.

I called the Reverend Fernando Wilkens and spoke to three people before he came on.

"Yes?" he said hopefully.

"If things go right," I said, "I'll have August Zink at that meeting by midnight. Stall."

"Won't be that hard unless the others know the way Zink plans to vote. They want him there too."

"I'll have someone call and say Zink is being held up by a flat tire," I said.

"Bring him, Fonesca."

"I'm pumping as fast as I can," I said.

I had Flo call the mayor, one third of the solid three. The mayor was a woman. She was all business and thought that Democrats were a little lower than University of Florida graduates. The mayor was a proud grad of Florida State University. Only the people in Florida and those who followed college football knew that there was a difference.

"Beatrice?" Flo said, sounding remarkably sober. "This is Flo Zink. Just got a call from Gus. He told me to call you and say he's on his way, but he'll be very late for the meeting. He said to tell you he knows the vote is important and he'll be there if he has to hijack an eighteen-wheeler."

Flo hung up before the mayor could ask any questions.

"Gus did hijack an eighteen-wheeler when he was about twenty-two and we were first married," she said with a smile. "Gus and a friend. That load of camera equipment gave Gus his start toward respectability. 'Course if you ever tell anyone, I'll say you're lyin'."

I crossed my heart.

"You can have the four thousand you saved me," she said.

"If we get your husband out and he makes it to the council meeting to vote, I'll take it," I said.

I stood and we shook hands.

We drove back to my office to wait until eleven. Eb or Wilkens might call and I wanted to be there to get the message. When I had told her I had no liquor where I lived and worked, she nodded and brought her own bottle and glasses. She also got the five thousand out of a safe somewhere deep in the house where I didn't follow and brought it.

Flo didn't seem to notice the stale smell of my office, the clatter of my air conditioner, or the cursing of the kids in the DQ parking lot. She drank and talked. I learned the life history of Gus, Flo, Flo's mother, father, and sister, and what she thought of every president of the United States, starting with Woodrow Wilson with leaps back to Jefferson, Grant, and Teddy Roosevelt.

I watched the clock, and we left a little earlier than we had to. We were across from Nils Anderson's impressive iron gate and high brick wall a little before eleven. I didn't stop. I drove around the neighborhood and came back on the dot, at least according to my watch. There were no other cars on the street of big houses, all of which had driveways and large garages.

Then I heard Eb's motor scooter coming. It was like a call to the curious. When he stopped behind me and turned the bike off, I was sure we had only minutes before we would be surrounded by police.

Eb and a very thin, very small, very nervous black man wearing a pair of dark pants, a black T-shirt, and a battered fedora that would have been the envy of Indiana Jones stopped me before Flo and I could get out of the car.

"Snickers," said Eb.

I shook hands through the window, and Snickers waved to Flo, who reached over and handed him five hundred-dollar bills. He kissed each one, pocketed the quintet, and motioned for us to get out of the car.

"The trunk," he said.

We moved behind the car and I opened the trunk. Since the car was a rental, the trunk was empty.

Snickers pointed at Eb's scooter.

"Inside," he said, standing back and looking both ways down the street, constantly adjusting his battered fedora.

Eb, Flo, and I managed to get the scooter in the trunk. Half of it hung out. Eb had a bungee cord and expertly tied the scooter down.

"Back in the car," Snickers whispered.

We all got back in. From the back seat, leaning over my shoulder, Snickers, who could have used a healthy dose of Scope, guided me slowly to a driveway two estates over from the Anderson place.

"They ain't home," said Snickers. "Go right over

the lawn. Lights out. Park near the pool. Don't drive in. Cops won't look. Someone stays with the car. Back in front of Anderson's in fifteen minutes. Eb comes to back me up. Lady comes to tell me which guy we're pulling out."

"I think I . . ." I tried.

"Do it his way, Lew," said Eb.

I nodded, and the bizarre trio got out of the car and disappeared through a clump of bushes behind me. I sat watching the moonlight in the pool and checking my watch. Fifteen minutes took about three days. When the second hand made the call, I was around the house, Eb's scooter bouncing in the trunk, and then back across from Anderson's.

They weren't there. Suddenly the back door of my car opened and I turned around.

"What took you?" asked Snickers, as he and Flo helped August Zink into the car.

"I'm on time," I said.

Zink needed a shave. He also needed some clothes. He was barefoot and wearing pajamas.

Zink sat between Eb and Flo in the back seat. Snickers got in, patted me on the shoulder, and pointed down the street. In my rearview mirror I could see Zink, who muttered, "That bastard."

Flo smiled.

"Bastard kidnapped me," Zink went on. "Couple of Cuban giants stood outside the bedroom door. Wouldn't let me out."

Snickers did three things to reward himself. First, he tipped his fedora back. Second, he held his hand out to Flo, who filled it with five more hundred-dollar bills. Third, he took out a giant-size Snickers bar, peeled back the paper, and began to eat it.

"Mr. Snickers is a genius," said Flo. "Got a ladder from somewhere. Boom, we're inside and no dogs, no guards. Lights on, but Mr. Snickers takes us in back and up some stairs to the roof. Attic door opens slow and quiet."

"What about the Cubans?" I asked.

A very large old six-shooter jutted in front of my face. It was in the hand of Flo Zink.

"They're either considerin' a new career or makin' love in the very small closet where we locked 'em in after Eb tied them up. Best time I've had since we kicked crap out of those kids who tried to hold us up in Manhattan back in '63."

" '62," Zink corrected. "I think I'm gonna have Anderson killed. Hell, I'll kill him myself. What've I got to lose?"

"Hey, I know a guy . . ." Snickers began.

"Forget it," Flo said. "No hits. No runs. No errors. Do what you got to do, Gus, and let's tear ass out of this town. How you feel about dyin' in Texas?"

"I think I prefer Vermont," said Zink. "You can move to Texas when I'm gone."

There was silence as we drove, except for Snickers' happy munching. About a block from the town hall, I stopped. We got the scooter out. It looked all right and started without trouble.

"I can walk to Edwardo's from here," said Snickers, waving and wandering down the street.

"Call me tomorrow, Eb," I said. "Better yet, stop by."

Eb nodded and putted off into the night.

When I got into the hearing room, where almost all the faces in the audience were black, it was nearly midnight. Reverend Wilkens saw me and came to meet me at the back of the hall while a well-dressed young black man addressed the bored council members on the need for a library in Newtown.

"You found him?" whispered Wilkens.

Heads were turned toward us.

"Yes," I said, "but he needs a suit of clothes and a pair of shoes and socks."

Wilkens looked around the audience and waved at a man and woman near the front of the room. The couple came to join us. Now everyone was looking our way.

The discussion was fast. Five minutes later, still in need of a shave but wearing the white shirt and slacks of the man we had just spoken to, August Zink entered the hall with his wife.

The black man in the suit was still seated facing the council, which watched as Zink pulled himself together and marched down the aisle and took his seat at the table.

"Time," said Mayor Beatrice McElveny, looking at her watch.

The speaker rose and returned to his seat. I stood at the rear of the room with Flo Zink. A uniformed officer with arms folded stood next to us.

"It's late," said the mayor with a smile. "We've heard you. We've heard others. We have considered the advice of our planning committee and their consultants, and we think it is time to move into the future on this issue. I call for a vote on the branch library location. Objections?"

Patormi, the old radical, looked for a second as if he were going to speak, but something about the nearly bearded Zink changed his mind.

"In favor of the Newtown site?" the mayor asked.

Patormi and Wilkens' hands went up.

"Opp . . ." she began and stopped in horror as Zink's hand went up.

"Councilman Zink," she said. "Please wait till I finish asking for those opposed."

"I'm voting in favor of the Newtown site," said Zink. "Are you going blind in your old age, Bea?"

The crowd went wild.

The mayor found her gavel and pounded for quiet.

"Quiet, please," Reverend Wilkens said.

Patormi was grinning and shaking his head.

The audience went silent.

"Madame Mayor," said Patormi, "I believe we just passed a motion."

The mayor looked confused.

"The way it works now, you hit the gavel," said the old man gleefully. "And then you say, 'The motion carries.' You've been doing that for almost a year. It shouldn't be that hard."

The mayor tapped the gavel and, her voice breaking, said, "The motion carries."

There was a celebration party late into the night at Edwardo's, but the Zinks didn't stay and I did little more than put in an appearance.

When I got back home, I found an envelope in my pocket. It contained four thousand dollars in hundred-dollar bills. I offered Eb half the next day, but he said he hadn't done two thousand dollars work for it. He did, however, accept three hundred.

The Zinks were packed and gone the next day. There was a hotly contested special election to fill Gus's place on the council. One of the biggest voter turnouts in Sarasota history. A Hispanic named

Gomez who owned a big auto repair business was elected, and life went on.

Shortly after the election, I got a postcard in the mail. On the front was a photograph of the Alamo. On the back in neat letters was: "We had two good months together in Vermont, and now I'm doing what Gus and I both wanted me to do. Watch your ass."

It had no signature.

Poor Lincoln

Dorothy Cannell

"Barbara, darling! What a marvelous surprise!"

I was waiting to be seated for lunch at Harrods, no doubt looking conspicuously dowdy in my old navy blue coat, when I heard the rumble of an all-too-familiar voice and turned to see my ex-mother-in-law bearing down upon me. To my admittedly jaundiced eye she was a five-foot troglodyte, swaddled in a mink coat that, like the voice, was a couple of sizes too big for her. Several people, who were probably thinking about roast beef and Yorkshire pudding, stepped smartly aside to avoid being enveloped in her furry arms.

"It's been an age since I last saw you!" She took hold of my elbow, effectively preventing escape. "Darling!" The word vibrated off her tongue. "You must tell me every single, tiny detail of what's been happening in your life since you and Gerald went your separate ways." She elbowed aside two pleasant-faced women in tweeds who were having a nice talk about doing the flowers for their church altar. "It seems only yesterday, sweetie, but I suppose it must be three or . . . could it possibly be four? . . . years since the divorce."

"There's not a lot to tell, Cassandra," I replied, feeling like a talking wooden soldier.

"Mumsie, darling!" She clasped a pudgy hand (which flashed with enough diamonds to light up London during a power cut) to her mink bosom. "You really must go back to calling me Mumsie."

"I'm working at an art supplies and framing shop in Chelmsford," I told her. "Today is early closing, so I came up to have a browse around the shops." Then quickly, in order to forestall her asking whether there was a new man in my life, I inquired after her husband.

"Popsie? Rubbing along much as usual. He misses you, of course, quite dreadfully." Her voice throbbed with emotion. "Only this morning he said to me, 'I do hope that gal Gerald was married to finds some decent chap to . . .' "

"And what about your mother, how is she doing?" Here my interest was not entirely fabricated. I had been rather fond of the old lady, who was a kindly, comfortable sort of person who looked the way grandmothers used to look before they started joining health clubs and wearing miniskirts.

"I'm sorry to say, Barbara, darling"—emotion played havoc with the lines on Mumsie's face—"that Grandma began to let herself go after turning eighty last year. It was quite a shock, really, when Popsie and I realized she couldn't continue living alone in that house in Warley."

"Oh, I am sorry," I said. "Did you bring her to live with you?"

"Darling, much as I longed to do so, it just wouldn't have worked." Monumental sigh. "Popsie and I are always on the go, a month or two in the London flat, then off to the house in Devon, and after that away to our sweet little villa in Florence. All things considered, I'm sure we made the best possible decision about Grandma."

"Which was?" I asked, hoping I wasn't going to hear that Grandma had been put to sleep.

"To have Lincoln move in with her, darling!" Mumsie patted my arm. "I don't suppose Gerald talked about him much. We're only distantly related, cousins two or three times removed. You know the sort of thing. And of course Lincoln is older than Gerald. In his fifties at least. Rather a shy sort of man, which naturally wasn't helped by his getting into that spot of bother."

"No, I don't suppose so!" I didn't try very hard to sound interested. Five minutes in Mumsie's company had always been more than enough for me, and I was now determined not to get stuck lunching with her. I would have to escape to the powder room, before the dreaded words "A table for two?" rang in my ears.

"People tend to be so judgmental. Don't you think so, Barbara?" Mumsie gave a lighthearted chuckle. "As if we all haven't made the occasional mistake along the way. Really, one's heart breaks for Lincoln! I'm sure it must be the easiest thing in the world for an accountant to make a mistake with his adding up or taking away and be accused of fiddling the books. To send a man to prison for a little slip of the pencil—well, it doesn't seem right, does it, darling?"

I was speechless, but that was all to the good. Mumsie was now in full flood. "As I said to Popsie and Gerald, it's like living under the Gestapo. But thanks to some exertion on my part, things have worked out. Grandma couldn't be happier having

Lincoln in the house, he is devoted to her, and my mind is at ease."

"It's certainly a solution," I agreed.

"The ideal one, if I do say so myself." Mumsie removed a powder compact from her alligator handbag and snapped it open to inspect her face in the mirror. "There's no need for you to worry, sweetie, that Grandma's fondness for Lincoln might lead her to do something silly like leaving everything to him, and us in the lurch. It can't happen—trust me, Barbara!" Her voice dropped several octaves and she popped the compact back into her bag. "The money, the house, and all important pieces of jewelry come to me by way of a trust my father set up years before he died. The only items Grandma has leave to dispose of as she chooses are the household furnishings. Believe me, there are no valuable antiques, darling! Absolutely nothing I'd want from that house in Warley. Indeed, I encouraged Grandma to leave the lot to Lincoln." Mumsie did an excellent job of looking magnanimous. "He can sell everything when the time comes or take some of it with him when he moves into a boardinghouse, or wherever he goes."

I took the dismissive tone in Mumsie's voice to indicate that she was done with the topic of Lincoln. But I quickly realized that, having succeeded in claiming my full—one might say stunned—attention, she was also done with me. In the twinkling of an eye she had spotted a tall woman in a flowerpot hat and lots of flowing scarves exiting the restaurant.

"Darling, it's been delightful—indeed, one might say it was meant to be. Fate and all that sort of thing! But I mustn't be selfish and keep you when I'm sure you're meeting someone." So saying, Mumsie blew me a haphazard kiss and charged toward her new prey, furry arms extended, diamonds flashing. "Lady Worksop-Smythe! How absolutely marvelous!"

From the back Mumsie looked more than ever like a bear who had escaped from the zoo, and I was left with the disoriented feeling that comes with abruptly imposed freedom. Should I proceed to have lunch here as planned and risk hearing rumbles of that familiar voice emanating from behind every potted plant? Or should I plan on an early-afternoon tea and meanwhile take a look around the housewares department?

It wouldn't have surprised Gerald, who had often criticized me for acting on impulse, that ten minutes later I was in my car edging out into bumper-to-bumper traffic. I told myself that I was simply no longer in the mood for an afternoon at Harrods, that I would go directly home to Chelmsford and share a boiled egg with my cat, Sunny. But before I had gone through the first traffic light I knew that I was going to see Grandma.

She lived in a house called Swallows Nest, set well back from the road behind a tall hedge, in Warley, which was no distance at all from where I lived. Unfortunately, I took a couple of wrong turns after exiting the motorway, and relief was uppermost in my mind when I negotiated the last bend in the tree-shaded drive. But as I climbed from the car onto the broad concrete sweep, I did have second thoughts about appearing in true long-lost-relative fashion on the doorstep.

It would have been politer and made more sense to phone in a day or two, if I still felt the urge. Why had I conjured up a picture of Grandma wilting away in bed while this Lincoln person who was supposed to be looking after her sat frozen in an armchair, mourning his fall from grace? Probably because Gerald had been right in accusing me of having too much imagination. In all likelihood, Lincoln was a perfectly sensible man who enjoyed living a normal life once more. And in appreciation, he would always make sure that Grandma knew where to find her slippers and never lacked for a hot meal or was left to sit by a dying fire.

The house certainly looked reassuring. Autumn flowers bloomed in the well-tended beds and, although a stiff breeze rustled the trees, the sky was clear. Afternoon sunlight stippled the rose-colored bricks with gold and sparkled on the latticed panes of the dormer windows that jutted out from the steeply pitched roof. Slipping the car keys into my coat pocket, I squared my shoulders and mounted the stone steps to the front door. The knocker was in the shape of a swallow, and I rapped it briskly, suddenly eager to see Grandma again and make Lincoln's acquaintance.

Several moments passed, and I was about to beat another tattoo when the door opened a cautious crack.

"Who is it?" came the hesitant inquiry.

"Barbara," I replied in my most nonthreatening voice. "Do you remember? I was married to your grandson Gerald."

"Oh, what a lovely surprise." Grandma opened the door wide and ushered me into a hall with a dark oak staircase running up one side. "And how very kind of you to come and see me." She looked the way I remembered, a solidly built, white-haired old lady. The intervening four years had taken no visible toll, I thought as she hung my coat on the hall tree. If anything, she seemed to move more briskly. Really, she was amazing for over eighty. I explained about meeting her daughter at Harrods and apologized for coming on the spur of the moment.

"I'd glad you did, dear. I've often thought of you." She smiled kindly at me. "Tell me, did Gerald let you keep the cat when you divorced?"

"Yes, I have her," I said, feeling extremely touched that she remembered Sunny.

"Isn't that good!" She squeezed my hand. "I must say I've always been fond of cats myself. But I couldn't possibly have one now. It's a pity"—her voice dropped to a whisper—"but poor Lincoln is afraid of cats. And it's important to consider his feelings after everything he's been through."

Before I could respond, Grandma turned from me to glance over at the staircase. There was no one standing on its oak treads. But when my eye shifted to the open gallery above, I thought I saw a shadow edge around a corner of the back wall.

"I hope you'll get to meet Lincoln, he's such a dear." Grandma's face creased into a fond smile. "But you'll understand if he stays out of sight while you're here, won't you? He's such a sensitive man, shy to the point of being timid, one might say. But I'm sure my daughter told you all about him."

"Not a lot," I said. Which was true. Mumsie hadn't gone into details, such as on which side Lincoln parted his hair or whether he preferred cricket to soccer.

"Really it was very kind of Cassandra," Grandma was still looking up the stairs, "I mean—suggesting that Lincoln move in here so I wouldn't be alone if I ever needed a little help."

"Very thoughtful," I said.

"So much nicer than putting me in a home."

And probably a lot cheaper, I thought, as Grandma took hold of my elbow and shepherded me down the hall.

"I've told my daughter I bless the day she came up with the idea. Dear Lincoln has been such a gem. Nothing is ever too much trouble. Would you believe he went out this afternoon even with that nasty wind blowing? Just to buy some pots of paint because he wants to give the dormer windows a fresh coat inside and out. I told him it wasn't necessary and we don't have a ladder, but I'm sure he's hanging out of a window painting away for dear life at this very moment." There was a suspicion of a break in her voice as Grandma led the way into a large sitting room.

This was made cozy by dusky-rose walls and faded mole-colored velvet curtains. The furnishings were comfortably old-fashioned, with lots of dark wood and plenty of roomy seating.

"Why don't you take this one, Barbara?" She patted the back of an armchair and while she was settling herself across from me I looked at the picture of horses pulling a hay cart along a country lane above the mantelpiece, very much aware that on the bookcase to my left there were several photos of Mumsie and Popsie and, inevitably, my ex-husband. "I'm so sorry about the divorce," said Grandma.

"Don't be." I undid the top buttons of my cardigan because the central heating at Swallows Nest was more than adequate. "Gerald and I weren't at all suited, and I'm enjoying my new life."

"That's good to hear. And, you know, Barbara, I've always been inclined to think that bad things so often happen for a reason." Grandma sat comfortably, hands folded in her wide lap, nodding her head wisely. "It's like that problem with the car, just a few months back."

"Really?" I said.

"Lincoln had taken me into town—he's so good about that sort of thing. Always so willing. I'd wanted to do a little shopping and decided we should stop at the bank first. It's right at the top of Queen Street, which is very steep. Always has been. Children used to go sledding down it in winter years ago." Grandma's face clouded. "Dear Lincoln, ever the gentleman! He leaped out of the car the moment it was at a standstill so as to race around and open my door. And I don't know how it happened (perhaps the hand brake slipped), but suddenly the car took off at breakneck speed down the hill."

"What a dreadful thing!" My hand went to my throat as I pictured the scene.

"Dreadful is the word. Poor, dear Lincoln! He was absolutely beside himself when he reached me. Couldn't hold back the tears even though I kept telling him I was as right as rain. Not so much as a bump or a scrape because, miraculously, the car had swung into a curve at the bottom of the hill and come to a standstill within inches of a shop window. I told Lincoln he had absolutely nothing to reproach himself for; accidents, as we all know, will happen."

"Absolutely," I agreed, letting out a breath.

"It seems to me that what we must do is learn from these experiences." Grandma looked pensive. "And of course what I discovered that day is that I have never known, will never know, anyone of Lincoln's sweetness and deep sensitivity. And does he ever put me to shame." She got to her feet. "Here I am talking your ear off, Barbara, when you must be longing for a cup of tea."

I protested that I wasn't in need of refreshment, but Grandma took off, back into the hall, and I found myself trotting at her heels. The kitchen, like the sitting room, had obviously not been done up in years—the appliances were at least thirty years old—but there was the same feeling of easy livability. Grandma soon had the kettle filled and began rattling about with cups and saucers. "Such a nasty drive down from London, all that heavy traffic and never knowing when it might come on to rain." She added a sugar bowl and milk jug to the tea tray. "And sometimes when you're shopping there isn't time to stop and eat. I often used to plan on having lunch at Harrods when I went up to town, but something always seemed to get in the way."

"It so often does," I replied.

"Meaning you haven't had a thing to eat since setting out this morning." Grandma made soft clucking noises as she filled the teapot. "And I'm sure a piece of fruitcake won't bridge the gap. How would it be," she said, peering into a cupboard, "if I opened a tin of soup and heated that up for you? I've got tomato if you like that."

"It's my favorite," I assured her, knowing I shouldn't put her to the trouble but suddenly aware that I was very hungry.

"Mushroom was always my favorite." Grandma had produced a saucepan and was making headway with the tin opener, her expression intent. "But of

course I could never have it in the house again, not
after what happened. Oh, it was the saddest thing!
Seeing poor Lincoln so upset. Of course I told him
he mustn't blame himself, but there was no getting
through to him."

"What happened?" I asked, availing myself of a
chair.

"It was all out of the goodness of his heart." Grandma
paused in the act of putting the saucepan on the
stove to wipe away a tear that plopped down on her
cheek. "Knowing how fond I was of mushroom
soup—really, it was my fault for always going on
about it—he went to all the trouble of making some,
using proper stock and everything. You wouldn't believe the hours he spent stirring away. And the dear
man doesn't even like mushrooms, never eats anything with them in it. You would have been so
touched, Barbara, if you had seen Lincoln ladling that
soup into my bowl and hovering over me like an
anxious mother as I took my first spoonful."

"Was it good?" I didn't know what else to say.

"Oh, delicious, so much better than the tinned
stuff!" Grandma came round to the table with my
tomato soup. "And really, when my tummy started
hurting afterward it wasn't all that bad. It just
seemed to make sense to send for the doctor and by
the time he got here I was in bed. Well, I'm never
one to stay up late at the best of times, but of course
Lincoln got himself worked up to a froth, even
though Doctor Wicker said I was the most resilient
old woman he'd ever looked after. A positively
amazing constitution, is what he said, and that I
would be as right as rain in the morning." Grandma
interrupted herself to ask if I would like a slice of

bread and butter with my soup, but I declined, no longer feeling quite as hungry. "Poor Lincoln, he just couldn't restrain his sobs," she continued, "and it was days before I saw the glimmer of a smile from him. Doesn't that just break your heart?" She sat down across from me.

I managed to nod my head and continued spooning away at my soup, without really tasting it, until the bowl was empty. After that, I asked Grandma how long it had been since Mumsie, Popsie, or Gerald had come down to see her. But it was clear she didn't want to discuss them, either because I had rubbed a nerve or because she wanted to get back to talking about Lincoln.

"I do wish he'd come down for a cup of tea." Grandma glanced upwards as if hoping a foot would tentatively appear through the ceiling. "But he's just so shy. I think it comes," she smiled mistily, "from his once having spent quite a time cooped up with strangers."

"Cassandra did mention something about that," I began, only to be kindly but firmly cut off.

"Yes," Grandma permitted herself a grimace as she gave the contents of the teapot a stir before filling our cups, "I'm sure Cassandra has told a whole lot of people, but I can't see that poor Lincoln has any reason to feel ashamed. A lot of boys can't settle at boarding school and want to go home to their mothers. He told me all about it. I remember the evening." Her voice grew reminiscent. "We had such a lovely time chatting by the fire. It was the perfect night for that sort of thing. The rain hadn't stopped all day and it was so cozy with the curtains drawn and our mugs of cocoa in our hands. Such a shame that afterward there was that unfortunate little incident with the lift."

"The what?" I was beginning to think that there was no keeping up with Grandma.

"Dear Lincoln had suggested we have one put in." She spooned sugar into her tea. "He was so worried about my using the stairs, especially the ones down to the cellar—even after I told him I never go down there anymore. Luckily, we didn't have to knock the house about when having the lift installed. There was an alcove in the hall and another directly above it on the landing, right next to my bedroom, just suited to the purpose. And there was loads of room in the cellar, seeing that I only use it to store odds and ends. Even so, I'm sure it would have been a much more expensive proposition if Lincoln hadn't worn himself to the bone doing most of the work himself." Grandma's eyes had misted over. "Was there ever anyone more thoughtful?"

"Probably not." I knew I didn't sound 100 percent convinced.

"Despite everything Dr. Wicker said, about my being as healthy as a woman half my age, there was no talking away Lincoln's anxieties, and so I agreed to the lift. And I must say I really did enjoy the luxury of being taken up and down in style, until that night—the one when we had such a lovely fireside chat." Her voice cracked. "Lincoln was pushing me in the wheelchair . . ."

"Why the wheelchair?"

"Again, that was dear Lincoln being protective." Grandma refilled my cup. "He decided I would recover faster from that business with the mushroom soup if I kept right off my feet. Dr. Wicker said I had bounced back like a two-year-old and what I needed was more, not less, exercise. But the important thing in my eyes was to make sure Lincoln didn't make himself ill worrying about me."

"You were saying," I prompted, "that he was pushing you in the wheelchair one evening . . ."

"Yes, across the hall to the lift." Grandma nodded. "The doors opened, just like always, and Lincoln sang out, 'Heave Ho!' as he always did. Only this time the lift wasn't there—or the floor wasn't—if you know what I mean, Barbara!"

"I think I get the picture!"

"I'm ashamed to say I screamed." Grandma gave a rueful shake of her head. "The panic of the moment! And really it was nothing more than a moment, because the instant the front wheels started to tip, I reached up and grabbed hold of the rim, or whatever you call it, above the doors. It was like clinging to the mast of a tiny boat that was being blown about in high winds. Really, rather a thrill for a woman of my age." Grandma smoothed back a strand of white hair that had inched over her left eye. "It so happens, Barbara, that I was quite a gymnast in my youth, so there wasn't any real danger of my falling. All it took was a good swing, forward and back, and then a jump to the safety of the hall floor."

"You could have been killed!"

"Oh, no, there was never any danger of that, I'm sure," Grandma replied briskly. "What bothered me was realizing that while everything was happening I didn't give a thought to poor Lincoln and how awful it must have been for his nerves when he heard the wheelchair crash into the cellar. It made the most unholy noise, although I can't say I was fully tuned in at the time. And then, of course, being Lincoln, he became so distressed that I thought I should have to send for an ambulance. Such a state he was in! Oh, it was piteous to hear him sob." Grandma dabbed at her eyes with her hanky. "And nothing I said could comfort him, not even when I told him that far from blaming him because the lift didn't work once in a while, I owed him more than I could ever hope to repay. His coming to live with me has given me a whole new lease on life."

"But Grandma . . ." I began.

"Oh, dear, I have been droning on, Barbara," she said, sounding thoroughly embarrassed. "Keeping you sitting on a hard kitchen chair when you must be tired out from all the driving you've done today. Let's go back into the sitting room where it's comfortable." She was already bustling towards the hall door. "You can tell me more about what's been happening to you. Did you say you have a job?"

I wasn't sure whether I had or not, but I explained that I was working in a picture-framing and art supplies shop, and she responded with great enthusiasm.

"Well, if that isn't a coincidence, Barbara," she said as I followed her into the sitting room. "I've a picture that I think would look better in a different frame. It's that one with the hay cart, hanging over the mantelpiece. Cassandra can't stand it; she calls it chocolate box art, but I've always liked Constable. And Lincoln is an ardent admirer."

"It is a nice print," I replied, looking up at the picture from the hearth rug.

"Oh, but it isn't a copy, dear." Grandma spoke matter-of-factly. "It's a proper painting. I had to sell all the family jewelry to pay for it. I suppose you could say that was wrong of me, because according to my late husband's will each and every bauble was to go to Cassandra after my day. But with all the jewelry she has accumulated I can't see how she could possibly wear any more. No, I really don't think I have to worry about Cassandra." Grandma settled herself comfortably in a chair. "She will do very well when my time comes."

"And she doesn't know that the Constable is genuine?" I remained standing motionless on the hearth rug.

"Not a suspicion." Grandma now sounded a little anxious. "And you won't say anything, will you, Barbara? I know it's an old lady's failing, talking too much. I haven't stopped since you got here, but I know I can trust you, dear, because you know my daughter and how she can be, well . . . a little difficult at times. That's why I had copies of the jewelry made—so that if Cassandra ever asked to see it there wouldn't be a scene. You do promise, dear, you won't let slip a word?"

"Of course," I replied, feeling like a villain, because surely it was my duty to make haste and report to Mumsie that not only had her mother recently suffered three life-threatening accidents, she also owned an extremely valuable painting that she just might have been persuaded to will, along the rest of the furnishings at Swallows Nest, to her faithful companion. Or was it possible Gerald had been right when he accused me of having an overactive imagination?

Grandma, seeing me still standing as if rooted to the spot, leaped to the conclusion that I was studying the clock on the mantelpiece. And she hastened to assure me that whilst she would have loved me to

remain for hours, she did realize I had to drive home
and was probably getting jumpy at the thought of
leaving my cat unattended for so long. We therefore
proceeded back into the hall and when passing
alongside the staircase I again thought I saw a
shadow figure go crouching around a corner of the
open gallery above.

"Oh, I do so wish you'd got to meet Lincoln,"
Grandma said as we went out the front door and
down the steps. "I just know the two of you would
have hit it off like a house afire, but you'll understand from everything I've said, Barbara, that being
so painfully shy and sensitive, he prefers to stay in
the background."

We were now standing alongside my car and I, at
a loss for words, nodded agreement while looking
back towards the house that presented such a safe
and cheerful face to the world. Following my glance,
Grandma perhaps thought I was admiring the flower
bed under the sitting room window. At any rate, she
asked if I could spare a few moments to take a look
at her chrysanthemums, which had been extraordi-
nary this year. And after that, everything happened
in a rush of merging shapes and colors.

One of the dormer windows set in the steeply
pitched roof opened, and within its framework appeared the top half of a man holding something in
his hands. The chill that crept down my spine was
explained by the breeze that was already plucking at
my hair. I can't say I experienced a sense of im-
pending disaster. It wasn't until I saw the figure
squeeze itself half out of the window and drop a gallon
pot of paint, that I dredged up speed I did not know I
possessed, threw my arms around Grandma, and

dragged her to safety before the thing landed on her head. What came next seemed to happen in comic slow motion. The figure at the window had leaned out too far for personal safety and now came sliding spread-eagled, and without making a sound, down the roof to land face down on the concrete.

And I stood there in my dowdy navy blue coat, staring at the inert huddle, waiting for a foot to move or a hand to twitch. But even his hair lay perfectly still. At last Grandma freed herself from my protective arm and took half a dozen tottering steps to stand looking down at him. "Oh," she said in a broken voice, "poor Lincoln!"

Plumbing the Depths

Charlotte MacLeod

The flowers that bloomed in the spring of 1932 probably didn't have anything to do with the case. But they were there, and Phil the plumber was glad to see them. Despite the sullen economy of the Depression years, Phil was glad more often than not. Furthermore, he didn't give two hoots and a holler as to what he was glad about, just so long as the sun was still rising without his having to get out there and help Old Sol push.

It was bliss to sniff the fragrance of the coffee in his thick white mug with the blue stripe around it and to see the sugar in the bowl ready to sweeten his day. He was glad that this time he'd remembered to bring home the bacon, and even gladder that his neighbor who kept hens had swapped him half a dozen fresh eggs in return for his cleaning out a drain that had got clogged with chicken feathers.

This was a fair swap. Phil and his neighbor spent a few minutes congratulating each other on two jobs well done, as why should they not, and then got on with their respective day's work.

With a hearty breakfast of eggs and bacon under his belt, Phil sallied forth to meet the glad new day, carrying his tool bag, his fire pot, and his blowtorch, brave symbols of the *Artifex Plumbarius*. He didn't know what he'd be in for on the new job that he was about to tackle, but whatever it was wouldn't faze him a jot now that he and his helper had finished the job at Mickleton.

The Mickleton Apartments, as they were grandly called, comprised a long row of connected buildings that stretched all the way along the swankiest avenue in town. There was a mall down the middle, planted with exotic shrubberies and guarded by a man who came around twice a day with his handcart, wielding a pointed stick to spear the tattered newspapers, the candy wrappers, and other trash before it could get scattered around the mall and lower the tone of the sandstone griffons and concrete gargoyles that added so much elegance to the avenue and so many cricks to the trash gatherer's aching back.

There were still swell people on the avenue. It was something to see the ladies in their furs and jewels and the faultlessly tailored men in their rakishly classy fedoras or their sedate black derbies, with the doormen rushing up to see them safely through the huge plate-glass doors and into their limousines. Little did the swells know that Phil the plumber and his helper had for the past weeks been waging a war against almost but not quite impossible odds. What would the upper crust have thought, or perhaps even said, had they but known that the laundry rooms and coal cellars of their magnificent habitations were infested with millions upon millions of fleas?

It must have been a long time ago that the fleas set up housekeeping in the vast, cavernous, and un- wholesomely dank basements; there they prospered. Knowing this, Phil had brought along a helper to shoulder a fair share of his burden. But this was not to be. The helper made it all too plain that he did not like the fleas. Even worse, the fleas did not like the helper. In phalanx upon phalanx, they hopped over to Phil's side of the new piping that he was trying to install and dined sumptuously on him.

Phil was not a big man, but he was well muscled from lugging bathtubs and water closets up and down many flights of stairs. Freed at last from his ordeal by flea, he washed every stitch of his working clothes in a magical solution guaranteed to rid him of every flea in the county. He then borrowed a couple of flatirons from the laundry room, ironed his garments dry, and presented himself to his wife and family all spruce and snappy and ready to join them around the kitchen table.

Phil was just finishing his supper and about to take the children outdoors for a jolly game of leap-flea when the fire alarm rang out from the belfry of the Congregational Church. Being a volunteer fireman, he made sure the children were kept well back from the fire line, then rushed forward with his comrades to do what must be done.

The fire was soon out, but the real problem was what to do about Chief Flicker. Hannibal Flicker had served manfully for more than a quarter of a century. During his long and generally successful reign among the hose carts and ladder trucks, Chief Flicker had accumulated a vast reservoir of information on subjects ranging all the way from Arson to the Zealousness that he manifested at all times. This particular time, the entire fire department was in a quandary as to what should be done. The gist of the problem was that in gathering to himself so much learning, he had also collected far more poundage than Mrs. Flicker thought he should be carrying.

The event proved Mrs. Flicker the winner, but a rueful one. Like any good fireman's wife, she had come out to watch what was happening. She was just in time to see her respected husband take a giant step backward, not realizing that he had planted his foot on the decayed wooden cover of a long unused cesspool. Before his crew could haul out the excessively weighty chief, he was up to his armpits, still wearing his good blue uniform with the brass buttons on it that had been shining brightly only a step ago.

Cries of anguish and dismay filled the air as the situation became increasingly dire. The only voice not adding to the din was that of Phil the plumber. He nipped over to home for a minute or two and hurried back carrying a short but sturdy length of planking, lifted the mortified fire chief out of the noisome cesspool all by himself, sluiced him off with one of the fire hoses, and steered him away from the scene of the near-tragedy.

While Chief Flicker squished off homeward without pausing to say thanks and the other firemen milled around wondering what to do next, Phil effaced himself and went home to get his wife's can of brass polish. He burnished every one of the chief's buttons, of which there were quite a few, and left them all present in perfect working order.

Rather than spend the money to have the chief's uniform dry-cleaned, Mrs. Flicker took the chance of washing it at home. At first she was horrified to see how it had shrunk; then Mrs. Phil reminded her gen-

tly that she'd been nagging her husband for months
to take off some weight.

And how right they both were. After a period of
making do, Chief Flicker lost just enough pounds to
fit into his shrunken uniform. It all came out in the
wash and nothing was lost except a smell from the
old cesspool that passed away when a heavy metal
cap was fitted over the top of the well, soldered to
the rim, and bolted down tight as a drum, or even
tighter. It was, of course, Phil himself who did the
soldering and bolting, at no charge to his fellow
townsfolk.

It need hardly be said that Phil loved his work
with a fervor that passed all understanding, though
relatively few of his family, friends, and neighbors
were able to pierce the curtain into his magical realm.
He had risen with amazing rapidity in the ranks of
his chosen field, from Journeyman to Master
Plumber. He knew his handbooks forward and backward. There were times, however, when Phil got so
carried away by the poetry of his art that certain
discrepancies spontaneously arose.

For a master like Phil, it should have been almost
laughably difficult to commit a slip of the grip; but
such situations did come about on rare occasions.
One of them was inspired by a fellow plumber's
ownership of an electric drill that weighed forty
pounds and had a torque of three hundred. This
meant that the driller might, if he wished, either use
the electricity or drill a hole two inches in diameter
through a heavy timber using a hand bit with a lead
screw sometimes called a worm. Phil chose the former course.

All would have gone well had Phil not been so

totally immersed in his art. Forgetting the warning
he had received against using so large a drill without
first shutting off the power, and exalted by the poetry
of his craft, he started to drill without taking his finger off the switch.

Of course he should have remembered, but it was
too late now. All of a sudden, Phil began spinning
around like a whirligig, his body parallel to the concrete floor and his legs straight out in the air. He was
well on the way to describing a perfect circle when
it occurred to him that it might not be a bad idea to
take his finger off that switch button. Immediately
the momentum died. Phil found himself sitting grog-
gily on the floor looking silly as a coot but seeing
the funny side—and feeling it, too.

This was a bagatelle compared to a contretemps
that occurred soon after that. Phil's penchant for exploring new paths, coupled with his eagerness to
open new doors for his family, led him to the outdoor market that came to the city every Friday and
Saturday. It was a colorful spectacle and a fine
chance to dicker with the vendors for good food at
small cost, which they all enjoyed, particularly Mrs.
Phil.

Sometimes the whole family went together in the
car. Sometimes the parents went together, leaving a
young neighbor who was studying to be a musician
to keep an eye on the children in exchange for being
allowed to practice on their piano. Sometimes Phil
took Mrs. Phil's grocery list with him and did the
marketing alone.

Phil's expertise in plumbing took him to jobs both
in the city and out in the suburbs, not that many of

his customers knew what a suburb was. Usually they just called it the sticks. One night he got held up on a job in the city and didn't get through until it was almost time for the weary pushcart vendors and the thrifty customers to get on the ferryboat or the streetcar, or walk home with a baby carriage full of good buys if they lived close enough. Workmen like Phil really needed their cars; they also needed to eat before they started home.

Phil had already been introduced to a kind of sausage called salami by one of the vendors, and he found it good. Tonight he got into a chat with a fellow who showed him an innocent-looking little bulb called garlic. The fellow claimed it was a vegetable somewhat like an onion but different, fine to eat and good for what ailed you, whoever you were.

There hadn't been much left to eat in the pushcarts by the time he started home, so Phil was still hungry, but he didn't want to bother his wife to fix him a snack. He was no great chef, but he figured that it might not be a bad idea to give the stuff a try. So he fried up a panful of the little bulbs and ate them all with a few hunks of bread and a cup or two of the strong black coffee that he'd gotten used to drinking at any hour of the day or night. Then, shedding his working clothes and putting on his threadbare pajamas, he crawled into bed beside his wife.

Mrs. Phil loved her husband, but she was not about to sleep with someone who didn't have brains enough to keep away from whatever was making that unearthly stink. For a whole week and a few days over, Phil was banished to sleep on the downstairs couch. Gradually, however, he began sneaking little bits of garlic into the family menu and they got so after a while that they actually liked it. But Mrs. Phil saw to it that he didn't go unchaperoned again to the pushcarts.

That was no tragedy. Phil could always think up more interesting things to do than sit around and grouch. In fact, there was very little grouching done, even on rainy Sunday afternoons when they took off the parlor lamp shades and hung up a sheet so that they could make shadow pictures with their fingers of everything from a butterfly to a raging dragon. And it hardly cost a cent on the light bill.

Card playing on Sunday was forbidden, with the one exception of cribbage, which Phil considered to be educational—though it was whispered among his children that their father sanctioned cribbage on Sunday solely because he liked to play cribbage. That was fine with them. They played four-handed until the rain stopped and they could go out in the yard to watch their father cement a patch on the inner tube of his right-hand front tire.

This was quite a ceremony. First, the front end of the car had to be jacked up, the wheel taken off, and the inner tube removed from the outer tire. Then the inner tube had to be carefully inspected for any flaw, from a slow leak to a puncture or a blowout.

If the tube was too badly damaged, there wasn't much that Phil could do but go down to the junkyard and see whether his friend the junk man happened to have a tube that would serve his purpose. If not, he might have to dig down into his wife's secret cache for the price of a new one, which would mean their having to put off a couple of less urgent purchases for another couple of weeks so that he could keep the car on the road and not have to ride the streetcar with his fire pot, his blowtorch, and various other necessaries festooned around him in various interesting and decorative ways—Phil being Phil.

If the tube was not too badly damaged, Phil would stop in at the hardware store and buy a small cardboard tube into which were packed a couple of rubber patches and a tube of rubber cement. The lid of the package was an efficient scraper that roughened the side of the patch that was going to be stuck down with the rubber cement once Phil had decided precisely how he could trim the corners of the patch in the most artistic way.

After the white cloth backing had been peeled off and the abraded rubber tubing given a light coating of rubber cement, the tube was allowed to set for a few minutes. Then Phil would partially inflate it with his hand pump and push it back inside the tire.

Now came the grand finale.

Having got the tire positioned to his satisfaction, Phil would finish inflating it and put it back on the wheel. He would then let the jack down very, very gently, having first made sure that all the lug bolts were firmly in place. And the mended tire was again ready to roll, though who could say for how long? These were exciting times; anything might happen and often did when Phil was around.

Not all weekends had to be given over to practical matters. If there was enough gas in the car's tank, Phil would treat his wife and the three children to an outing, usually to some historic site where there was a story to be told and himself ready, willing, and able to tell it. On the way home, Phil would hand out to each one a block of excellent chocolate, not forgetting Mrs. Phil and himself.

Once in a blue moon, Phil's much older brother, a fat little man with a fat little wife and two fat Scottie dogs, would stop by in their seven-passenger limousine. The dogs' names were Sis and Maggie; they were not allowed near the children because they growled and barked and carried on ferociously and had to be kept on their leashes so that they wouldn't leap out and bite somebody and get Uncle Archibald sued for damages.

Uncle Archibald and Aunt Bedelia growled and barked much as Sis and Maggie did, but they reserved their strictures for each other. On the avenue near which they lived there were two sizable red brick buildings, one on each side of the street, directly across from each other. Everything about these buildings looked attractive and well kept, yet there was a sadness about them. On each of the spacious green lawns there stood a handsomely painted sign, black with gold lettering. The one on the incoming side read ASYLUM FOR WOMEN. The one on the outgoing side read, ASYLUM FOR MEN.

Invariably, as they passed between those two havens for the incapable, Uncle Archibald would point to the right-hand sign and proclaim, "That's for the women." Aunt Bedelia would point to the left-hand side and retort, "That's for the men." Perhaps they thought it was funny, but even Phil could find little to joke about here.

Paradoxically, Phil's next job was an emergency on the grand scale, and it took place right there on the premises of the asylum. Somebody in a terrible tizzy, who might have been one of the patients but turned out to be the groundskeeper, had sounded the alarm. A main conduit that fed water through all the buildings and grounds had broken and water was bubbling up out of the ground at a rate that might dry up the whole area if the flow was not stopped soon enough.

The most tedious and backbreaking part of the job was already under way by the time Phil had gotten his tools together and gone to the scene of the trouble. The foreman in charge had described his role as being short and easy. All he had to do was to reach the shutoff valve, fashion a wooden stopper big enough to stem the flow of water until the plug was firmly in place so that Phil could fix the uncooperative valve, and go on back home rejoicing, with a nice day's pay in his pocket.

The hitch was that Phil would be working some five feet or more below the avenue, in a welter of liquid mud and a space roughly four feet wide by seven feet long. The laborers would have to do the filling-in after Phil had got the valve back in business—but that was more easily said than accomplished.

All that water sloshing around made his task a nightmare. Accidentally dropping a wrench could mean a dismal period of groping around up to the elbows in runny gook before he could get on yet again with that allegedly simple little job that he'd been hired to do.

By the time Phil's part in the mud wrestling was over, he was caked with mud from head to toe and perhaps even farther because it was pretty hard by this time to distinguish him from the shovelers and even from the shovels.

The water was now under control for as long as it needed to be, and he could wend his way homeward. But how? When he'd gotten that urgent plea to heed the call of duty, he'd put on the oldest and worst of his already threadbare clothes, not realizing at the time that he would need something to go home in.

Somewhere down there under the sidewalk, the clothes he'd been wearing had fallen into rags and tatters. He absolutely must have something to cover his nakedness, but who was going to let him have it? Things being as they were in these hard times, nobody was going to fork over so much as a handkerchief out of the goodness of his heart. All Phil could scrounge were a couple of towels, courtesy of the hospital.

The towels were big and soft and strong enough to serve his purpose. And, after all, he would be inside his car, so who was going to see him? He did wonder a bit, though, because woven into the fabric were the words "For incapables and incompetents only. No trespassing." Phil was not about to get into a fight with a couple of bath towels; he only wanted to go home and put his next-oldest pants on.

Just this past weekend, his brother had got somebody with a tow truck to hitch up the old Packard and haul it to Phil's yard without even asking. The incorrigible Scotties had eaten practically all the upholstery and done terrible things to the floor. The engine refused to do anything at all because it had been so dismally mistreated for so long a time.

Phil's brother had assumed, of course, that the Packard was no longer usable. He'd suggested that what was left of the car might still be put into service as a hen coop, thus saving his younger brother from having to buy eggs at the store. Phil would, of course, give the biggest eggs to his brother before taking his own share.

The elder brother had made a great to-do of handing the car over to Phil and pointing out what a great benefit he was bestowing on Phil's young family. He'd made very sure that the legal documents gave Phil sole title to the Packard so that he himself would not get stuck with the useless car. As usual, Phil had been glad to oblige.

After dumping the old Packard in Phil's backyard, the elder brother made himself scarce. Phil knew full well what his brother was up to and did a little chuckling of his own for the next few days as he tinkered with the fine old engine, which was gradually coming out of its long imprisonment.

There was still a lot of work to be done, but work was what Phil loved to do. Having taken care of the descent into the netherworld, he was on his way home, wondering whether in fact he owned a next-oldest pair of pants.

No matter; all was for the best in the best of all possible worlds. He was riding along in his towels, enjoying the sunlight, the heartening gasps and chugs being emitted by the handsome limousine to which he'd been so glad to fall heir, and life in general, when he heard the fretful wail of a siren and an irate policeman pulled up at his side.

"Halt, you loony! You can't go joyriding around with nothing on and your roof flapping. It's against the law."

"My roof?" said Phil. "I wondered where that flapping noise was coming from. I've only had the car since Sunday."

As he spoke, the flapping noise became more urgent. The great black rectangle that was the roof of the car had wrenched its two front fastenings asunder from the windshield, and the roof was standing straight up like a Viking ship under sail.

Forgetting everything else, particularly his scanty attire and the inscription on the borrowed towels, Phil darted out into the home-bound traffic, joyously waving a spool of strong though slender wire. As the policeman dashed up waving his truncheon, Phil tucked his lower towel more snugly around his hips, secured it with a piece of the wire, and began struggling to get the roof down where it belonged.

Once the strong arm of the law heard Phil's story about the underground leak with all its ramifications, he broke into wild hilarity and willingly joined Phil in the struggle to get the roof wired down firmly enough to keep it from flapping again.

All was now gas and gaiters. Phil's brother had been too lazy even to glance at the wooden supports that were supposed to hold up the roof; consequently they had rotted through unbeknownst, as anybody with half a brain could have told him if he'd only taken the time to notice.

By this time, motorists were coming down out of their cars and adding their muscle power. A ring of enraptured spectators formed around the car, the cop, and the happiest plumber in the county as they wired down the roof and burst as one great voice into the strains of "London Bridge is falling down." Then some wag changed the key word from "bridges" to "britches" and the party bade fair to be a humdinger until a curmudgeonly old spoilsport in a rented limousine came bowling along with smoke puffing out of his ears and was pinched by the policeman for blocking traffic.

The interloper was, of course, Archibald trying to

fix on some desperate stroke that would get the Packard back, but it was too late now. In his eagerness to cheat Phil out of the car, he had dashed in front of a milk wagon and been dealt a lethal blow by a kick from the milkman's horse.

As for poor old Sis and Maggie, Bedelia had never liked them very much and did not care to take them with her when she went home to her mother, as she had long wished to do. There was nothing left to do but to adopt them.

They were glum and surly for the first week or so, then they began to feel at home with the Phils and join in the family's usual pre-suppertime treats such as *Little Orphan Annie, Tom Mix, Renfrew of the Mounted,* and other programs of an interesting and educational nature.

Their shaggy coats got thicker and glossier with frequent brushing, their appetites improved, they began to take short walks with the children, and even struck up an acquaintance with a gentlemanly spaniel who, like them, was gray around the muzzle and not much inclined toward violent exercise. But their greatest delight was to be taken for a ride with the family in the Packard limousine. Good things did happen to good people,

And also to good dogs.

Body in the Potty:
The Ultimate in
Locked-Room Murders

Marlys Millhiser

Before the 727 crossed the San Bernardinos coffee, booze, fruit juice, or a combination thereof had severely stressed the bladders of the tightly seated fun seekers aboard.

"Now what you gotta remember," Richard Morse told Charlie Greene for what had to be the hundred and eleventh time, "is plan on losing only so much each day. You lose it all on day one, whatta you going to do day two?"

Room service on the agency and sleeping in sounded good. But Charlie told her boss, "Spend the time trying to convince Georgette to finish her novel? So Wayne can write the screenplay and you can get Cyndi Seagal the lead?"

"That's what's wrong with you career chicks, you don't know how to have fun." Richard snorted, and his head continued to nod long after he'd made his point and looked away to the faces crowding the aisle in front of them. He was the Morse in Congdon and Morse Representation, Inc., a talent agency on

Wilshire in Beverly Hills, and Charlie was his lone literary agent.

Richard controlled his hair color, eye bags, tan, figure, and (if you believed his bravado) libido to appear younger than he was. But short-term memory loss gave him away. And the twitches.

Their plane had snoozed in the runway gridlock of a Los Angeles morning fog longer than its scheduled flight time to Las Vegas. The drink cart on the gamblers' special was in evidence almost before the seat belt signs signed off.

Even the alcoholic beverages were on the airline this morning as an apology for the delay, which wasn't the airline's fault. But it was necessary to keep up the party mood that kept these planes overbooked.

Charlie, Richard, and the dozing gentleman in the window seat were situated in the last row, directly across the aisle from one rest stop, with another behind the partition that abutted their seat backs. They could afford to watch the discomfort of their fellows with detached amusement, since they'd been first in line to use the aircraft's cramped amenities.

This was a tax-deductible pleasure trip with a mad dash of business planned. Charlie squirmed with anticipation tingles while those standing and facing her squirmed for other reasons.

She loved the challenge of Vegas—not the loss of money but the thrill of winning initially. Charlie Greene usually lost her winnings and more before she left town. But the excitement, the stunningly tacky glitz, the clink of coins and the calliope *bleeps* of the slots, the *zit-zats* of the levers—it was simply an escape like no other. The blinking, glittering lights, the dice bouncing off green felt . . . well, Georgette really did need to finish that book. She was a year and a half past her deadline and Bland and Ripstop Publishers were threatening a lawsuit.

The lady second in line for the flying can wore a diamond-looking stone in her ring that could have bought several Third World countries. Then again, zircons looked the same to Charlie and they couldn't buy dinner. She hoped the lady had the real stone in a safe-deposit box.

The lady's hair, chin and neck tucks, and face-lift were the best money could recycle, so Charlie figured she had a fair-size stash. The woman turned to the man behind her, who twitched like Richard Morse but had much less hair. He had to look up at the lady with the expensive face, but his demeanor did not look up to her. The guy behind him winked a savvy eye at the lady in question and bit his lip. He was taller than anybody in the line and good looking in a nonprofessional way—made for some woman's bed, not the silver screen or even the tacky TV screen.

And the guy behind *him* looked big enough to play for the Raiders or maybe even to chaperon the team. But the three in front ignored his growly look. Charlie, ever the pragmatist, would have tallied the odds and given up her place in feminism to step out of that line.

And the woman behind *him* looked vulnerable and desperate.

Charlie relaxed as best she could thousands of feet above the earth, carefully avoiding a glance past her somnolent neighbor and out the window. Her stressed-to-the-max life placed her in planes far more than she liked. She always asked for an aisle seat. But Richard's legs were longer and thus he needed it more. Right? At least he'd arranged seats as far back as possible, in the part of the plane where the survival rate might be better.

Charlie needed this brief break. She was hanging on to sanity by her fingernails at home and had just sent a rebellious daughter off to cheerleader camp this weekend. At work, several promising projects had paid off in cold ashes.

Charlie's boss watched the slow-moving line, also thinking of other things. One eyelid and cheek twitched with fast-moving thoughts. Finger ends drummed on a bobbing knee. Was he pumping his self-esteem to out-threaten the competition for chips, stretch limos, shapely women with stretch legs, power, glory?

Too powerful in Charlie's life, Richard Morse was touchingly vulnerable in his own.

The lady in front of the one with the true-or-false diamond stepped backward to allow the door to open. The gentleman stepping out collided with the man leaving the head behind Charlie's seat row.

They did a small dance that flattened the woman first in line behind the door, knocked Richard's elbow off his armrest, and thus separated his chin from his fist, throwing his head over into the aisle space. Where it was bumped back into Charlie by the desperate-looking woman who broke from the line. She successfully claimed the back potty against all odds and caused an interesting interplay of expressions among those remaining in line.

Since it was not too long before the old 727 was due to land at McCarran (next to takeoffs and bumpy air, landings terrified her the most) Charlie filled her mind with questions about those assembled in the aisle in front of her. They acted peculiar, as did the geezer in the window seat next to her. He'd come alive, suddenly captivated by the people waiting to relieve themselves.

Charlie had hardly noticed the woman in front of the woman with the expensive ring and skin—who slid into the front potty out of turn. She realized why when the door closed on the latter, exposing the former as small, gray, embarrassingly inept. The kind of person it's too painful to notice—like homeless persons.

The balding guy shoved her none too gently back into place at the head of the line. The cute guy and the snarly guy exchanged glances. Charlie could see only the expression of the grouchy linebacker type, but his mood was deteriorating. He even shot a venomous look at the geezer next to Charlie. The one by the window, not her boss.

It was like watching the shuffling of chips at the roulette table. The unnoticeable woman replaced the desperate woman in the rear john while the bald guy replaced the ring lady in the one across the aisle from Richard's seat. The good-looking man replaced the unnoticeable woman in the rear head, and then so did the linebacker.

Meanwhile, the rest of the line backed up behind the drink cart, with the people wanting to return to their seats crowding the aisle behind it. The congestion brought to mind the Santa Monica Freeway.

The older gentleman next to Charlie twisted in his seat, his whole body twitching instead of just his face. She hoped he wasn't feeling the need for sudden access to the metal bench with the sickly blue-green flush under its inadequate opening.

Directly in front of the side head across from Richard was one of the plane's two galleys. A flight attendant tried to leave it with a coffeepot and three sample-size bottles of booze. A colleague tried to distribute breakfast-in-a-bag to whomever she could reach and ended up handing the bags to people in lines coming or going, who good-naturedly passed them along. A bagel with cream cheese, an apple, and a frosted thing that looked more like dessert than breakfast.

Relief came when some authority up front backed that line far enough ahead to temporarily displace the drink cart from the aisle to the front galley, allowing those behind to regain their seats and those heading to the back johns to regain the aisle behind the beverage of your choice.

Charlie ate the bagel without cream cheese and handed the rest of her breakfast over to her boss.

She pushed her tray table up, unconsciously reading the comforting message on the back of it (LIFE VEST UNDER YOUR SEAT), just as her elderly neighbor made *achhh*ing sounds and went headfirst into his frosted breakfast thing.

Charlie and Richard attracted the attention of a distracted flight attendant over the stream of people lining up for the back john, where the click of the door lock at regular intervals at least signaled some progress there.

At the same time another attendant banged on the door across the aisle from Richard.

There were at least two doctors on the Vegas flight that morning. Two that got the word. But probably more. American physicians tend to be plentiful at most vacation destinations.

The geezer was dead, of either a heart attack or the airline bagels. There was no place out of sight to treat him (physicians are nothing if not thorough). So they hauled him to the small aisle space behind Charlie and Richard's seat row, abutting the rear potty.

The aisle ended in an emergency exit door with SAIDA and EXIT boldly emblazoned above a crank handle with a curved arrow, below which appeared ABRIR and OPEN. All of which made Charlie pray that, if she needed her life vest, the plane would somehow have been diverted over water in Mexico.

The problem now seemed to be that both cans were blocked. Those who needed one still were panicked by the voice from the cockpit assuring them that the temperature and smog and traffic were idyllic on this wonderful day in Sin City. And surely even more good luck awaited their descent. Which, by the way, had begun some time ago. So would everyone please regain their seats and seat belts and would the flight attendants prepare for landing?

When the cockpit finally got the word, there was more confusion and much circling above before permission came from below for the aircraft to land.

Which gave the drink cart time to park in the front galley, the attendants time to gather food and beverage containers, and another attendant time to figure out which passenger was missing from a seat and therefore was the one locked in the potty across the aisle from Richard and Charlie.

Charlie could have told them. Or at least described the short, balding fellow who so despised the ring lady and who Charlie figured helped her form a not-very-satisfactory couple.

Even with the unpleasantness in the rear of the plane, the excitement in the rest of it rose to a palpable hum as the pyramid and sphinx of the Luxor, the metallic green of the huge MGM Grand, the castle turrets of the Excalibur, and the new skyline of New York, New York, rose to greet them with the earth.

But once they were on the ground, without requiring Charlie to take the "brace" position in her seat (it would ever be the "crash" position to her) or to don the life vest under it (scarce security on the Nevada desert), there was more waiting still.

The voice from the cockpit announced that, due to "the unfortunate circumstances on board," there would be a slight delay in "deplaning" this morning.

The circumstances in question turned out to be not the dead body the physicians were still trying to resuscitate (de-dead) in the aisle end behind Charlie. It was the fact that the plane was not allowed to taxi to its appointed gate with someone still in the lavatory.

"FAA law," the attendant, who could raise no one inside the forever "occupied" head, informed Richard, who was getting fed up with all the interruptions to his tax-deductible holiday.

He helped the attendant try to force the damn door. A boy with bars on his sleeve exited the cockpit and strode down the aisle toward them.

He couldn't get the door open either. One of the physicians took a breather from saving the dead to help.

"Shit, there's got to be a way to unlock this in an emergency," Richard voiced Charlie's thoughts.

"What if some kid locked herself in and panicked? Or some weirdo with a bomb?"

The attendant showed him the special metal doo-hickey meant to do just that. It resembled a miniature jimmy with a claw on the end. Then she showed him how she couldn't get it to work. Then the Morse in Congdon and Morse Representation, Inc., showed the attendant how he couldn't either. And the kid pretending to be a pilot (real pilots had gray hair, right?) demonstrated that he couldn't also. And, of course, the second physician had to follow suit.

The flight attendant rolled her eyes at Charlie and sat in Richard's seat while the big guns got their act together and forced the door open. One little door, five guys. Don't ask.

The man inside would scorn no woman again. He sprawled against the inner wall of the fuselage. Mouth and eyes agape. But fly zipped.

Two bodies on one short flight on one plane. Charlie knew the deplaning was going to be postponed some more. She just hoped the physicians didn't try to de-dead this guy too.

Although the agony on the balding man's face might indicate death by natural causes, the blood still spreading across his shirt front signaled murder.

If Richard hadn't opened his inherently big mouth, Charlie would have been off to the slots and the blackjack tables, the glitter and calliope *bleeps*, with the other passengers. Being female, she didn't expect anyone to be interested in her suspicions about the body in the potty unless she were a relative or an acquaintance, which would make her a suspect. Having survived the dangers of Hollywood, and with no personal involvement with either body, she frankly didn't feel that responsible.

But the boss had to point out every facet of her suspicions, which she'd revealed in good faith while awaiting the authorities and permission to deplane. And then he had the nerve to admit where these ideas came from. She could have killed him.

Charlie Greene and Richard Morse sat in a darkened booth over drinks and sinful hors d'oeuvres. Surgically empowered bodies in body stockings equipped with sequined G-strings kicked and squirmed to canned music on a stage alive with honest-to-God fireworks and elephants. Can't nobody out-tacky Vegas.

And nobody could out-morose Richard Morse. All the stretch blondes were on the stage and he was stuck with Charlie.

"You're the one that had to explain murder to Metro Homicide." Charlie had no sympathy for grandstanders. "Lucky they let us off that plane without handcuffs."

"I was simply being a good citizen."

"Well, you didn't have to involve me." The real problem was that they'd been detained as witnesses most of the day and missed their separately scheduled activities and dinner. They'd had lunch—sandwiches and coffee—compliments of the Metro P.D.

Richard had tickets for this show but hadn't been able to contact his date when they were finally told they could go on their way. Charlie didn't miss seeing Georgette Millrose to the same degree.

The hors d'oeuvres were rich pâtés with salty butter crackers, hunks of iced shrimp, lobster, and crab waiting to be dunked in braziers of naughty sauces.

And the wine was excellent. Richard had prepaid for tickets and reluctantly invited Charlie at the last minute.

Here he sat with a protégée and, even worse, female employee, trying not to appreciate the slender thighs and plump, rounded buns that suddenly left the stage and parked on his lap. Their owner's face squirmed a grin while her eyes mirrored thoughts of another life.

Most of the light came from either the stage or the tiny fires under the braziers at the tables. Richard ignored the hardworking woman and met Charlie's eyes over the feathered, gyrating shoulder.

"I don't know why they do this," he said sincerely. "Women just seem to like me."

Growing old must be harder than it looked.

Charlie had seen Vegas, white tigers and elephants and railroad trains on Rollerblades. But nothing with drinks and food this lavish.

The "chick" went to perch elsewhere, leaving Charlie's boss red-faced and gasping. In a booth seat what goes on under the table is very private.

But onstage even the sequins were coming off and only the elephants got to view the surgeon's scars close up. And not one of the pachyderms took a dump up there. This place was class all the way. Rich people sure knew how to live.

"So," Richard said, when he got his voice back, "how did you figure out the murder, the timing, and the motive so fast? I mean, without having special psychic powers like you claim you don't? And I don't want to hear no 'but it's elementary, my dear Watson,' okay?"

"I didn't, and I still don't. All you gave Metro

Homicide was conjecture." And Charlie reached across the table to lift one of the red feathers from the chick's headdress off Richard's short, wiry curls, where gray was allowed only at the temples. "*My* conjecture."

Another feather lay on the table, and he played with it absently. She brandished the first so he couldn't ignore it.

"The cops seemed pretty interested," he said. "And we were in an ideal position to see what went on with the two cans at the back of the plane. But I saw the same thing you did."

"We could have interpreted what we saw differently, though. Since we are so different."

"We're both Hollywood, right? What's to be different?"

Charlie looked around at the darkened booths. This place was so pricey, few of the men even bothered to darken their gray hair and she couldn't see one female companion over twenty-five. "Gee, I don't know, boss."

"Yes, you do. You're female and I'm not, right? You got to get over this feminist shit, Charlie. It don't play in Poughkeepsie, it don't play in D.C., and it sure as hell don't play in Studio City. And tell you something else, babe, you are ageist."

"And you are sexist."

"I hired you, didn't I? Now talk to me. If I wake up tomorrow and read that your 'conjecture' was on the money and I don't know why by then, you are fired—count on it. And don't give me no whining about power. Guys got to deal with guys who got power too."

A comedian who had somehow replaced the elephants leered at all who were not onstage, "Welcome to Sin City, folks." He leaned forward to squint at the booths that made a semicircle around him and the leer expanded to a knowing grin. "Ni-i-ce, yeees. Nice to see all you guys taking your daughters out for a night on the town."

Cheers, jeers, whistles, hoots, laughter all around them. Richard Morse appeared not to get the word.

"So, Charlie, talk to me. What's so different about a few hundred people trying to fit into two johns? And how'd you know the old guy wasn't just too old for the excitement of anticipating Vegas?"

"I didn't. I don't. I was just what-ifing. Like my writers do. And you had to go tell the cops. Not my fault we had to sit in a police station all day."

"You want to keep your job, Toots, you'll explain to me the what-ifs." An index finger drummed the table and the feather flew off onto the floor. "Now."

"Toots?"

"Charlie," he warned.

And so she did. Hey, she loved her work and she had a kid to feed. Okay?

Since half the people in line for the cans seemed to know each other and at least one seemed to know the geezer and the geezer got real upset with the unexpected change in the lineup, what if the two deaths were related? The one a heart attack or stroke because the intended victim went into the wrong potty?

What if a timed mechanism in the Occupied/Vacancy door latch was set to send some small deadly missile into said intended victim (the mechanism also intentionally or not keeping the airline doohickey from being able to override the lock) but instead took out an unexpected one? Causing the geezer who'd hired it done to die of stroke or heart attack or extreme disappointment?

"Where do you get this stuff?" the boss asked. "Innocent chick like you? Jesus, you're somebody's mother."

"The stuff that crosses my desk makes this look like nothing. Writers can't seem to avoid murder by odd means anymore. Richard, I am neither psychic nor a trained homicide type. I was merely passing the time by what-ifing. But when it turned out the unnoticeable woman was married to the geezer, it all really sounded possible."

"Keep it coming."

"Well, it was all family, Richard, except for the linebacker, the handsome guy, and the desperate woman behind the linebacker."

"I didn't see any handsome guy." The incredible display of female, youth, and genitalia on the stage took Richard Morse's mind off murder. And Charlie could relax, enjoy the food and wine.

Richard called her the next day as she luxuriated over a late room-service breakfast of poached eggs on corned beef hash, on the fourteenth floor of the Las Vegas Hilton.

"Hope you didn't order room service," he said. "They charge the earth for a tumbler of water here."

Charlie moved her tumbler of water next to her tumbler of fresh-squeezed orange juice. They were the same size, heh-heh. "You ought to see what they charge for a whole pot of coffee."

Richard had taught her more than he had meant to about "the business of the industry."

"You ordered room service," he said without a question mark.

Charlie could hear silverware hitting his plate too. She snuggled deeper into the center of the king-size, hardly disturbing the tray sitting on its legs across her lap. Between the wall-to-wall window of her room and the distant mountains, sun glinted off a steady stream of incoming planes and high-rise glass.

Richard didn't hang up, but stayed silent on the line—chewing. Charlie repunched the mute button on the remote and heard his TV echo the local news on hers.

An elderly newscaster chided the viewers for getting up for their morning news at noon and missing half a day of good luck at the tables.

"This being the town that never sleeps. And neither does Lady Luck." He turned to his co-anchor, a young blonde who bore a disturbing resemblance to Charlie Greene's illegitimate daughter.

She gave him the requisite adoring smile but turned hard eyes on Charlie. "Yesterday morning, the early charter flight from Los Angeles, Sin City Flight 107, arrived at McCarran with two aboard dead. Now Metro Homicide has uncovered one of the most bizarre stories this side of a Hollywood soap opera."

"One of those deaths was a murder," the male anchor took over. "Both were male. They were father and son-in-law. The elderly man, seventy-five-year-old . . ."

"He looked older. That's not so old," Richard mused in her ear.

". . . Morton Clayfish, patriarch of the wealthy Clayfish clan of Thousand Oaks, died in midflight of what appears to have been a heart attack, while his son-in-law, architect Donald Hanson, died of a mysterious projectile embedded in the lock of the airplane's lavatory door.

"Authorities believe the projectile had a poisoned tip and also a timing mechanism that allowed it to load and fire after the lock had slid into place several times. An informed source maintains that the speculation is that the wrong person was killed due to the crush at the lavatories after a long delay in taking off from LAX."

Charlie finished her breakfast/lunch, only half listening as pictures of the prominent family, the 727, even of her and Richard—but from a merciful distance—displayed themselves across the screen in the wardrobe at the foot of the bed. There might be time to lose the seventy dollars she'd won at video poker after the girlie/elephant show last night. And to see her client, Georgette Millrose, before catching the evening plane out.

"Morton Clayfish's daughter, Estelle Hanson, was on board as were her husband, Donald, and her reputed lover, Chris Benight. Alice Clayfish, shown here—the small woman walking between two of Metro's finest—and the wife of Morton and mother of Estelle, is thought to have been the intended target of the poisoned-dart attack. She apparently suffers from a bladder disorder."

"See? They're taking our word for it," Richard sputtered in her ear from his suite.

"They probably did some follow-up first." But Charlie had become increasingly convinced that, like the White House, police officials watched TV news for the latest developments. They might, even now, be reassessing matters.

Pulling off the oversized man's undershirt that she preferred for sleeping, Charlie headed for the shower, only to remember she hadn't hung up the phone. When she got back to it, the boss was carrying on in high form, talking ostensibly to her but in reality to himself. She gave a listen-in.

"So how did you figure out the victim and the tall broad were married? And don't give me no feminine intuition."

"I didn't. I just couldn't see anything else powerful enough to win such total disdain from him."

"She was obviously a twit. No spring chicken either," he added almost automatically.

"Now who's being sexist *and* ageist?"

"That's what's wrong with you feminists."

"What?"

"Uh . . . I forgot. But anyway, nobody could miss the big guy. I didn't see him do anything that even hinted he was a hit man. Looked more like a football player to me."

"There was something about the look he gave old man Clayfish that made me wonder—problem is, how could the hit man have put the murder weapon in place from that far back in line?"

"Gotcha," Charlie's boss fairly purred with triumph. "He'd already visited that can. I noticed. You didn't. Stick with me kid, you got a lot to learn."

Charlie relaxed, knowing she wouldn't lose her job. Well, not this weekend at least. "You mean—"

"I mean, I noticed the dude coming out of that can earlier and going to the back of the line instead of back to his seat. Figured he had the trots or something. Still doesn't tell me why Clayfish wanted to off his wife. Frankly, her I never saw. Didn't know she existed until you—"

"Mrs. Clayfish," said the male newsperson on the TV in the wardrobe, "was allegedly not only the intended victim but also the true heir to the family fortune. That fortune was handed down by her father, Millard Ambrose Clayfish, on the condition that her husband take the family name, should he wish to inherit if she preceded him in death."

Apparently he did. Charlie could only hope the unnoticeable woman finally got the word. And a little stiffening of her spine.

Where's the Harm in That?

Gillian Roberts

My mother always said, "Girls who are too picky about who they marry eventually find the pickings gone."

Luckily for me I never had time to be picky, or anything to pick over. My prince showed up right away, in high school. Prince Hal, I called him, and I wrote "The End"—and a happy ending it was—to my personal fairy tale.

But I remembered my mother's warnings when I met Amber for dinner. Amber and I went way back, but since I married nineteen years ago, we'd gone our separate ways. She was a big success, with her own company—image consultants, whatever that was. She was the city mouse. I was the country mouse, with kids and a part-time job selling glue sticks and appliqués at Krafty Korner.

Every so often, we tried to find common ground, but it was always on "her" side of the city boundaries. Amber wouldn't dream of venturing out to the boonies if she could help it. That was as close as we were able to get to compromise. I was always the one who had to travel the farthest, literally and figuratively.

But it was worth the trip, as a reminder to me,

because for all her sophisticated and glamorous life, her elegance and accomplishments, her travel and adventures—Amber was unhappy. You can bet that her mother hadn't warned her about being too picky, the way mine had. So now, as we stood on the far edge of our thirties, the great forever after on the horizon, Amber was in a state of wide-eyed panic.

"Don't you know anybody?" she asked. Amber wasn't the sort to whine, but there was an edge of desperation to her voice that I'd never heard before.

But I had heard the question before. From Amber. And I had searched my soul and my Rolodex and hadn't come up with even one solitary male who was single, straight, available, and functioning. Plus, Amber wanted him tall. And solvent.

On her behalf, I had monitored my friends' marriages, searching for signs of rot, ready to pounce if they fell apart. But their marriages, like mine, seemed to have reached equilibrium, or simply a state of resignation, and not a one of them collapsed. Well, two did—George and Harriet's, and Merle and Paul's—but they didn't count, because George left Harriet for Paul, which rendered both former husbands ineligible for the Amber sweeps.

"Anybody?" she repeated. "Where *are* all the good men?"

I knew the answer to that, not that she was really asking. She never wanted to hear about my life. Acted like it was boring. Like nothing happened. But out there in the boonies, that's where the good ones were, the ones with staying power. With me. And what was left for Amber were the boys you never had wanted to date, only they were old now.

Amber had tried them all. Scheherazade's Thousand

and One Nights were no more than a long weekend compared with Amber's accumulated nights and nightmares.

"I don't want to go to bars, I can't afford a marriage broker, I won't attend one more of those dreadful singles' outings—they're all women, anyway—or sign up for another of those dating services. They are absolutely the worst. I could tell you stories . . ."

She had. Hal said I had no imagination, so maybe that's why I loved being told stories, particularly Amber's grown-up versions of fairy tales about ogres and monsters and horrid things that lived under bridges. They were fun because unlike Amber, I didn't have to date the trolls.

Amber poked at her seared tuna. She constantly sliced, rearranged, and mashed food, none of which, as far as I could tell, went into her mouth. That's another bad thing about staying single. Makes you think you also have to stay a stick-figure adolescent with wee budding breasts, flat stomach, pipestem appendages.

"You have no idea what it's like out there," she said. "You and your perfect marriage. You're so sheltered, so innocent!"

"Just because I'm married doesn't mean I've been living in a cave for the last two decades," I snapped.

"Might as well, as far as men are concerned. Have you even ever *known* a man besides Hal?"

"What do you mean, 'known'?"

"Hah!" She plunged her fork into the tuna and mashed half of it down. "I thought so. Your high school love, your one and only! I can't believe it. Little Mrs. Faithful!"

"Is that suddenly a crime? Am I on trial?"

"Sorry." Her shoulders slumped inside her perfectly cut suit jacket. "I'm jealous."

As well she might be. But even so, she had no business deriding my happiness just because she was miserable. She'd been too good for everybody who wanted her, until, just as my mother said, the pickings—and my patience—were both gone. "How about ads?" I asked, deciding that this was my last suggestion and the last time I wanted to talk about Amber's social life, unless it changed a whole lot. "You know, where you specify what vintage, style, and special accessories you want."

"I couldn't," she said. "It's . . . demeaning. Tacky. Needy. Desperate. And dangerous. What if they turn out to be serial killers seeking victims?"

"Why should an ad-placer be more dangerous than guys you get fixed up with or meet at work? Take a chance now and then!"

"That's great advice, coming from you," she snapped. "Mrs. Play-It-Safe. When have you ever taken a chance on anything more serious than a raffle ticket?"

I spluttered and protested, but the truth was, I couldn't think of a single time.

All of a sudden I wasn't hungry anymore.

"Besides," Amber said, "the people who write those ads must be weird, or why'd they need to place one?"

I pondered how to phrase the obvious answer. Amber stomped all over my feelings, but I tried to protect hers. Because I had the benefit of a stable home life and true love, I could be more considerate of her emotions. "Maybe they're good people, like you. And they don't want to go to bars or join singles clubs, like you. And maybe their friends don't know any good single women." I thought maybe that last idea was pushing it too hard, since the world was crawling with terrific women who'd been dumped, traded in, exchanged, or ignored. The thing was, they were all around my age, and therefore invisible to men blinded by the thought of a perfectly stuffed bikini.

"And you know what they mean by 'long-term relationship'?" she asked. "Overnight on the first date. It's all a lie, a fake, a come-on. I'm too depressed to try."

"You're self-defeating."

Amber shook her head. Her hair was the color of burnt sugar, and her skin radiated a bright heat, as if she'd spent the day in the sun, which she never did. But I could see her light dimming. Her fuel was a special kind of hope, the expectation that she would get whatever she wanted, and it was running low.

Frankly, I was tired of Amber's self-centered romantic woes. I had a life, too. And worries of my own. Two of the kids needed braces, my part-time job at Krafty Korner was shaky, as was the business itself. And Hal worked too hard, flying all over and exhausting himself to keep us afloat. But none of that ever came up at these dinners. All we talked about was how she hadn't found a husband yet.

"I simply couldn't go through the ads," she said, "picking and choosing like a beggar in a used-clothing bin."

"Amber, sometimes you make me so mad, I want to shake you. If you liked being single, that'd be okay." Unfathomable but okay. "But you hate it. You tell me you want to meet somebody, and you say it's impossible. I may be an innocent housewife, but I know you have to do something—flag down Prince Charming before he gallops out of sight."

"You don't know what you're talking about. Those ads . . . the things some of them want! The arrangements they propose! People like you—married women seeking a man for an hour a week. Or a man and a woman. Or a man and a woman and chains and sticky tape or God-knows-what."

"Not people like *me*," I said. "If you don't want it, you don't buy it. What's so hard about that?" She stared at me, as if she couldn't understand that basic law of shopping.

I took a deep breath and admitted to myself that once again, if I wanted something done—like an end to Amber's table talk—I'd best do it myself. "All right, then," I said. "I'll do your searching. I'll read the ads, pick out only those that meet your criteria, and toss the rest. I am a smart shopper and you won't do better than me. Beyond that, I have absolutely no suggestions."

She agreed to my clipping service. I wasn't surprised. Amber was always happy to benefit from somebody else's work. "Only please, please," she said, "don't tell a living soul what we're doing. I'd die of shame. Honestly."

We made our list of particulars, what she had to have and what was optional. This shopping list was going to provide a whole lot more fun than looking for the best buy on facial-quality tissue. I could feel long-dormant juices activate as I thought about what was ahead. A hunt. A quest. A mission. A purpose.

* * *

I was thrilled to become familiar with the new language. SWF and DWM and ND/NS for "nondrinker/nonsmoker," ISO for "in search of" and LTR for "long-term relationship." I felt initiated into a secret society and looked forward to each day's new paper and prospects. I'd save the personals for last and carefully examine each listing.

It was true, what Amber had said of me with such disdain. Hal, my One True Love, had been my One and Only . . . anything. Not that I've wasted time regretting that, or being curious about what else there might be. All the same, it became increasingly obvious that there was a whole lot else out there.

I discovered that the weekly papers, the alternative presses, had even more interesting ads, and I expanded my research.

Even Hal noticed a change in me, and he wasn't an overly observant man, if you know what I mean. "You seem . . . happy," he said one morning.

I was shocked to hear him speak. "Not a morning person," he had long ago declared himself, and that had been that. He didn't do more than grunt till midday. It used to make me sad, to tell the truth. I wasn't asking for tap dances and songs, just a greeting aimed in my direction. And the shame of it was, during the hours that he was talkative and interesting, clients saw him at business dinners and meetings. I didn't.

But you adjust, get over things. That's reality. That's marriage.

I kept my promise to Amber. I scouted and circled and mailed off the winners and never let my family know what was going on. I honored her shopping

list, too, as I roamed through "Men Seeking Women"
and honed the candidates down to those seeking
LTRs. Of course, they had to be STD-free.

I also winnowed out the ones with bad grammar,
like the one who wrote, "I love intimacy, slender and
aware." No parallel construction, no shot at Amber.
I also tossed the one who said, much too vaguely, "I
have movie-star looks." He didn't say which star or
movie; for all I knew, he was a double for the raptor
in *Jurassic Park*. Another wanted "an unblenchable
spirit." I had no idea what it meant to blench, but
thought it might involve turning pale and burping,
and that didn't sound like Amber. Nor did the slew
of men touching their "child within," which sounded
unhygienic to me. Adios as well to the "spiritually
evolved" fellows when I realized that both Jesus and
Gandhi would have failed to meet Amber's criteria,
being neither tall nor solvent. Plus, they wouldn't
have advertised themselves as spiritually evolved.

And since Amber was an inside kind of woman,
who favored artificial light and climate control, out
went the excessively athletic—the sky divers, mara-
thon runners, and wilderness trekkers.

Amber wound up with one or two. I spent time
with them all, the ones who made the cut and the
ones who didn't. I loved speculating, imagining, dis-
carding. At first I was embarrassed. I thought of myself as—face it—the personals pimp. A procurer. But
then I admitted that Amber was only an excuse. This
was *my* adventure. I was doing this for me. Suddenly, my low-key life didn't seem at all without
event, and the imagination I hadn't had—or so Hal
said—was getting itself born, flexing its muscles, having an aerobic workout. Where's the harm in that?

I sated myself with the outdoorsy and the indoorsy, with men looking for someone wonderful. Someone a whole lot like me, if you must know.

". . . looking for female interested in nude sunbathing and hot-oil massages . . ." Just because I hadn't thought about that till now didn't mean I wasn't extremely interested.

". . . seeking adventurous lady to climb the High Sierra and scale even more heights under the stars." I could be adventurous. It had simply never been suggested before.

But precisely what heights was he talking about? What hadn't I found out about? And was it too late to do so?

I took a deep breath and caught myself. I was a happily married woman. I had one of the few good men in America. Ask Amber. I had to squelch these thoughts, these immoral, wrongheaded ideas. But I couldn't. I positively buzzed with them and felt more alive than I remembered ever feeling.

I decided to bring the thoughts home, where they belonged. I planned a fantasy evening with my One True Love.

"Hey," Hal said after I'd kissed him. He held me at arm's length to study me. "What's come over you?"

"The children are asleep," I said in a low voice, "and you've been gone for days. Welcome home, darling." I was wearing a new nightgown and perfume. "I've warmed oil, and I'd like to massage your—"

"Jesus," he said, "what is wrong with you? All week I've dragged my ass from city to city, waiting to get home and rest, and you want fun and games?

I'm not a young man anymore. Do you have to make me feel bad about it with crazy demands?"

At first his words hit me like a mallet. I felt crushed inside and out, literally. But after I realized that I'd been thinking only about myself, and then considered how Hal must have felt while I carried on, I tried to be more considerate. I knew how fragile a man's ego was.

From then on, I kept the ideas I got from my reading to myself. The personals were my hobby, I told myself. Harmless. A diversion. I would never jeopardize my life, never hurt Hal and my marriage and my family . . .

But, what if there were no consequences? After I warmed up by shopping for LTRs for Amber, my eyes wandered from "Men Seeking Women" to the "Alternate Lifestyles" column. No LTRs here. No Rs, except of the most primitive kind. Instead, a meaningless—thrilling—universe of short-term encounters and experiments.

Dangerous territory. Off-limits. But I couldn't stop.

"Secure male seeks underloved lady for thrilling daytime rendezvous. I'm safe and full of energy."

Tears pricked my eyelids, surprising me, because what did I have to cry about? Underloved? A man was devoting his life's strength to me and our kids!

Full of energy. Well, in that department, Hal wasn't a contender, but it wasn't his fault. We weren't getting any younger. So it was shabby of me, unworthy, to moon over ads advocating boundless energy in meaningless relationships.

"Seeking discreet lady for daytime rendezvous."

These ideas! These were lazy, delicious cover-up words, verbal slipcovers for bad things—adultery, illicit business, the making of videos, the shameless baring of everything with a stranger. These ads violated everything I stood for, everything I'd based my life on. And I could not stop reading them. They were my reason for waking up each morning.

"I have a great sense of humor, am financially secure, and I know how to treat a lady."

I realized I was weeping. I did that a lot lately.

And I was speculating. I did that even more.

". . . fun. Are you as sensual and uninhibited as I am?"

"How would I know?" I asked the question out loud, heard it bounce off my countertops, the coffeemaker, and the hood of the range, echo back over all the years of my marriage. "How would I know?"

"Great listener," another one said, and my vision blurred. It wasn't that Hal meant to ignore me. It was life. Time. You couldn't expect nonstop romance. But all the same, "I would love to hear your private thoughts and fantasies, or you mine. And then . . ."

And I lusted for an orgy of words touching more than touch could, of exploring the innards of each other's selves. Something I'd never known.

Then Hal came home, exhausted, the lines on his face deeper than ever, and I was consumed with shame for my terrible thoughts, the infidelities of my mind.

I vowed to stop, but I was too far gone.

". . . zest for life a must!"

More tears. I had a routine. I had a life. But zest? The only thing close to it was this, the daily readings. They alone got my blood going enough to survive. Was that anything like zest?

Was that anything like a life?

And then Amber called one morning. "You were right," she said. "Let me be the first to admit it and to thank you."

It seemed I'd "introduced" her to a "perfect" man, a widower with grown children, affluent, unencumbered, tall and handsome. He was funny, she said, needing to tell me everything. They'd been dating for a week, every night, and he was fascinating—been everywhere, knew everything. Loved to travel and wanted her along. She knew it was going to last. "And in bed . . ." Thankfully, she left the rest of that sentence to my imagination. My fevered, overheated, hyperactive, newly discovered imagination.

"Consider yourself retired. With honors."

The newspaper was in front of me, the section with the ads put aside, like dessert, for last. Except—my job was done.

My hands trembled. No reason now to open the paper? To read the ads? To live them?

Then the real meaning of Amber's call became obvious. The ads had worked their magic for her and now—now it was my turn.

So with a sigh of pleasure, I skipped the LTRs altogether and sank into the featherbed dreaminess of "Alternative Lifestyles."

And then I opted for complete honesty. I stopped pretending that I was satisfied skimming the surface of my ads, imagining the men and the pleasures. I wanted to—I was going to—experience them. And I grew amazingly calm—an exciting, anticipatory sort of calm—as if I'd been waiting for this admission all along.

I went shopping. For myself.

" . . . what you want . . ."

".. . what you want . . ."
".. . what pleases you . . ."
".. . what you want . . ."

I rented a P.O. box in a different zip code so that
neither Hal nor the children could find out. And I
carefully chose an ad. He was discreet, knew what
women liked, had boundless energy, a pied-à-terre,
and a few free hours in the late afternoon.

I told myself that nobody would ever know. That
I'd be a better wife for getting this out of my system.
A less restless wife. That I'd stop making excessive
demands, humiliating Hal, damaging his masculine
confidence.

The more I thought about it, the more it seemed
a way to help my marriage, because with my new
knowledge, with my brand-new sense of self, of enti-
tlement, of my hitherto unsuspected passionate ca-
pacities, I knew that what Hal and I had wasn't much
more than two kids, a long history, and habits. So,
really, where's the harm in that?

The man responded by return mail, on thick, impressive stationery. Told me the address, set a date
and time that were perfect, because Hal would be
out of town, in Kansas, and he said he'd have chilled
wine, hot oils, and infinite patience and energy waiting. Those were his precise words. I know, because
I repeated them to myself like a mantra through the
next three days. And each time I liked how they
sounded.

I decided to dress the part too. Go all the way with
my fantasy. For the first day of my secret life, I
bought a great black sweep of a hat that I wore tilted

at an angle, like the heroine of a thirties movie. I looked smashing. I felt better than I ever had.

His apartment was in the city, in an expensive residential neighborhood, an area of weathered brick, climbing ivy, mullioned windows, and great discretion. All the setting lacked was background music.

I carried a bottle of chilled champagne, to show that this was my idea too, that I, too, had style.

Then suddenly I was nervous. I rode the elevator, my heart beating so furiously I nearly turned back. But of course, I couldn't. I'd come too far for that.

By the time he answered the bell, my throat and mouth were so dry I was unable to speak.

"Ah," he said with audible pleasure. "You're here."

I kept my head down, the hat my last screen and defense as he closed the door behind me. The enormity of what I was about to do, of what I was risking, had suddenly hit me.

"Come in, please," he said. "Make yourself comfortable. I can see you're nervous, but please, don't be."

His words were soothing, his voice comforting, sensual and soft.

And utterly, horrifyingly, familiar.

My head jerked up, my face no longer hidden by the discreet broad brim of my hat, and I looked directly into the face of my husband. *"You?"* I screamed.

"You!" he shouted. "What the hell are you—"

"This place—this is your place—you put ads in—you—"

"What kind of woman—I thought—I trusted—"
He went on the attack, as if I alone stood in a moral

pit. Then I couldn't hear his words, only a roaring in my ears. This was *Hal*, my husband, my lodestone, he whom I was afraid to burden with myself, my too eager demands. *Hal*, who was too tired, who barely heard me but placed ads as a great listener with great energy. *Hal*, who complained about every penny I spent but maintained an apartment for his daytime dalliances. *Hal*, who was supposedly in Kansas at this very minute!

With each thought and pulse, my arm lifted, gained leverage and position until it—I—swung back, then forward, into Hal's temple, with all the weight of the very good bottle of champagne.

He didn't make a sound. Just dropped. Bump, like that, a look of amazement on his face as he hit the carpeting. It was lush, expensive carpeting, so he barely made a sound.

And then he made no sound at all.

Dead. *Dead!* But I controlled the reflex urge to scream.

Dead.

I bent over him, but could feel no breath. I touched his neck for a pulse, then realized I still had my kid gloves on. I took my compact out of my pocketbook and held the mirror in front of his mouth. No fog. No breath. Nothing.

So I left, taking my champagne with me. I left the door open, so somebody'd find him.

Late the next day, as I sat in my living room still wearing my Krafty Korner apron after a hard day's work, the police arrived. It had taken them a while to track down who Henry Plantagenet, the name on the apartment lease, really was. Prince Hal.

The police were apologetic and embarrassed. "A lot of crazies wandering around the city," they said. "Your husband just probably took some foolish chances and . . . we're real sorry for you."

"I thought he was in Kansas," I said. They were very sympathetic.

As soon as I'd seen the reality of who was behind the ad, it was over with the personals. I was sad to give them up, but the good news was the discovery of my talent. Hal had been wrong about a lot of things, but the one that turned out to be most important was his low opinion of my imagination. I now knew that not only did I have one, but I had one that worked a whole lot better than reality did.

Think about it—I'd been married to a figment of my imagination, a totally imaginary husband, for nineteen years. I'd spun a story about happiness with a somebody named Hal and created my own reality. A virtual marriage, I guess you could say. And I'd been great at it.

That's when I started writing fiction. So it's fair to say that in stopping Hal's career, I kicked mine into gear.

I had and have no guilt. Why should I? I killed a man who wasn't there, a man who was a good listener with boundless energy and splendid technique, a man who knew what women wanted and respected it.

A man who was no more than words on newsprint.

He never existed, and he continues not to.

Where's the harm in that?

A Mother Always Knows

Gar Anthony Haywood

It happened in Amarillo, Texas.

Nothing *ever* happens in Amarillo, Texas, from what I understand, but leave it to Joe and Dottie Loudermilk to liven up the place. We're trouble magnets, Big Joe and I. Sometimes I think we could roll Lucille, the Airstream trailer home we've lived in ever since we retired and ran screaming from the clutches of our five grown children, out into the middle of the Mojave Desert, not another living soul around for miles, and within fifteen minutes, a full-scale riot would break out. Teenagers chugging Molotov cocktails, National Guardsmen firing tear gas canisters into a hostile crowd—the whole nine yards.

Generally, we have to be traveling with somebody for real disaster to strike—either one of our aforementioned adult children or one of the adorably destructive grandchildren a pair of them have given us (Joe likes to call these little people Pit Bulls in Osh-Kosh)—but sometimes we can stumble onto a potentially catastrophic situation all by ourselves. As we did in Amarillo. True, we wouldn't have *been* in Amarillo if we hadn't just come from visiting our son Walter in Albuquerque, where a musical he was backing, entitled *Malcolm X and Mister T in the Key of*

G, was making its off-off-*off*-Broadway debut (please don't ask), but that's beside the point. What happened in Amarillo we brought upon ourselves, no familial assistance necessary.

Joe says it happened because I had to go to the bathroom, but the truth is, we would have been in the clear if he could have mustered the willpower to wait until our next food-and-gas stop to buy himself a 3Musketeers bar. It's a point of debate that we go around and around about every time one of us tells this story, but he really knows it was his fault. He doesn't go inside that Sunoco gas station's mini-mart at two in the morning so he can feed his face, we don't get trapped in there when Lewis Daniel Ryback decides to hold the place up. It's as simple as that.

I came out of the bathroom and there was Joe, standing in a long line in front of the cashier, two candy bars in hand. Had he been outside in the truck where I'd left him, neither one of us would have been around to see Mr. Ryback shove a gun under the horrified cashier's nose and demand every dime in the cash register. But Joe wasn't. So we were. We were about four positions back in the line, but we could see everything perfectly. Joe said later the gun Ryback was waving around was a Smith & Wesson Model 586, a .357 somethingorother, but all I knew was that it was big, and black, and looked like it could put a hole in a bank vault at fifty paces. There were nine people in all inside the mini-mart when Ryback made his move—Ryback himself, a woman and small infant hovering at his elbow, the cashier, myself and Joe, and three others, two men and one woman, I believe it was—and the sight of that gun just seemed to suck the life out of everyone. I mean, our feet froze to the floor like flesh to dry ice.

"Gimme the money," was all Ryback said. No real menace in his voice, just an unmistakable urgency. It was what a man always sounds like when he's reached the end of his rope.

And Lord knows, Ryback looked to be at the end of his. He was a long-haired, rail-thin white man in a sleeveless green T-shirt and well-worn Levi's, with a narrow face in need of a shave and eyes that couldn't sit still in their sockets for longer than two seconds. The gun said he was angry, but everything else about him suggested he was merely tired, maybe as tired as any man who had ever lived.

The cashier didn't move.

"I said give it up," Ryback told her, pushing the barrel of his gun closer to the heavyset woman's nose but not really raising his voice. He didn't seem to have the strength to do the latter.

I felt Big Joe stir beside me, and I put a hand on his arm, having known he'd get around to trying something foolish eventually. Before his retirement, my husband worked for the El Segundo Police Department back in California, and sometimes he forgets that his badge is gone and his authority to fight crime wherever and whenever he sees it is gone with it. I have to constantly remind him that, big and muscle-bound as he is, he can't talk his way out of a gunfight the way he once could. Without the uniform, his intimidation factor just isn't the same.

I looked up at him and shook my head. Don't you even think about it, my eyes said.

"Oh, my God!" the woman standing directly behind us exclaimed, starting to cry hysterically. I'd been wondering when somebody was going to do that.

Her wailing was all the cashier needed to hear. Suddenly energized, she popped the cash drawer open and began emptying it, her hands shaking so bad it pained me to watch them.

Ryback turned to the woman standing beside him, the short, freckle-faced butterbean holding the sleeping baby, and said, "Go get some food. Much as you can carry."

Like the cashier before her, she stood there like she hadn't heard him speak. She didn't look much more than nineteen or twenty years old, and she carried the same pall of melancholy weariness that Ryback himself did. "Honey, please," she said, her baby-girl voice just above a whisper.

"We don't have time to argue, Cee," Ryback said, firmly but without much anger. "Now go on. Get everything you can carry and let's go, we got to hurry."

The woman remained motionless for a second longer, mulling over her options, then she shuffled off to do as she'd been told.

Right about then, a Texas state trooper pulled up in the parking lot outside.

Ryback saw him right away. We all did. The front of the mini-mart was all glass, and our view of the parking lot and gas pumps beyond was almost completely unobstructed.

"Shit!" Ryback said.

"Oh, thank God," the woman behind Joe and me said, wiping her face dry with the palms of both hands. She thought it was okay to stop crying now; the cavalry had arrived. I think she was the only one in the building who didn't expect what happened next.

The trooper got out of his car and headed toward us, too busy adjusting his hat to notice what kind of trouble lay ahead until he'd practically stepped right into it. By the time he looked up to see what was happening, Ryback was already barking orders at him.

"Stop right where you are, mister! You step through that door, boy, I'm gonna start some serious shootin' in here!"

The trooper reached for the gun at his side instinctively, then froze. Just as he had to everyone on our side of the mini-mart's glass facade, Ryback sounded to him like a man who meant every word he said.

"Now, just hold on—" the trooper said, searching desperately for the right thing to say.

"No, *you* hold on! Get the hell away from that door! Right now, goddammit!"

"Son, you've got to give this up," Big Joe said, talking to Ryback the way I'd heard him talk to his own sons a thousand times before—with quiet calm and aged wisdom. "It's all over. Put that gun down before somebody gets hurt, okay?"

He'd held his tongue for more than ten minutes now, and he was all through playing the silent observer. He isn't the stand-back-and-let's-see-what-develops kind of guy, my husband. He takes a hand in things. No matter how close that sometimes brings me to full cardiac arrest. I tell him just because he's insured, that doesn't mean he has the right to make me a widow anytime he pleases.

"Shut your mouth, old man!" Ryback told him, his eyes still on the state trooper outside.

"I second that motion," I said, tugging on Big Joe's arm.

The woman behind us was crying hysterically again.

"And *you*! I told *you* to get the hell away from that door!" Ryback snapped at the trooper, who was still standing just on the other side of the mini-mart's glass doors, as frozen to the spot as an abandoned mannequin. Ryback actually tapped the cashier on the top of her head with the nose of his gun, just to make her cringe for the trooper's benefit, and said, "You want me to take this girl's head off? That what I gotta do to make you move?"

"All right, all right! I'm goin'!" the trooper said, showing Ryback the palms of his hands as he slowly backpedaled, moving in the general direction of his car. "Take it easy, take it easy!"

Ryback watched him retreat, then spun around when one of the men in line took a hesitant step toward him. "I tell you to move, mister? I don't remember tellin' you to move!" He was pointing his gun directly at the bearded potbellied man's startled face.

The man shook his head and stepped back to his original position in the line.

"Lewis, let's go," Ryback's woman said, sounding so hurt and fearful for him, it almost broke your heart. "You gonna get yourself killed!"

"Ain't nobody gonna get killed. We gonna get what we came here to get an' leave. Right now." He had said it not so much to quiet her but to soothe her nerves. His tone with her was light and gentle, like he was talking to a child who's just awakened from a bad dream.

It was suddenly hard to tell which of these two people loved each other more.

"Son," Big Joe said, as Ryback snatched the money out of the cashier's hand and shoved it into his pants pocket, "your woman there's right. You go on with this, you're gonna get yourself shot. That trooper out there's calling for backup right now. In about thirty seconds, this place is going to be crawling with police. Now, you give yourself up before they get here—"

"I told you to shut up, old man," Ryback said.

"Lewis, please! Listen to him!" Cee pleaded.

"Honey, it's gonna be okay. Trust me. We're gonna take one of these folks along, and we're gonna walk right out of here. I promise."

"Oh, my God!" the crybaby behind Joe and me bawled. Like there was one chance in a million that Ryback would take *her* hostage—the most woeful and annoying woman in the entire state of Texas.

"You. Come over here," Ryback said. He was looking straight at me.

"Me?"

"Yeah, you. Get over here. Hurry up."

I started to comply, but Joe put an arm out to stop me cold and said, "You're gonna take somebody, son, you're gonna take me. Not her. She's not goin' anywhere with you."

Ryback's eyes lit up like a pair of road flares. Up until now, I'd had my doubts he could shoot anybody, but those eyes made me reconsider. Judging by the look on his face now, he was capable of almost anything, if properly provoked.

"Joe, it's okay. I'm going to be all right," I said,

lifting my husband's massive arm away from my chest so that I might step around it.

"Dottie—"

"He's not going to hurt me, we do what he says. But if we don't . . ."

"If you don't, I'll kill you both right now," Ryback said, trying to divide his attention evenly between us and the trooper outside. It didn't sound like a bluff to me.

"Then that's what you're gonna have to do," Big Joe said.

"Joe, *no!*" I protested. "Just because we're prepared to die, that doesn't mean all these other people are. This man starts shooting in here, he may never stop. We have to do what he says."

I moved away from him before he could stop me again and went over to where Ryback was standing. I didn't want to, but I did.

"You're a smart lady," Ryback said. He looked over at his lady friend, Cee, and said, "Forget the food, honey. We gotta go now—"

The wide-eyed look of surprise that suddenly came over her face caused him to turn, just in time to see two blue-and-white police cars pull into the gas station's driveway, dome lights flashing like crazy. A pair of uniformed policemen poured out of each vehicle, three of the four men brandishing shotguns, and immediately began to confer with the state trooper, who had rushed over to brief them on the situation.

We all knew this was only the first wave of an onslaught yet to come.

"Lewis, we got to give up," Cee said, her eyes filling with tears. "There's too many of 'em out there now. They gonna kill you for sure, we don't give up."

"No. No! It's gonna be okay. You'll see." He pulled her to him and said, "Now, come on. We're gettin' out of here."

"But, baby—"

"You hush now, woman, and come on."

Ryback put his gun to my head and said, "You go first, grandma. So they can see I mean business."

He tried to guide me toward the door, but I stayed where I was, turning around to take a good hard look at his face. Maybe it was a little late to be getting cold feet, but I had them all the same. I didn't want to go out there with this man until I was dead certain I had no other alternative, that he really would shoot me if I didn't.

It was a hard call to make.

My intuition told me Ryback was more harmless than he was letting on, but intuition is not an exact science. It's fine for choosing boyfriends for your daughters and spotting surprise birthday parties coming a mile away, but it's nothing any sane woman would wager her life on. Sensing Ryback was putting on an act, and *knowing* he was, were two completely different things.

"I said let's go, lady," Ryback said, nudging me in the back with his free hand. "Don't make me tell you again."

"I don't believe you'd really shoot me," I said, holding my ground. I could actually hear my husband mumble "Jeez Loweez" under his breath, his favorite expression of disbelief whenever I do something he thinks is reckless or irresponsible. Or just plain stupid. He says it a lot when I do something stupid.

"You don't, huh?" Ryback asked, pressing the business end of his pistol right up against my forehead, then pulling the weapon's hammer back with his thumb. The *click* it made sounded as loud in my ears as a freezer door slamming.

"Dottie," Big Joe said, "for God's sake—"

"No. I don't," I said to Ryback.

When I'd agreed to be his hostage earlier, I'd liked the odds of him letting me go, safe and sound, once he had put enough distance between himself and the Texas state trooper to make himself feel comfortable. But now the situation had changed. Now there were five law enforcement officers out there bracing to bar his way, not one, and the chances of his escaping the gas station without some kind of gunplay breaking out had been greatly diminished. Again, if I was going to subject myself to that kind of risk, he was going to have to convince me right here and now that he was ready and willing to kill me if I refused to play along with him.

And so far, he was doing a pretty good job.

"Listen to me, you old fool," Ryback said, mustering as much patience as he could manage under the circumstances. "We been on the road a long time, my family an' me. I'm hungry, an' I'm tired, an' I don't much give a damn if I live to see tomorrow or not. So I'm tellin' you straight, so help me Jesus: You don't turn around and go out that door with us right now, I'm gonna shoot everybody in this goddamn room. Includin' this baby girl right here." Without taking his eyes off mine, he brought his pistol around to point it at the infant in his woman's arms, the gun's hammer still cocked and ready to fire.

To this day, it remains one of the most chilling things I've ever seen a man do.

"So what's it gonna be?" Ryback asked me, returning the muzzle of his pistol to its earlier resting place against my forehead. "You gonna go with us, or not?"

"No," I said flatly.

Then I went to the door on my own, opened it wide, and waved the police inside, assuring them Ryback was ready to give himself up peacefully.

When I turned around again, Joe was standing there with Ryback's gun in his hand, looking at me like I'd just jumped off the Golden Gate Bridge and lived to tell about it. Behind him, Ryback was in a heap on the floor, where Joe had apparently left him after disarming him. Cee was standing over him, asking him over and over again if he was all right, but he looked to be too busy shaking the cobwebs out of his head to answer her.

"I know you've got a reason for what you just did," Big Joe said as the police began to pour into the mini-mart, "but whatever it is, I don't want to hear it. All I want at this moment is a divorce. You understand? I want a divorce!"

He was only joking, of course, but it took him close to an hour to admit it.

The Amarillo police officer who questioned me later was a redheaded, clean-shaven young pup named Bodine, and the first thing he said to me when we sat down to talk was, "You're a very lucky woman, Mrs. Loudermilk."

He told Joe and me that Lewis Daniel Ryback was a very dangerous man, an ex-con out of Arizona with a number of violent offenses to his credit, and that it was nothing short of a small miracle that our chance meeting with him had ended as peacefully as it had. Ryback had never actually shot anybody before, Bodine admitted, but he certainly had demonstrated the willingness to do so on more than a few occasions. Why he hadn't put a few rounds in me when I'd turned my back on him, to summon the police, Bodine said he'd never understand. So he asked me to try and explain it to him, if I could.

And I could.

"His gun wasn't loaded," I said simply.

"How did you know that, ma'am?" Bodine asked.

"She doesn't," Big Joe said.

"Yes, I do," I said.

"You *think* you do."

"No, I *know* I do. You think I would have done what I did if I hadn't been *certain* that gun wasn't loaded?"

"And what made you 'certain,' ma'am?" Bodine cut in, trying to seize control of an interrogation that my husband seemed intent upon running himself. "Was it something Mr. Ryback said, or did—"

"It was when he pointed the gun at that baby."

"Yes?"

"He put the barrel of that gun right up against that child's head, with the hammer pulled back and everything."

"I see. You thought he had to be bluffing, pointing a gun at his own child like that."

"No, I—"

Bodine looked over at Joe and smiled. It was the

smile men always put on their faces when they think a woman's done something so wrongheaded it's cute. "I got you. You figured if he was bluffing about that, he had to be bluffing about everything else."

"No. That's *not* what I figured," I said.

"It's not?"

"No. It's not. I never said I thought he was bluffing. I said I knew his gun wasn't loaded. There's a difference. For all I know, that man is perfectly capable of shooting his own child, he has a gun with some bullets in it. But he didn't. *That's* what I knew. Not that he was bluffing, but that his *weapon wasn't loaded.*"

"And how did you know that, ma'am? You still haven't said *how* you knew."

"Because I'm a mother, that's how. A mother always knows these things."

"Excuse me?"

"That man put the nose of that gun up against that baby's head and the child's mother never *flinched.* I was looking right at her, and she *didn't bat an eye!* Right then I knew, no way that gun had a single bullet in it. No way. There's not a mother in this world who'd just stand still like that while a man pointed a gun at her child unless she knew for certain that it wasn't loaded. Believe me."

"That was it? That's what made you take the chance you took? His wife's reaction to him pointing a gun at their baby?"

"Yes. She didn't *have* a reaction to it. Because that gun was empty, and she knew it."

I smiled and waited for Bodine to congratulate me. Score another one for old folks with smarts.

When he started to laugh, I was surprised. And

when he tried to stop laughing and couldn't, I began to worry.

"What?" Big Joe asked him, after training his patented What-Have-You-Done-Now glare on me for several interminable seconds.

Bodine wiped his eyes, tried to speak, and failed. Joe and I let him convulse without interruption for a little while longer, then he tried to speak again. This time he made it.

"Like I said before, Mrs. Loudermilk, you're a very lucky woman," he said, looking at me through a veil of tears, his head cocked playfully to one side.

"What do you mean?"

"I mean that that mother's intuition of yours is some powerful stuff, all right, but I'd make tonight the last time I bet the farm on it, I was you."

He started laughing again.

"You trying to tell us Ryback's gun *was* loaded?" Big Joe asked.

The Amarillo lawman nodded, once more struggling to compose himself.

"Jeez Loweez," Big Joe said. The shock made him sag like a slowly deflating party balloon.

Black people like myself can't turn white, per se, but we can change to a broad range of other sickly colors, something scares us enough. I think right about now I was something akin to chartreuse; it *felt* like chartreuse, anyway.

"But—"

"Oh, you were right about his wife, Mrs. Loudermilk," Bodine said, wiping tears from his eyes again. "She *did* think that gun was empty. Ryback hadn't had bullets in it for months, she said. Him, too. Hell, they were close to starving, who had money for bullets? But a couple days ago—"

"He bought some," Big Joe said.

"Yessir. Actually, he made a trade for some, is what he said. Gave somebody the spare tire out of his van for a box of shells down in Littlefield."

"Without telling his wife," I said.

"Yes, ma'am. That's correct. Seems she's been on 'im to clean up his act lately, and he didn't want to upset her. So"—he shrugged—"he let her go on thinkin' the gun wasn't loaded. I'm sure she would have had somethin' to say to him otherwise, just like you said, when he pointed that thing at her baby. But she didn't know. She thought the gun was empty, same as you."

"Then why—"

"Why didn't Ryback shoot you? Because he was bluffing, I imagine. Like I said, his missus had been on 'im a while to turn over a new leaf. Maybe he's done just that, in his way." He grinned at me and closed his little notebook, marking an official end to my questioning. " 'Course, there's no way any of *us* could've known that at the time. Some things, Mrs. Loudermilk, even a *mother* can't know. You take my word on that, okay?"

When he stood up and walked away, he was laughing all over again.

The next day, out on Interstate 40, on our way to Memphis, Tennessee, Big Joe and I were still discussing the close call we'd had in Amarillo, and whether or not anyone else besides the two of us ever needed to know about it.

"Joe, please don't tell the children," I was saying.

"They have a right to know. They don't know you're crazy, you could maybe get one of *them* killed someday."

"Nobody got killed."

"Besides, I need witnesses. I ever decide to have you institutionalized, which is looking more and more likely every day, I'm going to need a few voices to back me up. The more the kids know about what I have to put up with out here on the road with you, the better off I'm gonna be when that day comes."

"It'll never happen," I said.

"You don't think so, huh?"

"No. I don't."

"You think I love you too much to ever put you away, is that it?"

"Exactly. That, and the fact you're just as crazy as I am. Or do you think every Airstream owner foams at the mouth whenever somebody refers to their trailer home as a Winnebago?"

"I do not foam at the mouth."

"Okay. I tell you what. You bring one of our kids to the competency hearing, and I'll bring a Winnebago owner. See if you aren't wearing a jacket you can't take off before I am."

It took a while, but he had to laugh at that.

I did, too.

Tea for Two

M. D. Lake

The door opens and a tall, elegantly clad woman with sleek black hair strides into the restaurant. She glances around, spots Jane already seated at a table against the front window, and marches over to her. Other guests, mostly middle-aged women having late-afternoon tea, glance up at her as she passes and comment in undertones that she looks familiar.

"It's remarkable," she exclaims as she slides into the chair opposite Jane. "I recognized you the moment I came in. You haven't changed at all." She shrugs out of her mink stole, letting it fall over the back of her chair. "You should exercise more, though, Jane—as much for health reasons as for appearance. I exercise an hour every day—even have my own personal masseuse now, an absolutely adorable man!"

She peers into Jane's cup, sniffs. "What're you drinking? Herbal tea!" She shakes her head in mock disbelief. "Same old Jane! You were the first person I ever knew who drank the stuff—you grew the herbs yourself, didn't you? Not for me, thanks. Oh, well, since you've poured it anyway, I suppose I can drink a cup of it for old times' sake. But when the waiter gets here, I want coffee. What are these? Tea cakes?

I shouldn't, but I'll take a few. It's my special day, after all."

She puts some on her plate and one in her mouth. "Um, delicious! Did you make them yourself? Of course you did! It's just amazing what a clever cook can do with butter and sugar and—cardamom? A hint of anise? What else?" She laughs gaily. "You're not going to tell me, are you? Oh, you gourmet cooks and your secret recipes! Well, it would be safe with me, since I don't even know how to turn on the stove in either of my homes."

She eats another cookie, washes it down with a swallow of tea, and then makes a face. "Needs sugar. Oh, look! I haven't seen sugar bowls like this on a restaurant table in years. Nowadays all you see are those hideous little sugar packets that are so wasteful of our natural resources." She spoons sugar into her cup, tastes the result. "That's better," she says.

She looks at her jeweled watch. "Unfortunately, Jane, I don't have a lot of time. I told the escort to be back to pick me up in an hour—one of those damned receptions before the awards banquet tonight, you know. I don't know why I bother going to those things anymore. Vanity, I suppose, but this one is special, after all."

She glances around the room, an amused smile on her lips.

"So this is your little restaurant! Such a cozy place, just like you—and I mean that in the kindest possible way! You started out as a waitress here, didn't you? Then you became the cook, and finally, when you inherited some money and the owner died, you bought the place. See, I didn't cut *all* ties with you when

suddenly dropped out of my life, Jane. I've kept myself informed through our mutual friends."

She smiles. "It's ironic, isn't it? The author of cozy
little mysteries featuring the owner of a cozy little
restaurant quits writing and becomes the owner of a
cozy little restaurant of her own! You've turned fiction into reality, Jane, haven't you? It's usually the
other way around."

Becoming more serious, she goes on: "Oh, Jane,
I've wanted so much to see you again, to try to clear
the air and restore the trust that was lost twenty
years ago through misunderstandings—but I wasn't
sure you would want to, or that you were ready for
it. I was afraid that your wounds, real and imagined,
might never heal. But they have, haven't they?

"I can't tell you how happy I was when my secretary told me you'd called and wanted to get together
while I'm in New York. 'My cup runneth over,' I
thought—isn't that what they say? To get a lifetime
achievement award from my peers and, on top of
that, to see you again—all on the same day!"

She swallows a cookie, chokes on it, and tries to
wash it down with tea.

"It came as such a shock," she continues when
she's recovered, "when you threw your writing career away and went to work as a waitress! I mean,
over just one little rejection!"

She laughs. "If I'd known it was going to do that
to you, I might have accepted the manuscript. I
mean, you should have talked to me about it before
doing anything so drastic—we could have worked
something out. Our relationship, after all, was more
than just editor-slash-author. Much more—we were
friends!

"Your manuscript *was* bad, of course, but your track record was good enough that you could have survived one weak effort like that. Not that I don't think I was right to reject it! As an editor, I had an obligation to my company, and I couldn't let friendship cloud my professional judgment. I did what I thought was right, without considering the consequences. And damn, Jane, there wouldn't have been any consequences if you'd been strong! You could have taken the rejection as a challenge to rise to another plateau. And I thought you were strong—everybody did. 'Strong Jane,' we all called you. Quiet, unassuming—maybe even a little dull and drab—but strong. How wrong we were!"

She wags a long, slim finger playfully in Jane's face. "And I don't feel a single twinge of guilt. Don't think for a moment I do, Jane! I'm sure that the rejection couldn't have been the sole reason you gave up writing! Admit it! Doing something that drastic is a lot like suicide. Something had been building up in you for a long time, and my rejection of the manuscript was just the last, but not the only, straw that broke the camel's back. Am I right? Of course I am! You were burned out, or burning out, weren't you? I could sense it in the manuscript. No—no more tea for me or I'll be spending most of the evening in the Ladies, instead of at the head table as guest of honor! Besides, it's a little too bitter, even with the sugar. Well, half a cup, then, since my throat's so dry—probably because I've been doing most of the talking, haven't I? Well, you always were the quiet type, weren't you?"

She spoons sugar into the cup and stirs it, sips tea

and scrutinizes Jane across the table, a look of concern on her face. "Are you happy, Jane?"

She rolls her eyes and shakes her head in resignation. "Why do I ask! I don't think you were ever happy, were you? You always went around with a frown on your face, you were always concerned that you weren't writing enough, you were afraid you'd run out of ideas. You once told me you died a little every time you sent in a manuscript, wondering if I'd like it enough to buy it. Well, you look happy now—not happy, exactly, but content—even pleased with yourself, it seems to me. God, I'd give anything to be content! Well, not anything—I don't know any successful author who's content, do you? But you know what I mean. Here I am, about to receive a lifetime achievement award—a *lifetime* achievement award, Jane, after only twenty years, isn't that funny!—and I'm still not content. I don't think I'm writing enough, or good enough, and except for that first book, none of my books has been successfully translated into film. And I'm afraid I'm going to run out of ideas! I've pretty well taken up where you left off in the worry department, haven't I?"

Suddenly she leans across the table, rests one hand lightly on one of Jane's. "Look, Jane, I accepted your invitation this afternoon because on this, what should be the happiest day of my life, I don't like the thought that you might blame me for your career going into the toilet the way it did. I don't want that shadow over my happiness. I'm here because I want us to be friends again—you do see that, don't you?

"Don't frown at me like that! I know what you're thinking, but you're wrong! When I rejected the manuscript, I didn't have any intention of—of appro-

priating your plot! I rejected it on its own merits—
its own *lack* of merits, I should say."

She lowers her voice. "But then the plot began to
haunt me, you see. It was so original, so clever—and
you hadn't known what to do with it! You'd played
it out with such small people—your heroine, that
drab little owner of a cozy little restaurant, for Chris-
sakes! Her friends, the kitchen help, and her dreary
little husband—not to speak of her poodle and her
parakeet!"

She laughs harshly. "And all those suspects, the
sort of people who patronize restaurants like that—
cozy people with cozy middle-class lives and cares
and secrets! Who's going to pay good money to read
books about characters like that?

"I saw immediately that your plot could be applied
to talented and successful characters—characters who
were larger than life, the kind that most people want
to read about. Characters who own horses and big,
expensive cars—not poodles and parakeets! And I
took it from there, and it was successful beyond my
wildest dreams—and beyond anything you could
ever have achieved, Jane!"

She laughs a little wildly. "My God—even I'll
admit I've been living off that book ever since. One
critic actually went so far as to say that I haven't
written seventeen books, I've written the same book
seventeen times! That hurt, but there's some truth
in it. Even I'll admit it—as I laugh all the way to
the bank!

"Oh, I know, I can see that you've caught me in a
little contradiction. First I said I didn't have any intention of appropriating your plot and then I said I
saw immediately that it could be put to so much

better use than you'd put it to. But there's really no contradiction, Jane. Once I'd read your manuscript, I couldn't get the plot out of my head! It haunted me day and night. I couldn't sleep, couldn't think of anything else. I'd been trying to write a mystery for years—God knows, as an editor, I'd read enough of them to know how to do it—but after reading your manuscript my own seemed to turn to ash."

She arranges her mink stole around her shoulders, shivers. "It's cold in here. And where's the damned waiter? I'd like coffee. You'd think he'd be dancing attendance on us, Jane, considering he works for you."

She lowers her voice. "Was what I did so wrong? Your plot was like a succubus, eating away at my creativity. And since your creativity destroyed mine, didn't I have a right to steal from you? But I didn't think it would end your career! I assumed you'd go on writing those miserable little mysteries featuring Maggie O'Hare—or whatever her name was—forever, earning tidy little advances, a steady dribble of royalties, and tepid reviews. Damn it, Jane, I wasn't stealing *everything* from you—just that one brilliant little plot!"

A sheen of perspiration glistens on her forehead and upper lip, and she glances quickly around the room. "Sorry! I didn't mean to raise my voice like that. But you can see how aggravated it still makes me when I think of how you were going to waste it. I thought of you as a bad parent, Jane, and I felt it was my moral obligation to take your child from you to save it. You should have thanked me for that, not quit writing and disappeared without so much as a by-your-leave."

She picks up the teapot and starts to pour tea into Jane's cup, but, when she sees it's full, refills her own instead.

"And when your apartment burned down," she goes on after a moment, "and with it your computer and all the diskettes, it seemed to me that that was a sign from God—or whoever it is who watches over the really creative people in this world—that I should seize the moment! I mean, after the fire your plot was in the air, so to speak, wasn't it—just ashes floating in the air for anybody to grab who had the moral courage to grab it. And I did. I grabbed it, since I was left with the only copy of your manuscript still in existence!"

She dabs at her forehead with the napkin bunched in her hand. "Don't you think it's too hot in here?" she asks, shrugging out of her mink stole again.

"Even then," she continues after a moment, "I'm not sure I would have done it—taken your plot, I mean, changing the names and occupations of the characters—if it hadn't been for your husband. In fact, I'm not sure it wasn't Brad's idea in the first place! You see, he'd grown tired of being the husband of a plump, rather drab, lower mid-list mystery author, and one afternoon when we were lying in bed idly chatting about this and that, I happened to mention how possessed I was by the plot of your latest manuscript and how I thought it was bigger, much bigger, than your abilities to do anything with it. It needed larger characters and a larger milieu, I told him—perhaps a strikingly beautiful gourmet cook who has studied with some of the best chefs in France or Italy and is married to a remarkably handsome stockbroker—strong, self-possessed characters who move with casual grace in a world of money, power, and elegance!''

She smiles at a memory. ''And you know how it goes when you're lying in bed after sex with your lover. Brad remarked—in all innocence, I'm sure—that unfortunately you weren't equipped to write about such a world. You didn't know it. You only knew the world of the middle class.

''And then I said that, well, *I* knew the world of the beautiful people very well! After all, as an editor I'd had to attend the kind of literary soirees that now, as one of the world's best-selling authors of romantic suspense, I'm forced to attend all the time.

''And that's how it happened, you see, Jane. I rejected your book because it wasn't up to your usual standards, Brad and I discussed what I could do with its marvelous plot—and the next thing I knew, your apartment burned down with all your records! You were lucky to get out with your life, if I remember correctly—although you did lose the poodle and the parakeet you'd loved so much. I remember that because Brad hated them both and was glad they were gone, although he did feel badly about everything else you lost.''

She nibbles a cookie. ''And your miscarriage, of course,'' she adds. ''Brad was very, *very* sad about that, as was I. Brad had ceased to love you by that time, of course, but he still *cared* about you. *Deeply.*''

She smiles compassionately across the table at Jane. ''If you need money, Jane—for expansion or to get more help—and God knows you could use another waiter!—I'd be glad to give you some. I've got more than I know what to do with now. I'll even give you a little monthly stipend if you want it, even though

I don't have to and I certainly don't feel any moral qualms about what I did."

She picks up her cup and brings it to her lips, pauses suddenly, and then puts it down and stares at it thoughtfully for a long moment. Then she laughs uneasily, shrugs, and picks it up again and takes a big swallow.

"Funny," she says, "in your manuscript it's in a pot of tea that Nora Smith puts the poison that kills first her husband and then her husband's lover in Maggie—Margie?—O'Hare's restaurant. Do you remember, or has it been too long ago for you? I'd probably have forgotten about it myself except I had a big quarrel with my editor, who wanted me to make the poison a faster-acting one, cyanide or strychnine. I pointed out that if it acted that fast, the police would have no trouble tracing where the victims ingested it, but by making it take several days, nobody would know—until Maggie or Margie figures it out in the end, that is. Of course, by the time I rewrote it my way, it wasn't Maggie's—Megan's?—drab little restaurant anymore, it was the elegant bistro belonging to my heroine, Titania Oakes, a culinary artist, which attracted only the beautiful people—the trendsetters, the movers and the shakers. And the victims weren't a dowdy schoolteacher and an insurance salesman either—they were famous Broadway stars! That's how I made your wretched little story into a blockbuster, Jane! But I kept the poison the same as yours, except in my book it wasn't in tea, it was in a lovely risotto, for which Titania's restaurant was famous."

She frowns in thought, her eyes moving involuntarily to the teapot. "What was the name of that poison, anyway—do you remember? Something odorless and tasteless that leaves no trace, unless the medical examiner knows what to look for. I remember asking you where you got the idea for it and you said you'd had mushrooms like that growing in your backyard when you were a kid. Your mother had warned you against eating them. Once they got into your system, she said, you were done for—nothing could save you."

She shudders, picks up her teacup, and starts to take another swallow, then changes her mind and puts the cup down with a clatter.

"God, how you must hate me!" she whispers. "First I steal your husband and then your novel. Then you lose your poodle, your parakeet, and your baby—and finally your career. It sounds awful now, in the cold light of a gray autumn day in this cozy god-awful place—but it seemed so right at the time! And I didn't mean to hurt you, Jane! I expected you to bounce back stronger than ever. And probably meaner, too."

She tries to laugh but coughs instead. "I even imagined you'd write a novel in which you murdered me in the most horrible possible way! Isn't that ridiculous? Instead, you just dried up and blew away, didn't you?

"But you did get Brad back! When it didn't work out between us and I was forced to show him the door, right around the time my novel hit the *New York Times* best-seller list, he crawled back to you, didn't he? I seem to recall hearing that somewhere. As I said, I've kept track of you all these years, Jane. I don't know why. I guess I just don't know how to let go of a friend, even one who's turned her back on me the way you did. Call me a fool, but at least I'm a *loyal* fool!"

She frowns at a sudden memory. "But then Brad died, didn't he? I recall hearing that, too. First, you got remarried, and then, a year or so later, he came into some money. And then he died—suddenly, although he wasn't very old."

She's pale and breathing hard now, but she manages a ghastly smile. "Did you have him cremated, Jane?" she asks with forced humor. "So they'd never be able to find out if you'd put something in his food?"

Her voice rising, she asks, "What was it called again—the poison? There's no known antidote for it, is there? And a little goes a long way. Isn't that what your Megan or Maggie or Margie told the homicide inspector? 'No known antidote, inspector—and a little goes a long way.' " She laughs. "How much better that line sounded in my Titania's mouth than in—in your dreary little protagonist's!

"But once you've got it in your system," she goes on slowly, ominously, "it doesn't do any good to pump your stomach, does it? It doesn't do any good at all! Isn't that right, Jane?"

She jumps up and stares down at Jane in horror. "How long before you begin to feel the effects?" she shouts. "Do you remember? Of course you do—how could you forget? And the symptoms—chills and fever that mimic the flu, aren't they?" She wipes her forehead with her soggy napkin, stares at her shaking hand.

"And then, shortly after Brad died, the owner of this place died too, didn't he, Jane? Suddenly. And you bought the restaurant from his heirs with the money you'd inherited from Brad!"

She looks around the room wildly. "Why hasn't the waiter come over to our table? It's because you told him to leave us alone, didn't you? The tea and cookies were already here, waiting for me. It was in the tea, wasn't it? You never touched a drop of it. Or was it the cookies, or the sugar? Damn you, Jane, tell me!"

Without waiting for an answer, she turns to the others in the room and shouts, "She's killed me! As sure as if she'd pointed a pistol at me and pulled the trigger, she's killed me because I stole her plot, her story, her husband—everything—and she's never forgiven me! And I won't die quickly, either. No—it'll be tomorrow or the next day and I have to live with that knowledge and with the knowledge that it's going to be a slow and painful death. And I'll be conscious every moment of the hideous ordeal!"

She rushes around the table and throws herself on Jane. "Monster!" she screams. "Mass murderer! First your husband, then the owner of the restaurant, now me!"

The waiter runs over and pulls her off Jane. She struggles violently for a moment, then collapses onto the floor.

"Oh, God!" she whispers. "This was supposed to be the happiest day of my life, and now look what you've done! How cleverly you've plotted your revenge, Jane!"

Her face lights up briefly when something occurs to her. "But you won't get away with it this time. They'll do an autopsy! After my long, slow, agonizing death, they'll open me up and find what you murdered me with—and then you'll spend the rest of your life in prison—or worse!"

She chuckles madly and closes her eyes. "Will somebody please cover me with my mink stole?" she says plaintively. "But try not to let it touch the floor. Oh, how like you, Jane, to add insult to injury—poisoning me in such a grubby little place, among such drab people!"

She pulls the stole up over her face, after which her muffled voice can still be heard complaining that the pains have already begun, the poison is acting faster than Ms. Know-It-All thought it would.

As Jane waits for the ambulance and the police to arrive, she stirs sugar into her cold tea (she likes cold tea), helps herself to a couple of the remaining cookies, and begins planning tomorrow's menu. She remembers to turn off the tape recorder in her purse, too. That goes without saying.

Some Days You
Get the Bear

Lawrence Block

Beside him, the girl issued a soft grunt of contentment and burrowed closer under the covers. Her
name was Karin, with the accent on the second syllable, and she worked for a manufacturer of floor cov-
erings, doing something unfathomable with a
computer. They'd had three dates, each consisting of
dinner and a screening. On their first two dates he'd
left her at her door and gone home to write his review of the film they'd just seen. Tonight she'd invited him in.

And here he was, happily exhausted at her side,
breathing her smell, warmed by her body heat. Perhaps this will work, he thought, and closed his eyes,
and felt himself drifting.

Only to snap abruptly awake not ten minutes later.
He lay still at first, listening to her measured breathing, and then he slipped slowly out of the bed, careful not to awaken her.

She lived in one room, an L-shaped studio in a
high-rise on West Eighty-ninth Street. He gathered
his clothes and dressed in darkness, tiptoed across
the uncarpeted parquet floor.

There were five locks on her door. He unfastened them all, and when he tried the door it wouldn't open. Evidently she'd left one or more of them unlocked; thus, meddling with all five, he'd locked some even as he was unlocking the others. When this sort of dilemma was presented as a logic problem, to be attacked with pencil and paper, he knew better than to attempt its solution. Now, when he had to work on real locks in darkness and in silence, with a sleeping woman not ten yards away, the whole thing was ridiculous.

"Paul?"

"I'm sorry," he said. "I didn't mean to wake you."

"Where are you going? I was planning to offer you breakfast in the morning. Among other things."

"I've got work to do first thing in the morning," he told her. "I'd really better get on home. But these locks—"

"I know," she said. "It's a Roach Motel I'm running here. You get in, but you can't get out." And, grinning, she slipped past him, turned this lock and that one, and let him out.

He hailed a taxi on Broadway, rode downtown to the Village. His apartment was a full floor of a brownstone on Bank Street. He had moved into it when he first came to New York and had never left it. It had been his before he was married and remained his after the divorce. "This is the one thing I'll miss," Phyllis had said.

"What about the screenings?"

"To tell you the truth," she said, "I've pretty much lost my taste for movies."

He occasionally wondered if that would ever happen to him. He contributed a column of film reviews to two monthly magazines; because the publications were mutually noncompetitive, he was able to use his own name on both columns. The columns themselves differed considerably in tone and content. For one magazine he tended to write longer and more thoughtful reviews, and leaned toward films with intellectual content and artistic pretension. His reviews for the other magazine tended to be briefer, chattier, and centered more on the question of whether a film would be fun to see than if seeing it would make you a more worthwhile human being. In neither column, however, did he ever find himself writing something he did not believe to be the truth.

Nor had he lost his taste for movies. There were times, surely, when his perception of a movie was colored for the worse by his having seen it on a day when he wasn't in the mood for it. But this didn't happen that often, because he was usually in the mood for almost any movie. And screenings, whether in a small upstairs room somewhere in midtown or at a huge Broadway theater, were unquestionably the best way to see a film. The print was always perfect, the projectionist always kept his mind on what he was doing, and the audience, while occasionally jaded, was nevertheless respectful, attentive, and silent. Every now and then Paul took a busman's holiday and paid his way into a movie house, and the difference was astounding. Sometimes he had to change his seat three or four times to escape from imbeciles explaining the story line to their idiot companions; other times, especially at films with an enthusiastic teenage following, the audience seemed to have more dialogue than the actors.

Sometimes he thought that he enjoyed his work so much he'd gladly do it free. Happily, he didn't have to. His two columns brought him a living, given that his expenses were low. Two years ago his building went co-op and he'd used his savings for the down payment. The mortgage payment and monthly maintenance charges were quite within his means. He didn't own a car, had no aged or infirm relatives to support, and had been blissfully spared a taste for cocaine, high-stakes gambling, and the high life. He preferred cheap ethnic restaurants, California Zinfandel, safari jackets, and blue jeans. His income supported this sort of lifestyle quite admirably.

And, as the years went by, more opportunities for fame and fortune presented themselves. *The New York Times Book Review* wanted 750 words from him on a new book on the films of King Vidor. A local cable show had booked him half a dozen times to do capsule reviews, and there was talk of giving him a regular ten-minute slot. Last semester he'd taught a class, "Appreciating the Silent Film," at the New School for Social Research; this had increased his income by fifteen hundred dollars and he'd slept with two of his students, a thirty-three-year-old restless housewife from Jamaica Heights and a thirty-eight-year-old single mother who lived with her single child in three very small rooms on East Ninth Street.

Now, home again, he shucked his clothes and showered. He dried off and turned down his bed. It was a queen-size platform bed, with storage drawers underneath it and a bookcase headboard, and he made it every morning. During his marriage he and Phyllis generally left the bed unmade, but the day after she moved out he made the bed, and he'd persisted with this discipline ever since. It was, he'd thought, a way to guard against becoming one of those seedy old bachelors you saw in British spy films, shuffling about in slippers and feeding shillings to the gas heater.

He got into bed, settled his head on the pillow, closed his eyes. He thought about the film he'd seen that night, and about the Ethiopian restaurant at which they'd dined afterward. Whenever a country had a famine, some of its citizenry escaped to the United States and opened a restaurant. First the Bangladeshi, now the Ethiopians. Who, he wondered, was next?

He thought about Karin—whose name, he suddenly realized, rhymed with Marin County, north of San Francisco. He'd first encountered Marin County in print and had assumed it was pronounced with the accent on the first syllable, and he had accordingly mispronounced it for some time until Phyllis had taken it upon herself to correct him. He'd had no opportunity to make the same mistake with Karin; he had met her in the flesh, so to speak, before he knew how her name was spelled, and thus—

No, he thought. This wasn't going to work. What was he trying to prove? Who (or, more grammatically, whom) was he kidding?

He got out of bed. He went to the closet and took the bear down from the top shelf. "Well, what the hell," he said to the bear. (If you could sleep with a bear, you could scarcely draw the line at talking to it.) "Here we go again, fella," he said.

He got into bed again and took the bear in his arms. He closed his eyes. He slept.

*   *   *

The whole thing had taken him by surprise. It was not as though he had intentionally set out one day to buy himself a stuffed animal as a nocturnal companion. He supposed there were grown men who did this, and he supposed there was nothing necessarily wrong with their so doing, but that was not what had happened. Not at all.

He had bought the bear for a girl. Sibbie was her name, short for Sybil, and she was a sweet and fresh young thing just a couple of years out of Skidmore, a junior assistant production person at one of the TV nets. She was probably a little young for him, but not *that* young, and she seemed to like screenings and ethnic restaurants and guys who favored blue jeans and safari jackets.

For a couple of months they'd been seeing each other once or twice a week. Often, but not always, they went to a screening. Sometimes he stayed over at her place just off Gramercy Park. Now and then she stayed over at his place on Bank Street.

It was at her apartment that she'd talked about her stuffed animals. How she'd slept with a whole menagerie of them as a child, and how she'd continued to do so all through high school. How, when she'd gone off to college, her mother had exhorted her to put away childish things. How she had valiantly and selflessly packed up all her beloved plush pets and donated them to some worthy organization that recycled toys to poor children. How she'd held back only one animal, her beloved bear Bartholomew, intending to take him along to Skidmore. But at the last minute she'd been embarrassed ("Em*bear*-assed?" Paul wondered) to pack him, afraid of how her roommates might react, and when she got home for Thanksgiving break she discovered that her mother had given the bear away, claiming that she'd thought that was what Sibbie had wanted her to do.

"So I started sleeping with boys," Sibbie explained. "I thought, 'All right, bitch, I'll just show you,' and I became, well, not promiscuous exactly, but not anti-miscuous either."

"All for want of a bear."

"Exactly," she'd said. "So do you see what that makes you? You're just a big old bear substitute."

The next day, though, he found himself oddly touched by her story. There was hurt there, for all the brittle patter, and when he passed the Ginger-bread House the next afternoon and saw the bear in the window he never even hesitated. It cost more than he would have guessed, and more than he really felt inclined to spend on what was a sort of half-joke, but they took credit cards, and they took his.

The next night they spent together he almost gave her the bear, but he didn't want the gift to follow that quickly upon their conversation. Better to let her think her story had lingered in his consciousness a while before he'd acted on it. He would wait another few days and say something like, "You know, that story you told me, I couldn't get it out of my mind. What I decided, I decided you need a bear." And so they'd spent that night in his bed, with only each other for company, while the bear spent the night a few yards away on the closet shelf.

He next saw her five days later, and he'd have given her the bear then, but they wound up at her apartment, and of course he hadn't dragged the crea-ture along to the Woody Allen screening or to the

Thai restaurant. A week later, just to set the stage, he'd made his bed that morning with the bear in it, its head resting on the middle pillow, its fat little arms outside the bedcovers.

"Oh, it's a *bear*!" she would say. And he would say, "The thing is, I've got a no-bears clause in my lease. Do you think you could give it a good home?"

Except it didn't work that way. They had dinner, they saw a movie, and then when he suggested they repair to his place she said, "Could we go someplace for a drink, Paul? There's a conversation we really ought to have."

The conversation was all one-sided. He sat there, holding but not sipping his glass of wine, while she explained that she'd been seeing someone else once or twice a week, since theirs had not been designed to be an exclusive relationship, and that the other person she was seeing, well, it seemed to be getting serious, see, and it had reached the point where she didn't feel it was appropriate for her to be seeing other people. Such as Paul, for example.

It was, he had to admit, not a bad kissoff, as kissoffs go. And he'd expected the relationship to end sooner or later, and probably sooner.

But he hadn't expected it to end quite yet. Not with a bear in his bed.

He put her in a cab, and then he put himself in a cab, and he went home and there was the bear. Now what? Send her the bear? No, the hell with that; she'd be convinced he'd bought it *after* she dumped him, and the last thing he wanted her to think was that he was the kind of dimwit who would do something like that.

The bear went back into the closet.

*   *   *

And stayed there.

It was surprisingly hard to give the bear away. It was not, after all, like a box of candy or a bottle of cologne. You could not give a stuffed bear to just anyone. The recipient had to be the right sort of person, and the gift had to be given at the right stage of the relationship. And many of his relationships, it must be said, did not survive long enough to reach the bear-giving stage.

Once he had almost made a grave mistake. He had been dating a rather abrasive woman named Claudia, a librarian who ran a research facility for a Wall Street firm, and one night she was grousing about her ex-husband. "He didn't want a wife," she said. "He wanted a daughter, he wanted a child. And that's how he treated me. I'm surprised he didn't buy me Barbie dolls and teddy bears."

And he'd come within an inch of giving her the bear! That, he realized at once, would have been the worst possible thing he could have done. And he realized, too, that he didn't really want to spend any more time with Claudia. He couldn't say exactly why, but he didn't really feel good about the idea of having a relationship with the sort of woman you couldn't give a bear to.

There was one of those cardboard signs over the cash register of a hardware store on Hudson Street. SOME DAYS YOU GET THE BEAR, it said. SOME DAYS THE BEAR GETS YOU.

He discovered an addendum: Sooner or later, you sleep with the bear.

It happened finally on an otherwise unremarkable

day. He'd spent the whole day working on a review of a biography (*Sydney Greenstreet: The Untold Story*), having a lot of trouble getting it the way he wanted it. He had dinner alone at the Greek place down the street and rented the video of *Casablanca*, sipping jug wine and reciting the lines along with the actors. The wine and the film ran out together.

He got undressed and went to bed. He lay there, waiting for sleep to come, and what came instead was the thought that he was, all things considered, the loneliest and most miserable son of a bitch he knew.

He sat up, astonished. The thought was manifestly untrue. He liked his life, he had plenty of companionship whenever he wanted it, and he could name any number of sons of bitches who were ever so much lonelier and more miserable than he. A wine thought, he told himself. *In vino stupiditas.* He dismissed the thought, but sleep remained elusive. He tossed around until something sent him to the closet. And there, waiting patiently after all these months, was the bear.

"Hey, there," he said. "Time to round up the usual suspects. Can't sleep either, can you, big fellow?"

He took the bear and got back into bed with it. He felt a little foolish, but he also felt oddly comforted. And he felt a little foolish *about* feeling comforted, but that didn't banish the comfort.

With his eyes closed, he saw Bogart clap Claude Rains on the back. "This could be the start of a beautiful friendship," Bogart said.

And, before he could begin to figure it all out, Paul fell asleep.

*   *   *

Every night since, with only a handful of exceptions, he had slept with the bear.

Otherwise he slept poorly. On a couple of occasions he had stayed overnight with a woman, and he had learned not to do this. He had explained to one woman (the single mother on East Ninth Street, as a matter of fact) that he had this quirk, that he couldn't fall fully asleep if another person was present.

"That's more than a quirk," she'd told him. "Not to be obnoxious about it, but that sounds pretty neurotic, Paul."

"I know," he'd said. "I'm working on it in therapy."

Which was quite untrue. He wasn't in therapy. He had indeed thought of checking in with his old therapist and examining the whole question of the bear, but he couldn't see the point. It was like the old Smith-and-Dale routine: "Doctor, it hurts when I do this." "So don't do that!" If it meant a sleepless night to go to bed without the bear, then don't go to bed without the bear!

A year ago he'd gone up to Albany to participate in an Orson Welles symposium. They put him up at the Ramada for two nights, and after the first sleepless night he actually thought of running out to a store and buying another bear. Of course he didn't, but after the second night he wished he had. There was, thank God, no third night; as soon as the program ended he glanced at the honorarium check to make sure the amount was right, grabbed his suitcase, and caught the Amtrak train back to the city, where he slept for twelve solid hours with the bear in his arms.

And, several months later when he flew out to the

Palo Alto Film Festival, the bear rode along at the bottom of his duffel bag. He felt ridiculous about it, and every morning he stowed the bear in his luggage, afraid that the chambermaids might catch on otherwise. But he slept nights.

The morning after the night with Karin, he got up, made the bed, and returned the bear to the closet. As he did so, for the first time he felt a distinct, if momentary, pang. He closed the door, hesitated, then opened it. The bear sat uncomplaining on its shelf. He closed the door again.

This was not, he told himself, some Stephen King movie, with the bear possessed of some diabolical soul, screaming to be let out of the closet. He could imagine such a film, he could just about sit down and write it. The bear would see itself as a rival for Paul's affections, it would be jealous of the women in his life, and it would find some bearish way to kill them off. Hugging them to death, say. And in the end Paul would go to jail for the murders, and his chief concern would be the prospect of spending life in prison without the possibility of either parole or a good night's sleep. And the cop, or perhaps the prosecuting attorney, would take the bear and toss it in the closet, and then one night, purely on a whim, would take it to bed.

And the last shot would be an ECU of the bear, and you'd swear it was smiling.

No, scratch that. Neither he nor the bear inhabited a Stephen King universe, for which he gave thanks. The bear was not alive. He could not even delude himself that it had been made by some craftsman whose subtle energies were locked in the bear, turning it into more than the inanimate object it appeared to be. It had been made, according to its tag, in Korea, at a factory, by workers who couldn't have cared less whether they were knocking out bears or bow ties or badminton sets. If he happened to sleep better with it in his bed, if he indeed took comfort in its presence, that was his eccentricity, and a remarkably harmless one at that. The bear was no more than an inanimate participant in it all.

Two days later he made the bed and tucked the bear under the covers, its head on a pillow, its arms outside the blankets.

Not, he told himself, because he fancied that the bear didn't like it in the closet. But because it seemed somehow inappropriate to banish the thing with daylight. It was more than inappropriate. It was dishonest. Why, when people all over America were emerging from their closets, should the bear be tucked into one?

He had breakfast, watched *Donahue*, went to work. Paid some bills, replied to some correspondence, labored over some revisions on an essay requested by an academic quarterly. He made another pot of coffee, and while it was brewing he went into the bedroom to get something, and there was the bear.

"Hang in there," he said.

He found he was dating less.

This was not strictly true. He no less frequently took a companion to a screening, but more and more of these companions tended to be platonic. Former lovers with whom he'd remained friendly. Women to whom he was not attracted physically. Male friends, colleagues.

He wondered if he was losing interest in sex. This didn't seem to be the case. When he was with a woman, his lovemaking was as ardent as ever. Of course, he never spent the night, and he had ceased to bring women back to his own apartment, but it seemed to him that he took as much pleasure as ever in the physical embrace. He didn't seek it as often, wasn't as obsessed with it, but couldn't that just represent the belated onset of maturity? If he was at last placing sex in its proper proportion, surely that was not cause for alarm, was it?

In February, another film festival.

This one was in Burkina Faso. He received the invitation in early December. He was to be a judge, and would receive a decent honorarium and all expenses, including first-class travel on Air Afrique. This last gave him his first clue as to where Burkina Faso was. He had never previously heard of it, but now guessed it was in Africa.

A phone call unearthed more information. Burkina Faso had earlier been Upper Volta. Its postage stamps, of which his childhood collection had held a handful, bore the name Haute-Volta; the place had been a French colony, and French remained the prevailing language, along with various tribal dialects. The country was in West Africa, north of the Equator but south of the Sahel. The annual film festival, of which this year's would be the third, had not yet established itself as terribly important cinematically, but the Burkina Fasians (or whatever you called them) had already proved to be extremely gracious hosts, and the climate in February was ever more hospitable than New York's. "Marisa went last year," a friend told him, "and she hasn't left off talking about it yet. Not to be missed. *Emphatically* not to be missed."

But how to bring the bear?

He obtained a visa, he got a shot for yellow fever (providing ten years of immunity; he could go to no end of horrid places before the shot need be renewed), and he began taking chloroquine as a malaria preventative. He went to Banana Republic and bought clothing he was assured would be appropriate. He made a couple of phone calls and landed a sweet assignment, thirty-five hundred words plus photos for an airline in-flight magazine. The airline in question didn't fly to Burkina Faso, or anywhere near it, but they wanted the story all the same.

But he couldn't take the bear. He had visions of uniformed Africans going through his luggage, holding the bear aloft and jabbering, demanding to know what it was and why he was bringing it in. He saw himself, flushing crimson, surrounded by other festival-goers, all either staring at him or pointedly *not* staring at him. He could imagine Cary Grant, say, or Michael Caine, playing a scene like that and coming out of it rather well. He could not envision himself coming out of it well at all.

Nor did he have room for a stuffed animal that measured twenty-seven inches end to end. He intended to make do with carry-on luggage, not much wanting to entrust his possessions to the care of Air Afrique, and if he took the bear he would have to check a bag. If they did not lose it on the first leg of the flight, from New York to Dakar, surely it would vanish somewhere between Dakar and Ouagadougou, Burkina Faso's unpronounceable capital.

He went to a doctor and secured a prescription for Seconal. He flew to Dakar, and on to Ouagadougou. The bear stayed at home.

The customs check upon arrival was cursory at best. He was given VIP treatment, escorted through customs by a giant of a woman who so intimidated the functionaries that he was not even called upon to open his bag. He could have brought the bear, he could have brought a couple of Uzis and a grenade launcher, and no one would have been the wiser.

The Seconal, the bear substitute, was a total loss. His only prior experience with sleeping pills was when he was given one the night before an appendectomy. The damned pill had kept him up all night, and he learned later that this was known as a paradoxical effect, and that it happened with some people. It still happened years later, he discovered. He supposed it might be possible to override the paradoxical effect by increasing the dosage, but the Burkina Fasians were liberal suppliers of wine and stronger drinks, and the local beer was better than he would ever have guessed it might be, and he knew about the synergy of alcohol and barbiturates. Enough film stars had been done in by the combination; there was no need for a reviewer to join their company.

He might not have slept anyway, he told himself, even with the bear. There were two distractions, a romance with a Polish actress who spoke no more English than he spoke Polish ("The Polish starlet," he would tell friends back home. "Advancing her career by sleeping with a writer") and a case of dysentery, evidently endemic in Burkina Faso, that was enough to wake a bear from hibernation.

* * *

"They didn't paw through my bag at Oooga-booga," he told the bear upon his return, "but they sure did a number at JFK. I don't know what they think anybody could bring back from Burkina Faso. There's nothing there. I bought a couple of strands of trading beads and a mask that should look good on the wall, if I can find the right spot for it. But just picture that clown at Customs yanking you out of the suitcase!"

They might have cut the bear open. They did things like that, and he supposed they had to. People smuggled things all the time, drugs and diamonds and state secrets and God knew what else. A hardened smuggler would hardly forbear (for*bear*!) to use a doll or a stuffed animal to conceal contraband. And a bear that had been cut open and probed could, he supposed, be stitched back together, and be none the worse for wear.

Still, something within him recoiled at the thought.

One night he dreamed about the bear.

He rarely dreamed, and what dreams he had were fragmentary and hazy. This one, though, was linear and remarkably detailed. It played on his mind's retina like a movie on a screen. In fact, dreaming it was not unlike watching a movie, one in which he was also a participant.

The story line fell somewhere between *Pygmalion* and "The Frog Prince." The bear, he was given to understand, was enchanted, under a spell. If the bear could win the unconditional love of a human being it would cast off its ursine form and emerge as the ideal partner of the person who loved it. And so he gave his heart to the bear and fell asleep clutching it and woke up with his arms around the woman of his, well, dreams.

Then he woke up in fact, and it was a bear he was clutching so desperately. Thank God, he thought.

Because it had been a nightmare. Because he didn't *want* the bear to transform itself into anything, not even the woman of his dreams.

He rose, made the bed, tucked the bear in. And chucked the bear under its chin.

"Don't ever change," he told it.

The woman was exotic. She'd been born in Ceylon, her mother a Sinhalese, her father an Englishman. She had grown up in London, went to college in California, and had lately moved to New York. She had high cheekbones, almond-shaped eyes, a sinuous figure, and a general appearance that could have been described as Nonspecific Ethnic. Whatever restaurant Paul took her to, she looked as though she belonged there. Her name was Sindra.

They met at a lecture at NYU, where he talked about Hitchcock's use of comic relief and where she asked the only really provocative question. Afterward, he invited her to a screening. They had four dates, and he found that her enthusiasm for film matched his own. So, more often than not, did her taste and her opinions.

Four times at the evening's end she went home alone in a taxi. At first he was just as glad, but by the fourth time his desire for her was stronger than his inclination to end the evening alone. He found himself leaning in the window of her cab, asking her if she wouldn't like a little company.

"Oh, I would," she assured him. "But not to-night, Paul."

Not tonight, darling. I've got a . . . what? A head-ache, a husband? What?

He called her the next morning, asked her out to yet another screening two days hence. The movie first, then a Togolese restaurant. The food was succu-lent, and fiery hot. "I guess there's a famine in Togo," he told her. "I hadn't heard about it."

"It's hard to keep up. This food's delicious."

"It is, isn't it?" His hand covered hers. "I'm having a wonderful time. I don't want the night to end."

"Neither do I."

"Shall I come up to your place?"

"It would be so much nicer to go to yours."

They cabbed to Bank Street. The bear, of course, was in the bed. He settled Sindra with a drink and went to stow the bear in the closet, but Sindra tagged after him. "Oh, a teddy bear!" she cried, before he could think what to do.

"My daughter's," he said.

"I didn't even know you had a daughter. How old is she?"

"Seven."

"I thought you'd been divorced longer than that."

"What did I say, seven? I meant eleven."

"What's her name?"

"Doesn't have one."

"Your daughter doesn't have a name?"

"I thought you meant the bear. My daughter's name is, uh, Paula."

"Apolla? The feminine of Apollo?"

"That's right."

"It's an unusual name. I like it. Was it your idea or your wife's?"

Christ! "Mine."

"And the bear doesn't have a name?"

"Not yet," he said. "I just bought it for her recently, and she sleeps with it when she stays over. I sleep in the living room."

"Yes, I should think so. Do you have any pictures?"

"Of the bear? I'm sorry, of course you meant of my daughter."

"Quite," she said. "I already know what the bear looks like."

"Right."

"Do you?"

"Shit."

"I beg your—"

"Oh, the *hell* with it," he said. "I don't have a daughter, the marriage was childless. I sleep with the bear myself. The whole story's too stupid to go into, but if I don't have the bear in bed with me I don't sleep well. Believe me, I know how ridiculous that sounds."

Something glinted in her dark almond eyes. "I think it sounds sweet," she said.

He felt curiously close to tears. "I've never told anyone," he said. "It's all so silly, but—"

"It's not silly. And you never named the bear?"

"No. It's always been just The Bear."

"*It*? Is it a boy bear or a girl bear?"

"I don't know."

"May I see it? No clothing, so there's no help there. Just a yellow ribbon at the throat, and that's a sexually neutral color, isn't it? And of course it's not anatomically correct, in the manner of those nasty dolls they're selling for children who haven't the ingenuity to play doctor." She sighed. "It would appear your bear is androgynous."

"We, on the other hand," he said, "are not."

"No," she said. "We're not, are we?"

The bear remained in the bed with them. It was absurd to make love in the bear's company, but it would have been more absurd to banish the thing to the closet. No matter; they soon became sufficiently aware of one another as to be quite unaware of the bear.

Then two heartbeats returning to normal, and the air cool on sweat-dampened skin. A few words, a few phrases. Drowsiness. He lay on his side, the bear in his arms. She twined herself around him.

Sleep, blissful sleep.

He woke, clutching the bear but unclutched in return. The bed was full of her scent. She, however, was gone. Sometime during the night she had risen and dressed and departed.

He called her just before noon. "I can't possibly tell you," he said, "how much I enjoyed being with you last night."

"It was wonderful."

"I woke up wanting you. But you were gone."

"I couldn't sleep."

"I never heard you leave."

"I didn't want to disturb you. You were sleeping like a baby."

"Hugging my bear."

"You looked so sweet," she said.

"Sindra, I'd like to see you. Are you free tonight?"

There was a pause, time enough for him to begin to regret having asked. "Let me call you after lunch," she said.

A colleague had just published an insufferably smug piece on Godard in a quarterly with a circulation in the dozens. He was reading it and clucking his tongue at it when she called. "I'm going to have to work late," she said.

"Oh."

"But you could come over to my place around nine-thirty or ten, if that's not too late. We could order a pizza. And pretend there's a famine in Italy."

"Actually, I believe they've been having a drought."

She gave him the address. "I hope you'll come," she said, "but you may not want to."

"Of course I want to."

"The thing is," she said, "you're not the only one with a nocturnal eccentricity."

He tried to think what he had done that might have been characterized as eccentric and tried to guess what eccentricity she might be about to confess. Whips and chains? Rubber attire? Enemas?

"Oh," he said, light dawning. "You mean the bear."

"I also sleep with an animal, Paul. And sleep poorly without it."

His heart cast down its battlements and surrendered. "I should have known," he said. "Sindra, we were made for each other. What kind of animal?"

"A snake."

"A snake," he echoed, and laughed. "Well, that's more exotic than a bear, isn't it? Although I suppose they're more frequently encountered than bears in Sri Lanka. Do you know something? I don't think I've ever even seen a stuffed snake."

"Paul, I—"

"Squirrels, raccoons, beavers, all of those. Little cuddly furry creatures. And bears, of course. But—"

"Paul, it's not a stuffed snake."

"Oh."

"It's a living snake. I got it in California, I had the deuce of a time shipping it when I moved. It's a python."

"A python," he said.

"A reticulated python."

"Well, if you were going to have a python," he said, "you would certainly want to have it reticulated."

"That refers to its markings. It's twelve feet long, Paul, although in time it will grow to be considerably larger. It eats mice, but it doesn't eat very often or very much. It sleeps in my bed, it wraps itself around me. For warmth, I'm sure, although it seems to me that there's love in its embrace. But I may very well be imagining that."

"Uh," he said.

"You're the first person I've ever told. Oh, my friends in L.A. knew I had a snake, but that was before I started sleeping with it. I never had that intention when I bought it. But then one night it crawled into the bed. And I felt truly safe for the first time in my life."

An army of questions besieged his mind. He picked one. "Does it have a name?"

"Its name is Sunset. I bought it in a pet shop on Sunset Boulevard. They specialize in reptiles."

"Sunset," he said. "That's not bad. I mean, there

but for the grace of God goes Harbor Freeway. Is Sunset a boy snake or a girl snake? Or aren't pythons anatomically correct?"

"The pet-shop owner assured me Sunset was female. I haven't figured out how to tell. Paul, if the whole thing puts you off, well, I can understand that."

"It doesn't."

"If it disgusts you, or if it just seems too weird by half."

"Well, it seems weird," he allowed. "You said nine-thirty, didn't you? Nine-thirty or ten?"

"You still want to come?"

"Absolutely. And we'll call out for a pizza. Will they toss in a side order of mice?"

She laughed. "I fed her just this morning. She won't be hungry for days."

"Thank God. And Sindra? Will it be all right if I stay over? I guess what I'm asking is should I bring the bear?"

"Oh, yes," she said. "By all means bring the bear."

Shaggy Dog

Margaret Maron

What you have to understand is just how much Arthur MacHenry and Gillian Greber loved Emily, okay?

And each other, too, of course.

Arthur is the successful, hard-driving owner of an earth-moving company, and I suppose you could say that Gillian is his trophy wife. She is certainly twenty years younger, five shades blonder, and three sizes slimmer than his first wife, who let her hair go gray and started wearing slacks with elasticized waistbands about the time Arthur and Gillian met.

This is not to say that Gillian's a trinket to be dangled from any man's key ring. She's an equally hard-driving stockbroker who ruthlessly fought off several other fast-trackers for the MacHenry account when it was up for grabs, and she didn't permit herself to fall into Arthur's bed until she'd upped the return on his investments by several percentage points, okay?

Arthur as much her trophy as she his—trim, distinguished, and as utterly besotted with her as she with him—a marriage made in heaven and blessed by Wall Street.

But not by children.

On this point they were both clear: no kids. She

claimed to have been born without a mommy gene and of his three grown children, one was into drugs, one was into a survivalist cult somewhere in Montana, and the third was convinced that her corporeal body was actually in an alien spacecraft on its way to Alpha Centauri and that what was still walking around on Earth was a telepathic projection.

As for his desire to take another swing at fatherhood, "Three strikes, I'm out," said Arthur.

The first few years of marriage were blissfully carefree. Their lifestyle was modestly lavish—a large Victorian jewel inside the beltway in the older part of town where hundred-year-old oaks arched above the streets, a weekly cleaning service, a yardman, catered meals that tasted almost homemade. She kept her name and job, his company won a major contract to clear and grade the land for a hundred-acre retirement village, and their combined personal portfolios topped the goal she'd set for them a whole year earlier than she'd planned. They scheduled quality time for each other in their calendars: they traveled when both could get away—Mexico or the Virgin Islands in the winter, wilderness adventures in the summer; they subscribed to the symphony; they attended the Episcopal church every Sunday morning and even based their tithes on actual income.

Until Emily showed up on their doorstep one day, they felt no lack in their lives. Once she was there, though, hoo-*boy*!

Overnight, those two objective, articulate, career-oriented adults morphed into baby-talking, overindulgent Mega-Mommy and Doting Daddy.

And for what?

Emily?

Even for a dog, she was a dog.

Beyond ugly.

Picture a thirty-pound cross between a spitz and a spaniel, with an uneven black and tan and yellow coat that had obviously been groomed with hedge trimmers. Picture hind legs slightly longer than the front ones so that she always looked ready to pounce. Picture the raggedy ears of a spaniel, the mouth of a Doberman, the nose of a poodle.

"Ah, but wook at dose big bwown eyes. Her's a shweetie, yes, her is," Gillian cooed, cupping the dog's homely face in her slender hand and kissing its poodle nose.

"Her's Daddy's clever widdle Emily," Arthur beamed as the dog obligingly fetched, shook hands or offered to share a squeaky rubber duck.

Clearly Emily was intelligent. I mean she *did* pick Gillian and Arthur's doorstep, didn't she? And she did know how to ingratiate herself instantly, didn't she?

Gillian and Arthur were smitten from the first, but being the decent, high-principled people they were, they tried not to become too attached too quickly. Such a lovable dog as this, they agreed, must have owners who would be grief-stricken to lose her. She wore no collar, so they notified the local animal shelter, put an ad in the Lost and Found column, and read every homemade LOST DOG sign they passed. They themselves posted a few FOUND signs at strategic crossings.

Nothing.

While they waited, Arthur bought a handsome red leather collar and leash so that they could safely walk her around the neighborhood and ask if anyone recognized her.

Still nothing.

Cautiously, Gillian bought a wicker basket with a goosedown cushion.

"Emily has to sleep somewhere."

"Emily?"

"She was always my favorite poet," Gillian said shyly.

That afternoon, Arthur visited the mall near his office and came home with a pair of beautifully engineered stainless steel food and water bowls and a leather-bound copy of Emily Dickinson's poetry.

"Something for both my girls," he said.

Both smothered him with kisses.

There was an upscale pet boutique near Gillian's office, and when an early frost was predicted the following week, she bought an expensive plaid coat and hat for Emily.

"The clerk said it was the MacHenry tartan," she told Arthur.

By Thanksgiving, it was as if they'd had Emily from puppyhood.

Gillian had never been particularly craftsy, but for Christmas, she knitted matching scarves for Arthur and Emily.

Not a week passed that one of them didn't bring Emily something special: buffalo hide chew bones, a raincoat, neckerchiefs, doggy shampoo, Velcro-tabbed boots to protect her paws from ice and salt, and dozens of toys.

Yellow rubber ducks were her favorite. She would toss them in the air, catch them in her Doberman teeth, and clamp down so quickly that the ducks

seemed to give a surprised *quack*. Occasionally a startled Gillian or Arthur would step on one of the
squeaky things by mistake, and Emily gave such a
wolfish grin when they jumped that all three enjoyed
the joke.

After a while they would find the ducks deliberately placed where they'd be sure to step on them.
"What a clever girl, her is!" they exclaimed, and
laughed together all the more.

Unfortunately, those sharp teeth meant a short life
span for the ducks. As soon as the toy had too many
tooth holes, Arthur would replace it so that Emily
wouldn't choke on pieces of yellow rubber. The pet
boutique began giving them discounts on ducks by
the dozen.

In the year that followed, Emily's morning and
evening walks introduced the MacHenrys to a different side of their neighborhood. There were the pleasures of being outside in all kinds of weather, of
greeting the morning when it was dewy and fresh,
of peeping through cozy lighted windows on frosty
winter evenings or greeting the humans attached to
Spike and Goldie, a grumpy English bulldog and a
sweet-tempered golden retriever.

(Spike's "daddy" invited Arthur to join his club.
Goldie's elderly "mommy" turned out to hold the
purse strings of a large cosmetics company that Gillian's company had been wooing. When Gillian
walked in with the account, she was promoted to
full partner.)

That summer, they took Emily hiking with them
in the High Sierra. For walking sticks, they ordered
a hand-carved alpenstock for Arthur and a sturdy
little shepherd's crook for Gillian. From the same chi-

chi outdoors catalog, they ordered a special salve to keep Emily's pads from cracking on the trail, a collapsible/inflatable water bowl and packets of freeze-dried sirloin.

The trip almost ended in disaster, though. On the second day out, Gillian glanced back to speak to Arthur and her foot came down on a twig.

Except that the twig writhed beneath her foot.

She looked down and froze as a young timber rattler gathered itself to coil for a strike.

Emily gave one sharp bark, then moved so rapidly that she was a blur of yellow, black, and tan. They could only watch in amazement as she slung the snake into the air as if it were a rubber duck, caught it by the tail and then slung it again so hard that it cracked like a whip and fell lifeless to the cliff below, broken and bloody.

"My God!" cried Arthur. "Are you all right, sweetheart?"

"She saved my life," said Gillian, throwing her arms around Emily. "Oh, you wonderful, brave baby!"

Since this trip had been planned before they found Emily, the MacHenrys were now firmly convinced that Fate had sent her to them as a guardian angel.

It was a lovely idyllic vacation after that and when the MacHenrys returned refreshed to town, they continued to carry their walking sticks on Emily's daily outings.

Living in one of the oldest, most historical sections of the city meant living not too far from some of the oldest, less desirable sections, and Goldie's owner had been mugged while they were away. She wasn't hurt, merely shaken up a bit, but it was enough to make everyone uneasy. A stout walking stick seemed a sensible precaution.

"Not that anyone would bother me with Emily," Gillian assured Arthur.

Golden retrievers were not much protection, Arthur agreed, and Goldie had lost most of her teeth anyhow; but Emily was young and assertive and her Doberman teeth were a formidable deterrent.

"Look at how she handled that rattler," they told each other. (The length and girth of the rattlesnake had increased with each telling of the story.)

So when Gillian went out that wet autumn night to walk Emily, she was not at first concerned with the man who stopped and stared at them from across the street as they passed beneath a corner light, even though the man's tight jeans and flashy jacket immediately signaled that he was not of this neighborhood.

Nor was she overly apprehensive when he turned and began walking along in the same direction as they, still staring.

When he crossed the street to intercept them, however, she shortened Emily's leash and tightened her grip on her sturdy shepherd's crook.

"Warty?" he said tentatively when he was only a few feet away.

"I beg your pardon?" said Gillian.

"I'll be damned," said the man. "It *is* Warty!"

He patted his thigh, inviting Emily to jump up on him. "Where you been, girl?"

Emily declined to jump, but neither did she growl as she normally would when Gillian drew back from strangers.

"That's my dog," said the man.

"*Your* dog?"

"Yeah. I lost her about a year ago. Right after we moved here." He gestured toward the east, where the large, carefully restored, turn-of-the-century homes gave way to a blue-collar neighborhood of bungalows and tract houses. "I figured Warty tried to get back to the guy up in Pennsylvania that gave her to me, but he said she never turned up. And here she is."

All the while he was talking, Gillian could feel him sizing her up, from her Italian boots to her English slicker.

"Can you prove this is the same dog?" she asked coldly.

The man snorted. "You kidding? You think there's another dog in the world like her, uglier than a wart-hog? It's Warty, all right. I'll show you. C'mon, Warty, shake hands."

Emily hesitated and then, with something very like a human sigh, she put out her paw.

Gillian felt her heart begin to break. Clearly the man spoke the truth, but just as clearly she knew she could not bear to give Emily up.

"Please," she said. "My husband and I— Could we buy her?"

"Gee, I don't know, lady." Again, that appraising stare.

"Oh, please. Any price. She's like a child to us and if you didn't have her long to begin with—"

"Five grand," the man said flatly.

'Five thousand dollars?" Gillian was taken aback. "But she's not purebred."

He gave a sardonic sneer. "She's one of a kind,

lady, and that's the going rate. You give me five thou, I give you a bill of sale."

It was extortion pure and simple, and they both knew it, but then Gillian looked down at Emily, who was looking up at her with such beseeching, humiliated eyes.

"Very well," said Gillian. "If you want to come now, we'll—"

"No checks," the man said sharply. "Cash."

"Then it will have to be tomorrow," Gillian said, just as sharply. "We certainly don't keep that much on hand."

A light mist began to fall as they exchanged names and addresses. He was Mike Phipps and Gillian saw that he lived about six blocks to the east of them.

"My husband and I will be home after six tomorrow," she told him and started to move away, but he grabbed Emily's leash.

"We'll see you at six-thirty, then," he said and, despite her protests and pleas, he hauled Emily away with him.

Emily tried to resist, but Phipps gave the leash a vicious jerk and the dog reluctantly heeled.

The mist had turned to rain by the time Gillian returned home, but her tears were falling faster. Arthur lowered his newspaper as she came into the den, took one look at her distraught face, and hurried to her.

"Sweetheart, what's wrong? And where's Emily?" Images of wet pavement, bad brakes, and a small shaggy heap of fur lying limply in the gutter flashed through his mind. "She—she isn't hurt, is she?"

"No, she's fine, but oh, Arthur!"

Between her sobs, she told him all that had happened. Arthur was indignant and outraged at the man's effrontery. "But if she *is* his dog—?"

Gillian nodded. "She knew him when he spoke to her."

"Then we shall just have to pay him. Cheer up, sweetheart. It's only money, and if it brings her back to us—"

"But he was so awful. You can't know. Poor Emily. No wonder she ran away from him."

Arthur went to the bank next day, and that evening they both came home early. It had been an unhappy twenty-four hours, but soon it would be behind them.

The doorbell rang promptly at six-thirty. Mike Phipps was on time, but he came alone.

"Where's Emily?" Gillian asked anxiously as Arthur ushered him into the den.

Phipps just stood in the doorway. His hands were thrust into his jacket pockets, but his greedy eyes touched every lovely object in the room with a pawnbroker's cold assessment.

"Well, it's a funny thing. I got her home, and it's like I forgot how much a dog can add to a man's life, you know?"

Bewildered, Gillian could only stare, but construction work had kept Arthur at street level. "How much?" he asked.

Phipps grinned appreciatively. "I like a man that can cut straight through the crap. Ten thousand dollars."

Arthur laid a stack of bills on the polished oak table. "There's the five thousand you and my wife agreed on last night. Either take it and bring the dog back or get out because we won't pay a penny more."

"Oh, I think you will. Look at your wife, man."

Gillian was white-faced, but her sense of right and wrong was just as strong as Arthur's and her chin came up bravely. "We will not be blackmailed, Mr. Phipps. You have our phone number. When you are ready to honor the bargain we made, call us."

Yet thinking of poor Emily alone with this awful man who would probably chain her up outside with nothing but scraps to eat, Gillian gathered up some of the dog's possessions—her wicker basket with the goosedown cushion, a bag of her special food and some of her favorite toys.

Phipps took them with a sardonic sneer. "You don't fool me, lady. You're bluffing, the two of you. You said Warty's like your child? So just think of it as her adoption fee."

"Warty?" asked Arthur when Phipps was gone.

Tears spilled down Gillian's lovely cheeks and she shook her head. It was bad enough that she had to know why Emily's owner had given her that ugly name; she could at least spare Arthur that indignity.

Next evening, there was a message from Phipps on their answering machine when they got home. It was not a message they wanted to hear. The man sounded drunk.

"Somebody here's missing her mom and pop. Say hey to 'em, Warty. Speak . . . come on, dammit, speak!"

There was the sound of something falling, a muffled curse, and then Emily gave a sharp yelp of pain.

"Hear what she's saying? You don't come up with her adoption fees, I might decide to donate her to science. Knew a guy once that washed out of vet school when he operated on a dog and the dog died."

"Sweetheart, please," Arthur said, trying to loosen her hand from his.

Gillian looked down and saw that she'd squeezed his hand so tightly that her nails had left little red half-moons on his palm.

Both of them had read of the experiments done on dogs and cats over the years in the name of science and cosmetics. That Phipps could even consider it—!

"He's just trying to scare us," she said, with a shaky little laugh.

"Of course he is," Arthur agreed briskly. "Pathetic really, trying to make us think he'd pass up our offer and just give her away."

"We were merely firm with him yesterday, weren't we?" she asked, needing reassurance. "He wouldn't feel that we tried to emasculate him, would he?"

"So that he'd give up five thousand on principle? Believe me, love—when it comes to money, men like Phipps have no principles."

He said it with more conviction than he felt.

"Be brave, sweetheart. We cannot give in to extortion. He'll come around. You'll see."

But Phipps's message left them with little small talk, and after dinner Arthur murmured something about contracts that needed his attention in his den.

"Maybe I'll take a walk," said Gillian. "Unwind."

"Shall I come with you?"

She shook her head. "I think I need to be alone."

He nodded so understandingly that she felt like a complete fraud when she stepped out into the autumn night.

A low-pressure system had hung over the city all week, bringing intermittent showers that left the sidewalks adrift in fallen leaves. She had picked up her shepherd's crook by habit and was glad for its support when her feet nearly slipped out from under her on the wet leaves.

The damp night air was chilly, and as she reached into her slicker pocket for gloves, her hand brushed the thick envelope that she'd hidden there. If she went through with this, it would be the first time she'd ever gone behind Arthur's back and the thought of deceiving him pained her intensely.

But what if Arthur's wrong, she thought. What if this Phipps creature *did* mean to carry out his threat? Could she stand idly by and sacrifice Emily for their principles?

It was a simple plan. She would go to Phipps and throw herself on his mercy. "Arthur will never pay you another penny," she would tell him. Then she would give him the five thousand in cash, which she'd drawn out of her personal account this afternoon, and beg him to tell Arthur that he had decided to accept their original offer after all.

Phipps would get his ten thousand, Arthur would retain his principles, and Emily would come safely home.

A simple plan—and yet she couldn't bring herself to do it. Indeed, she spent the first twenty minutes walking in the opposite direction from Phipps's house. Eventually, though, her feet turned eastward and less than an hour after she'd left her home, she found herself staring into the front window of a small bungalow.

The curtain hadn't been drawn, but there was no light in the front room, merely a dim glow from somewhere beyond.

She went up onto the dark porch and pushed the bell button, but it appeared to be broken, so she knocked with more confidence than she actually felt.

Immediately, she saw Emily race into the room. As soon as the dog caught sight of Gillian, she seemed to go mad with joy, leaping up at the window, thrusting her little poodle nose through the mail slot, giving soft little yelps until Gillian slipped her gloved fingers under the brass flap.

But where was Phipps?

Gillian rapped again. With all the noise Emily was making, surely he must hear her?

Emily was whining now, begging Gillian to dissolve the barrier between them.

Helplessly, Gillian touched the old fashioned latch and, to her surprise, the door swung open. Emily was all over her in an instant, jumping, dancing, racing in circles, tugging at her gloves.

"I know, lovey, I know," she whispered, calming the dog. "It won't be long, I promise."

A cold draft swirled through the house and suddenly, as if she'd forgotten an earlier appointment, Emily trotted across the dark room and into a narrow hall. After a moment of hesitation, Gillian followed, still clutching her shepherd's crook.

The light of the all-white bathroom dazzled her eyes at first. Emily was dancing in excitement again, and Gillian was dumbfounded by the man who crouched in front of the old-fashioned white porcelain sink. She gasped, and he pulled himself erect with the aid of his sturdy Alpenstock.

"Arthur?"

Then her eyes adjusted to the bright lights, and she saw that the dark object on the white-tiled floor beyond him was not a scrunched-up rug but the sprawled figure of Mike Phipps.

He lay face down in a puddle of blood.

Head wound, she thought automatically and looked at Arthur's stick.

"Is he—?"

"Yes."

"Oh, Arthur," she moaned.

For just a moment, his face was reproachful, as if it were her love of Emily and her love alone that had driven him to this.

"It's all right," he said decisively. "No one will think twice about it. They'll think he fell and cracked his skull on the sink or tub. An accident, pure and simple. My car's out back. I'll get Emily's basket, you find her leash and toys."

Quickly, efficiently, they cleared the house of all traces of Emily, then slipped the latch on both the front and the back doors and got in the car unnoticed by any of the neighbors.

Emily sat between them, blissfully happy even though her humans were silent on the circuitous drive home.

Gillian knew she should be shocked and appalled by what Arthur had done, but instead she felt an almost atavistic glow of pride. He was Man, she was Woman, and he had protected the clan of his cave with a primal club.

"Phipps was an evil man," Arthur said at last and reached past Emily to squeeze her hand.

"The world is better off without him," Gillian said, hoping that the squeeze she gave him in return would make it clear that she would never reproach him for this night.

He stopped on a deserted back road where there was a steep drop into a wooded ravine and reached into the back seat. A moment later, she heard the sharp crack of breaking wood, then the clatter of something hitting the rocks below.

But what—?

When Arthur got back into the car, she was touched to realize he was not quite as calm and efficient as he appeared. Somehow he had confused her shepherd's crook with his alpenstock. No matter, she told herself. She would take off early tomorrow evening, chop it into kindling with their camping hatchet and have a cozy fire warming their cave by the time Arthur came home.

Sex had always been good for them, but that night it was sensational.

Afterward, when they had let Emily back into their bedroom and all three were lying cozily in bed, Arthur said, "You didn't leave fingerprints anywhere, did you, sweetheart?"

"I had on gloves the whole time," she reminded him. "What about you?"

"I didn't touch anything except the doorknob and Phipps's neck to see if he was still alive." He pulled her closer with a satisfied sigh. "So we're safe then. Nobody will ever connect your crook to—"

She pulled upright. "My *crook*? But it was *your* alpenstock!"

"You mean you didn't—?"

"No. I thought it was you!"

"You mean it really *was* an accident?"

Curled up at the foot of their bed, Emily, the dog formerly known as Warty, sighed happily at the sound of her humans' laughter.

That last human hadn't laughed when his foot made her duck squeak. He jumped back, lost his balance, and fell heavily, and after that he never moved again. She certainly wouldn't want that to happen to *her* humans.

Something very like a resolution was forming in her homely, shaggy head: Never again would she leave a rubber duck where one of them might step on it.

If you can't be beautiful, then you'd better be smart.

Wake Up, Little Suzie

Ed Gorman

"Murder," she said.

"Murder?"

"Uh-huh," she said. Then, "Edsel."

Usually Pamela Forrest doesn't have any trouble at all speaking in complete sentences.

But at the moment her lovely mouth was filled with a piece of doughnut, a fact she was demurely trying to hide behind a napkin, and so of necessity she spoke in a kind of code.

"Somebody got murdered in an Edsel?" I said.

She said, "Trunk."

Murder. Edsel. Trunk.

It was starting to make sense.

"That's why the judge got me over here?" I said.

She held up one slender, elegant finger to indicate that I should indulge her a few more moments, and then she made a big show of swallowing the rest of her doughnut bite in a single gulp.

I suppose I should tell you right here that I'm in love with Pamela Forrest and plan to marry her someday. I also suppose I should tell you that Pamela Forrest is in love with Stew McGinley and plans to marry *him* someday. Cross-purposes, I think the term is.

"What Edsel are we talking about?" I said.

She said, "Stan, the Ford dealer?"

"Stan Winwood. Right."

"He had his unveiling yesterday."

He sure did. He even served beer at it, as I can testify, having swilled maybe a half dozen of the big paper cups myself. I had a good excuse: it's not every day that Ford Motor Company introduces a car that's going to revolutionize the auto industry as the Edsel is going to. All across the country, at more than three hundred dealerships yesterday afternoon, Americans got their first look at the Edsel.

"So Stan came to work—" I said.

"—and then he noticed this yellow Edsel he'd left out near the service garage overnight—"

"—and when he walked up to it and saw the trunk—"

"—there was blood all over it. So he opened the trunk and looked inside and—"

Now it all made *perfect* sense, what those sumptuous lovely lips had been telling me: Murder. Edsel. Trunk.

"He opened up the trunk and there was a body in it," I said.

"Exactly. And that's what the judge wants to talk to you about. And you're already—" She gave me a flash of her heartbreaking profile as she looked up at the wall clock. "—twelve minutes late."

"How's her mood?"

Pamela, never Pam, smiled at me. In her buff blue two-piece summer suit, with her soft blond hair pulled back into a loose chignon, she looked city-smart as all hell, like Grace Kelly in *To Catch a Thief.*

"How's her mood, McCain? When somebody's late? Are you kidding?"

Since I was already twelve minutes in arrears, I decided to gamble it all and be *thirteen* minutes late.

"There's a Tony Curtis double feature on at the drive-in tonight," I said. "I know how much you like Tony Curtis."

She sighed. "You never give up, do you?"

"You don't, either. With good ol' Stew."

"We had our time, McCain, and it just didn't work out for us."

"We had three weeks, and then you went right back to mooning over Stew."

"That isn't a very flattering word, mooning."

"You know what I mean."

"I'm in love with Stew. I can't help it."

"And I'm in love with you, and *I* can't help it."

"Poor you, and poor me. But you'd better get in there, McCain. She's really on the warpath."

"Tony Curtis," I said, and held up two fingers. "Two Tony Curtises, in fact."

Just then her intercom crackled to life and Judge Eleanor Whitney said, "Is he out there bothering you again, Pamela?"

She winked at me. "He never bothers me, Your Honor. In fact, in a kind of pathetic way, he's sort of cute."

"Tell him to get his butt in here."

"Yessir, Your Honor."

When the judge clicked off, I said, "Thanks for saying I'm cute."

She smiled and said, "I said 'sort of cute,' McCain. It's not exactly the same thing."

*   *   *

The last time Judge Eleanor Whitney was in a good mood, at least as far as anybody can recall, was sometime in June 1906.

In her first sixty-one years, she's buried three husbands, built herself four mansions, bought and paid for several local elections, and even managed to install a governor who, unfortunately, had to be recalled after it was proved he'd engineered a stock swindle in another state.

Other than that, she's a pretty typical Midwestern widow who flies her own Beechcraft-Bonanza, plays the occasional eight holes with President Eisenhower, and is a world-class fox hunter.

This morning she wore a white blouse that was frillier than she usually seemed to care for, a handsome and well-fitted blue skirt, and a scowl that would give men on death row the chills. For all her power, and occasional malice, she's actually a pretty woman, with a pert little face, a very well-kept and very tidy little body, and the wiles of a seductress when the circumstances require.

One other thing about her: she shoots rubber bands. Uses thumb and finger as a gun to launch them.

One sailed past me just as I stepped into her chambers and even before I could quite seat myself in a leather chair across from her desk, she was already loading up another round.

She came away from the window, seated herself in her magisterial high-backed leather chair, and said, "You know who he's arrested?"

"You mean Chief Sykes?"

"Of course I mean Chief Sykes. Who else would I

mean? And by the way, don't you think it's time you stop pestering Pamela?"

"In reverse order, (a) I'm not pestering Pamela. She's actually in love with me but she just doesn't know it yet. And (b) How would I know who Chief Sykes arrested?"

"Pentecost?"

"Lou Pentecost?"

"Lou Pentecost. Charged him with first-degree murder."

"You're kidding."

"Of course I'm not kidding, McCain. I never kid about Sykes. You should know that by now."

"But why would he charge Lou Pentecost?"

"Says that Pentecost was seen leaving the car lot around dawn this morning."

"Seen by whom?"

She had an impish and seductive smile. "Old Charlie Burton."

"Now you *are* kidding."

"That's what the esteemed chief of police told me on the phone this morning."

"But Old Charlie Burton—"

"—hasn't been sober since 1931. So as a witness, he's—"

"—totally unreliable."

"Exactly. That's why I want you to go to work on this, McCain. That poor man sitting in jail didn't kill her. I'm sure of it."

But she wasn't thinking of "that poor man." She was thinking of the Sykes clan.

During his four-year tenure as police chief, Cliff Sykes has indicted five people for murder. Every one of them was later proved innocent. I know, because

Judge Whitney hired me as an investigator to check out the cases myself. I'm a pretty good investigator, actually. In addition to my law degree, I've been taking criminology courses over at the state university, and during the summer I usually spend a couple of weeks auditing courses at the state police academy.

So why is Judge Whitney so obsessed with humiliating Chief Sykes? She's old money, he's new money. Her people came out here from Connecticut 160 years ago and settled this part of the frontier. They brought some formidable cash reserves with them. It was the Whitneys who built this town. And they ran it, too, for well over a hundred years, right up till the end of World War II. The Sykes family, prairie people as suspicious of "fancy folk" as they were of bathing, struck one of those wartime gold mines. Their very modest construction company got the nod from the federal government to build roads and airstrips out here. By the early 1950s, the Sykeses had even more money than the Whitneys. And they spent it just as the Whitneys had spent it—they bought themselves a mayor and a town council, and as soon as that council was installed, its first act was to appoint the eldest Sykes boy, Cliff, chief of police. In desperation, obviously hoping to frustrate the Sykeses in the only way she could, Eleanor Whitney got the governor to appoint her the local judge and fixed it so that Cliff Sykes always had to ask her for his search warrants, writs of habeas corpus, and so forth, a situation she relished and Cliff Sykes loathed.

Money hadn't changed the Sykes family any, Judge Whitney's friends liked to say. They were still the same mean, stupid, dishonest, and uncouth people they'd always been. And when Cliff Sykes Sr. built the tire factory, and became the biggest employer in Black River Falls, Iowa (pop. 20,457), the Sykes family took on the mantle of the respectable and the revered. Even if they still did smell a little bad when you stood downwind of them.

"You know, Judge, one of these days, Cliff Sykes Jr. is going to arrest the right man just to spite you."

"I probably won't live long enough to see it."

"And maybe someday my law practice will be able to support me and I won't have to run all over town making enemies."

"That's part of a lawyer's job, making enemies. Or didn't they teach you that in law school?"

I smiled. "That isn't exactly how they phrased it. I think they mentioned something about pursuing the truth."

"Well, in this town making enemies and pursuing the truth are very often the same thing, McCain. Now get the hell out of here. Court starts in fifteen minutes."

I stood up. "You mind if I tell you you look nice this morning? Maybe it's because there aren't any rattlesnakes around."

That's one other thing the judge does, she keeps a dozen rattlesnakes in glass cages in her mansion. That's why I'm always a little nervous when I'm out there.

"Why, McCain, you're young enough to be my son." But my words, and they'd been sincere, had put a dazzle in those green eyes that was nice to behold. "But I sure do appreciate the compliment. Now git."

And with that, she fired off another rubber band, missing my head by two inches.

* * *

I held up two fingers as I passed by Pamela's desk in the outer office. "Two Tony Curtis pictures, and they're having hula hoop contests on top of the concession stand between movies."

"Hula hoops," she said and shook her head. "This whole town has gone crazy. Did I tell you I saw Sister Mary Rosamund out on the convent lawn practicing with a hula hoop? I just wish it could be a little more dignified."

I smiled. "Like Liberace." I felt sorry for him, the way people made fun of him, but he sure was corny.

"Exactly," she said, being a longtime fan of the man's. "Exactly like Liberace."

When the Sykes clan took over the town council, one of the first things they did was alienate the county sheriff, a man who had previously been in the construction business and had bid against the clan on many occasions. His crew kept having "accidents," as did his trucks and road graders. Everybody knew who was making these accidents happen, but nobody could prove it. So the man, Ron Baynes, decided to give up his business and run for sheriff. But the Sykes clan hated him, and when they took over the council they laid down several demands on the sheriff that made him balk. As a consequence, Chief Sykes cleaned out the dusty, long-unused jail on the top floor of the police station and jailed his own prisoners. He sent nobody to county unless absolutely necessary.

Cliff Sykes Jr. sat with his size 14 DD cowboy boots up on his desk, his khaki uniform morning-fresh, and his gray eyes filled with scorn as he said, "This time she's wrong."

"She just wants me to talk to him."

"For what?" Sykes said.

"He needs a lawyer, doesn't he?"

"He didn't ask for you," Sykes said.

"He still needs a lawyer."

"He killed her."

"Maybe you're right this time, Cliff."

"I sure don't know why you'd want to work for somebody like her."

"She isn't so bad."

"We took that blood oath that time, the four of us in that Indian gang we started up, remember?"

"I remember." We'd been eight or nine years old, four scruffy small-town kids who'd decided to become Indians after seeing the fifteen-part serial *War Drums of the Mohawks* with Roy "Crash" Corrigan. Pete Himes went first, cutting his wrist with a pocketknife, but he teared up so bad the rest of us decided to forgo the pleasure of slashing our wrists, the way Crash had in the movie, and just sort of rub our wrists together.

"We said we'd always defend each other."

"Yes, we did, Cliff."

"Seems like to me you're defendin' her instead of me."

"I'm not defending either of you, Cliff. I just want to see the man and see if he'd like me as a lawyer."

"Daddy's gonna be real pissed if you get involved in this case. So's Luke."

"Your brother Luke?"

"Uh-huh."

"Why would Luke be pissed? He's the fire marshal."

"Yeah, but she kept Daddy'n him out of the country club. Personally, I don't give two raccoon turds if I ever get in that club or not. But you know how Luke's wife is. Real highfalutin and all. She still drives to Cedar Rapids twice a week to take those damned rhumba lessons. Now she's got Luke taking them." He frowned, all the little nicks and cuts on his face standing out in bloody relief against his pasty skin. Near as I can figure, Cliff Sykes Jr. shaves himself with a butcher knife. The tiny pieces of toilet paper absorbing the blood do not make him any prettier, either.

"I won't need more than ten minutes."

"He killed her. And I almost got a confession out of him, too, if that damned Ralph hadn't stopped me."

"Ralph, your deputy, stopped you?"

"Yeah, I had Lou Pentecost down on the floor, and I was pretendin' like I was gonna strangle him to death, you know, and Ralph starts screamin' like a woman and stoppin' me. All I was doin' was trying to scare Pentecost a little. Figured if he thought he was ready to die, he might just confess. And I could sense it about to happen, too. So I gnawed on Ralph real good and made him hand over every one of those books he's been readin', and I took them right out to the incinerator we got, and I burned the damned things."

"What books were those?"

"Those law enforcement books he bought. Filled with all this crap that Earl Warren's always talkin' about, the rights of the accused and all that baloney. I mean, if you can't do a little stranglin', how you ever gonna get a confession?"

"I couldn't agree more, Cliff. I mean, I think the Founding Fathers clearly had 'stranglin' in mind when they wrote the Bill of Rights."

"That darned Ralph. He even got my other deputies readin' those books of his."

"Good thing you burned them when you did, Cliff. Otherwise there wouldn't have been any stranglin' goin' on over here at all."

"I'm givin' you ten minutes with him, Cody, then I'm gonna kick your ass out of here. Understood?"

"Understood."

He opened the middle drawer of his desk and took out a key ring and said, "He did it, Cody. He did it, all right. No matter what Judge Whitney says."

"I want a simple answer yes or no, and I want it to be the truth. You understand, Lou?"

He nodded miserably.

"Did you kill her?"

He looked right straight at me and in a strong, clear voice said, "I don't think so."

"You don't think so? What the hell does that mean?"

"You know how I get sometimes."

"Lou, I *don't* know how you get sometimes. I barely know you."

"But I barfed all over the podium that night I was giving the speech at the Jaycees. You were there."

"Oh, God, that's right."

"All that potato salad I'd been eating."

"I get the picture, Lou."

"I just can't hold my liquor."

"And you were drinking last night?"

"Lots."

"Alone?"

"Sometimes. I mean, I was in and out of several taverns. I kept trying to get Suzie on the phone. I was pretty messed up."

"Why?"

"Because Suzie didn't want to see me anymore."

"Lou, I hate to remind you of this, but you're a married man."

His head dipped, and he pawed at his face with a shaky white hand.

The jail was six cells in a large square room with only two windows. Even the sunlight had a dank and grainy feel to it up here. The other cells were empty. Lou sat on the edge of a cot that looked as if it would collapse if he moved. He smelled of sleep and urine and sweat. On the floor in front of him was a tray with the remnants of breakfast, two pieces of toast untouched, an open container of orange drink, a cup of coffee he'd finished, and two pancakes he'd apparently done some nibbling on. Idly, almost unconsciously, he kept pushing the tray away with his right foot, then nudging it back to him with his left, as if it was all some kind of crisis he'd couldn't resolve. In high school, he was a state champion gymnast, so he could move foot and toe with great and graceful ease.

He said, "I know I'm a married man."

"With two kids."

"I just needed to sow some wild oats. That's all it was. I got married when I was eighteen, right after high school, and went to work over at the paint plant, and I never got a chance to run around."

"Neither did your wife, Lou."

"It's different with men."

"Yeah? You sure about that?" Then I said, "Your wife grew up down the street from me, Lou. I guess I still feel a little protective about her. She's a nice woman. But I don't need to give you a sermon, I guess."

"I've got a sermon coming, believe me."

"Old Charlie Burton says he saw you over at the Ford lot this morning."

"That's where she said to meet her."

"Suzie?"

"Uh-huh."

"So you remember talking to her?"

He thought a long moment. "I guess it was around three. I woke up in the city park behind the bandstand. Must've passed out there. Then I found a phone booth and called her. She sounded—funny."

"Funny?"

"Scared or something."

"She say why?"

"No. She just said she needed to get out of town and this was the last time I'd ever get a chance to see her." He shook his head again. "I guess I figured it was because she was going to miss me and all, her wanting to meet me in back of the Winwood lot— but that wasn't why at all."

"It wasn't?"

"She wanted me to give her all the money I had. She didn't give a damn about me at all."

"You seem pretty clear about all this."

"Yeah. I mean, I was sober there for a while. Maybe an hour after I woke up. But then I found my car and got in the trunk. I usually keep a pint of Jim Beam there. So I drank that and got good and drunk again."

"Then what?"

"Then I don't know. I mean, it's all pretty hazy."

"You remember meeting her?"

"I don't think so."

"You got any recollection of a yellow Edsel?"

"You see those damned things? Nobody's gonna pay good money for one of those pieces of crap."

"Right now, I just want to know about *one* Edsel, Lou. A yellow one near the back of Winwood's lot."

"That's where they found her, right? In that yellow one, I mean? In the trunk?"

"Right."

He looked at me and then he did it, just sat there and started bawling.

I'm not good around bawlers of either sex. I don't think it's unmanly, I don't think it's even especially embarrassing to watch. It's just that it makes me feel so damned *helpless*.

"Lou," I'd say every half minute or so. "Lou."

He just kept on crying.

"Lou."

And more tears.

"Lou, look, I've only got a few minutes before Sykes kicks me out. I've got to ask you another question."

He looked up at me with big silver tears hanging from his eyes like stalactites.

"You gonna ask me if I killed Suzie?"

"No. I'm going to ask you if you want me to be your lawyer."

"I'm just a working guy, Cody. I don't have any money."

"Right now I'm not worried about money. Right

now all I care about is if you want me as your lawyer."

He started sniffling, bringing his tears to an end. "Well, sure, Cody, I mean if you *want* to be my lawyer."

"You could use a lawyer about now."

"She used to have a crush on you, you know that?"

"Suzie?"

"No. Ida. My wife."

"She had a crush on *me*?" I said.

"She would've been a lot better off marryin' you than me," he said.

And then he started crying again.

I listened to a little Chuck Berry as I tooled my way over to Stan Winwood Ford and Lincoln. And now Edsel.

I was in my cherry-red 1951 Ford ragtop, the one all the teenagers crowd around whenever I pull into the A&W on a warm evening. I take better care of my ragtop than I do of myself.

You could see the debris of Edsel Day, yesterday, September 4, 1958, all over Stan's car lot. Pennants still snapped crisply in the breeze. Several dozen Dixie cups still needed to be raked up from the concrete. And the picnic tables and the folding chairs and the podium used by the local dignitaries (if that's not a contradiction in terms) still needed to be taken back to the rental place. The feeling around Stan Winwood's Ford and Lincoln this morning was that of melancholy.

I knew Stan well enough to walk straight back to his office. I was just about to knock on the closed door when I heard him shout into the phone, "Either that damned disk jockey of yours is fired or I'll never advertise on your station again, Pete!" And then a phone was slammed.

I knocked.

"Come in!" Stan shouted.

Actually, he already had a visitor, Bob Kenny, the owner of Kenny's Paints, where my spanking-new client Lou Pentecost was employed. At least had been, until he'd been charged with murder.

"Oh, hi, Code," Stan said, not sounding all that thrilled to see me.

"I'm a little busy right now, Code," Stan said. He's a chunky man who wears bright golf clothes all year round. He's bald and round-faced, and he'd probably be asked to play Santa Claus in the town pageant if he wasn't so crabby most of the time. He also always calls me "Code," as if that single extra syllable is just too much work for him to say.

"Hi, Cody," Bob Kenny said. Bob, on the other hand, is long and lean, with graying hair and the hard face of an evangelist who takes his work very seriously. He was dressed, as always, with a certain primness—dark suit, white shirt, dark tie, as if all dressed up for an emergency funeral he might have to go to. "You've heard about Lou Pentecost?"

"That's why I'm here," I said.

I guess I sort of invited myself in. Sat myself down next to Kenny, across the desk from Winwood.

"To hell with Lou Pentecost," Stan said. "How about my Edsels? That damned disk jockey at KSTB has been making jokes about them all morning long."

As had a good deal of the country, at least according to the *Today* show this morning (I don't care much for Dave Garroway, the host, but I do like his chimp). Ford's self-declared "Edsel Day" had been met with an unexpected amount of scorn and derision. One Ford dealer alone, somewhere in California, had spent $15,000 on fireworks last night. Automobile critics said it had not enough horsepower and too many gimmicks—push-button gears and a tachometer, among other features. But what bothered most people was the grille, which several men had whispered looked just like the female sexual organ. And it sort of did.

Apparently, like many of his fellow Edsel dealers across the nation, Stan Winwood had awakened this morning, read his newspaper, and learned that despite all the hoopla, the Ford Motor Company had created a car that a lot of people saw as something of a joke.

A knock.

"Mr. Winwood," said a very nervous mechanic, peeking in through the door, "one of the Edsels we sold yesterday?"

"Uh-huh?"

"Well, guy's been having some trouble with it and he wants to talk to you."

"What kinda trouble?"

"Said it rattles a lot."

"Rattles?" Stan Winwood said, vaulting out of his chair as if he'd been shot from a cannon. "Rattles? It can't rattle! It's only one day old!"

But in fact, the man from *Consumer Reports* whom Garroway had interviewed this morning had the same complaint. Test driving had shown inexplicable rattling and very bad steering.

"I'll talk to the sonofabitch all right!" Stan Winwood said, sounding as if he was going to beat the guy up for criticizing the car Ford Motors had promised would revolutionize the industry.

Then he was gone and Bob Kenny said, "Lou Pentecost is one of my best workers. I just wish he wouldn't have gotten involved with Suzie. He has such a fine wife."

"You're assuming he did it, then?"

He shrugged. "Right now I'm not sure what to think, I guess. You saw him?"

"For a few minutes. I'm going to represent him."

He smiled. "Judge Whitney wouldn't have anything to do with this, would she?" He didn't wait for my answer. "It's almost pathetic, isn't it?"

"What is?"

"Watching a woman of her intelligence and caliber going after a redneck like Sykes." Like much of the town's ruling class, he'd long ago sided with Judge Whitney. The thing was, he couldn't afford to cross Cliff Sykes Sr. A year ago, when Kenny's paint factory had burned to the ground after an electrical fire, he'd been forced to turn to Sykes Sr. for a low-interest quick loan. Sykes had given him the money in exchange for his tacit support in town matters. "But I suppose even Sykes can be right once in a while."

I stood up. "Guess I'll go out and look over the Edsel where they found her."

"I'll walk out with you," Kenny said.

Since his car was parked near the yellow Edsel, he walked over there with me.

Sykes had had sense enough to cordon the car off, but as all the footprints around the vehicle showed, he hadn't been smart enough to take any casts of the prints nor, from what I could see when I inspected the trunk, had he even dusted for fingerprints. He probably thought these ideas were too "newfangled." All a good lawman needed was to drag some poor wretch back to the jailhouse and do hisself a little bit of "stranglin'." Life was a pretty simple business for people like Sykes.

"Well, I need to get back to the plant," Kenny said. "Give Lou my best."

I spent twenty minutes going over the car. The trunk was bloody inside, and smelled pretty bad. She'd been stabbed several times.

I made notes in my little notebook, the way they'd taught us to in crim class, and then I snapped a few pictures of the trunk open and then the trunk closed, and then I started walking up and down the alley in back of the yellow Edsel. I had no idea what I was looking for. But it was a sure thing that Cliff Sykes Jr. hadn't done any kind of scientific investigation at all, not when he had stranglin' at hand.

I found footprints with a strange V pattern. The prints led from the cordoned-off area to the alley, where they started to disappear in the tire tracks of this morning's traffic.

Not until I followed them back to the yellow Edsel did I notice the barely microscopic flecks of red on the concrete around the car.

I got down on my hands and knees, like the human equivalent of a hunting dog, and followed the flecks back to the alley. The flecks were inside the outline of the shoes.

When I finally looked up, I saw a little girl standing next to her mommy. Mommy was talking to one of the Edsel salesmen. Little Girl was watching me, no doubt wondering why I was down on all fours.

As she stood there, in all her five years or so, a hula hoop went round and round on her little hips.

"You look funny, mister," she said.

I wanted to tell her that she looked funny, too, but I'm much too gallant to ever insult a lady.

About the time I reached Kenny Paints, the factory workers were taking their lunch break. Hot autumn lent the air a sweet perfume. I went out back, where Kenny had built picnic tables for his people. He paid good wages and was about as decent to his employees as employers ever got.

I spent half an hour asking questions of people talking around bites of Spam sandwiches, hot dogs, thermoses of soup, and lots of Hostess cupcakes. There were a couple of radios going, both playing the rock and roll station, "Yackety-Yak" by the Coasters having been voted the town's favorite hit of the day according to the disk jockey. Over beneath an elm tree two young women taught another young woman the intricacies of the Cha-lypso, which Dick Clark was pushing these days on *American Bandstand*.

Then I finally heard something useful from one of the workers.

"Davey?" the man said, biting into an apple carefully with what appeared to be a brand-new set of dentures.

"Davey?"

"Davey Hovis."

"I guess I don't know who he is."

"Works here." He smiled. "Part time, anyway. Spends most of his time working on his hair. Got

him one of those ducktails. He went out with her
a lot."

"I thought she was seeing Lou Pentecost."

He winked. "She was a busy gal."

Five minutes later, I said, "Davey Hovis?"

"Yeah, what's it to ya?"

My informant was right. I found Davey in the back
of the plant, in the area where winter coats were
hung and galoshes stored. A small, square, faded
mirror was hung behind the door.

"I'd like to talk to you."

"A lot of people would like to talk to me. Especially chicks."

He was a cutie, all right, kind of a pudgy version
of Elvis, the upturned shirt collar, the long, wide
sideburns, the Lucky Strikes riding in the rolled-up
sleeve, the calculated sneer.

"I'm told you went out with Suzie."

For the first time, his comb stopped raking his
wavy blond hair into a duck's ass. He looked at me
with great and practiced insolence. "I go out with a
lot of women."

"I'm also told she liked Lou Pentecost better than
she did you and that you didn't like that at all." I
hadn't been told that at all, but I thought it might
prompt an interesting reaction.

He went back to combing his hair. "He killed her,
didn't he?"

"That's what Sykes thinks, anyway."

"Oh, he killed her all right."

"What makes you so sure?"

He didn't say anything for a time. Just combed his
locks. "October fifth."

"What about it?"

"That's the day we were gonna get married."

"She told him?"

"Damn right she told him. And that's why he killed her. She prob'ly even told him about the song."

"The song?"

"Yeah. She thought I sounded a lot like Elvis."

"She did, huh?"

"Yeah, and she wanted me to sing at our wedding. 'Love Me Tender.' It was gonna be like my debut. I was even thinkin' of puttin' a little band together. You never know, I might pick up a record contract or something."

By now, I'd duly noted his dry eyes. If he was upset about his bride-to-be having been murdered, he was keeping it to himself.

Leather creaked. As he moved away from the mirror—a guy can comb his hair only so many hours a day—his brand-new tan cowboy boots made new-shoe noise.

When I looked down at them, I saw the red flecks instantly, all along the sides of the boots. The same red flecks I'd seen in the parking lot by the Edsel.

"You've got something on your boots," I said.

He looked down and said a nasty word. "Damned cleaning compound the janitors use on the floor at night. Sticks to your shoes all the next day."

The news didn't make me happy. With so many people tracking the compound all over town, its usefulness as any kind of clue was worthless.

"You book a hall for your wedding?"

He shrugged. "Didn't need one."

"Oh?"

"Just gonna have the JP marry us. Small ceremony.

Just havin my old lady and stepfather come over from Davenport."

I was wondering if he was just making up the wedding to give his competition, Lou Pentecost, a motive for murdering Sally.

"You talk to the JP about it?"

"I sure did. He was all set up for the fifth."

"That'd be JP Bauman?"

"Sure would."

He smiled. "You Lou's lawyer?"

"Yeah."

The smile became a sneer. "You got your hands full, man. He killed her for sure."

Suzie had lived in a three-story stucco box that had probably been an upscale apartment house back when President Harding was taking office. Now it didn't look so hot. Maybe it was the rusting Kaiser that was up on blocks in the front yard.

I found the door with the MANAGER sign on it and knocked. A man in an undershirt, suspenders, a massive belly, gray work pants, bare feet, and a terrible-smelling cigar opened the door of apartment 2.

In the background, I could hear Jack Bailey welcoming everybody to *Queen for a Day*.

"Yeah?"

I told him who I was and why I was here.

"She was a good-time gal, if you know what I mean. My wife said she was a hussy."

"A hussy. I see."

"She really means whore, but hussy sounds better."

"I see."

"We was always wonderin' where she got her money from."

"Money?"

"You should see her apartment."

"I'd like to."

A few minutes later, he turned the key to apartment 6 on the second floor, pushed the door inward, and then led us inside.

"Need to open these damned windows," he said. "Closed 'em after the rain the other night and forgot about the damned things."

Everything in the place was new and expensive, including the twenty-one-inch Zenith console TV and the two closets full of rather fashionable clothes. She had had taste, our Suzie. And money.

"And you don't have any idea where she got her money?"

"Well, she worked at the paint factory, but that sure as hell didn't buy her all this stuff," he said.

We were profaners, to be sure. Here was the apartment of a young woman and we were paying her death no honor at all. Indeed, we were dishonoring the woman's memory by making the worst sort of speculations.

"She saw a lot of men?"

"I thought of that, too," he said. "You know, a pross."

"Pross?"

"Prostitute."

"Oh."

"We used to call them 'prosses' over in the South Seas during the war."

"I see."

"But anyway, I sat down at the kitchen table one night and figured it out with a pad and pencil."

"Figured what out?"

"How many men she'd have to have over to make this kind of money. You know how many men she'd have to average a night? I mean, that console there alone cost six hundred dollars."

"How many men?"

"Six, seven a night. At ten dollars a throw."

"That's a lot of men."

"Wife says she couldn't have done it."

"Oh?"

"Female parts would've given her trouble, all those men like that on a regular basis."

"Yeah, probably."

"And we sure as hell would've noticed that many guys tramping up and down the stairs at night."

"Did you notice any men?"

"Just Lou and Davey. You can have Davey. Wife didn't approve of Lou, him bein' married and all, but he was a lot nicer guy than that Davey creep. I hear Sykes arrested Lou."

"Yeah."

"Sykes doesn't know his ass from a hole in the ground."

I had my usual late lunch of cheeseburger, fries, and cherry Coke over at the Rexall. The radio played the new Jerry Lee Lewis song while I read an article in the paper about Debbie Reynolds and Eddie Fisher and how they had one of the few Hollywood marriages that would really last.

Then I just sat there and smoked a couple of Pall

Malls over my cup of coffee and thought about the case.

It was time to talk to Judge Whitney. I'm not bad at gathering all the information, but Judge Whitney is particularly good at figuring out what it all means.

"Tony Curtis said he'd really like to see you tonight," I said to Pamela as I walked into the judge's office.

"Yeah, well, Marjorie Main said she'd really like to see *you*," Pamela said.

Marjorie Main being, of course, the grumpy "Ma" of Ma and Pa Kettle, and not exactly the kind of female that set innocent young hearts like mine aflutter.

"She in?"

"Uh-huh."

"How's her mood?"

"Well, she gave three defendants the maximum sentence this morning."

"Any death penalties?"

"No, and I think she was disappointed."

I don't think there are any words that fill Judge Eleanor Whitney with such warmth—at least when she's in one of her moods—as "hang by the neck until dead."

I knocked the way a supplicant would knock on the Pope's door and waited to hear her familiar bark. The bark barked, I went inside.

"You won't guess who's had three charges of public drunkenness against him dropped," the judge said as I sat down.

"Sure I can guess. Old Charlie Barton."

"Exactly. Sykes is rewarding him for testifying

against Lou Pentecost." Then: "So what did you find out?"

I told her everything, and when I was finished she said, "The apartment. All the new furniture. That's the part that puzzles me."

And with that, she launched a rubber band past my head.

"Could she have inherited it?" the judge asked.

"I did some checking. From what I could find, she hadn't come into any money that either the bank or her attorney knew about."

"Her attorney?"

"Hascomb. He handled her divorce two years ago."

"Where's the husband?"

"Germany. In the army."

"So she just mysteriously started spending money. It wasn't credit?"

"Checked that, too. The merchants I talked to said she always paid cash."

"She couldn't have been—"

I shook my head. "Thought of that, too. In fact, the guy who manages her apartment said that he worked it out on paper and she couldn't possibly have seen that many guys."

She was about to say something else, but then a quick, nervous series of knocks sounded on the door, and without waiting to be barked inside, Pamela put her lovely face between edge of door and frame and said, "Cliff Sykes, Jr. is on the phone, Cody, and he's screaming that he wants to talk to you."

The judge rolled her eyes.

I stood up and walked around on the side of Judge Whitney's desk and picked up the receiver.

"Hello?" I said.

"You sonofabitch."

"And a good day to you, Chief."

"You bastard."

"I didn't know you cared, Chief."

"You helped him escape, didn't you?"

"What the hell're you talking about?"

My sudden change in tone caused the judge to sit up straight in her chair and start watching my face closely.

"He jumped the guard who brought him his lunch and then somehow managed to wiggle through one of the barred windows."

We both had the same thought at the same time.

"He was a gymnast in high school," Sykes said. "Remember?"

"I didn't have a damned thing to do with him escaping, Sykes, and you know it. This is just about the worst thing an innocent man could've done."

"Yeah, well, you'll have a hell of a time proving he's innocent now, you sonofabitch."

And with that, Sykes slammed down the phone.

I haven't been on many manhunts in my life but the few times I've gone along, I've noticed the almost joyous air of the participants. It's like playing cowboys and Indians for real.

By the time I got over there, a posse had formed in front of the police station. Men with hunting dogs and shotguns were gathered around pickups and cars, ready to go.

I noticed that the posse included Kenny from the paint factory, who didn't seem to be carrying any sort of weapon at all, and Davey Hovis, who was hefting a double-barreled shotgun.

Chief Sykes even wore his Colt .45, worn gunfighter style low and to the left of his imposing gut.

He even used the word "reckon" a couple of times.

"I reckon you boys know the kind of killer we're up against here, so I don't reckon I have to tell you to shoot first and ask questions later. You know what I'm saying here."

"I reckon I do, Quick-Draw," I wanted to say, but I figured Sykes would find some reason for jailing me if I did.

The men then piled into their vehicles and took off for various parts of the countryside. Lou Pentecost had grown up here. He'd know a good number of hiding places.

Sykes came over and said, "You may get cheated out of your trial fee, counselor."

"Just remember he's probably unarmed."

"He wasn't unarmed when he killed Suzie."

"*If* he killed Suzie."

"If he didn't kill Suzie, he wouldn't have no reason to run."

I smiled haplessly at him and said, "I reckon you're right."

But he didn't get the joke. Which didn't surprise me a whole hell of a lot.

Then he was gone, too.

I was just walking back to my office when I saw Ida Pentecost, Lou's wife. She was pushing a stroller along the street.

"I appreciate what you're tryin' to do for us," she said. Ida wasn't a beauty, but she had a nice face and vivid brown, intelligent eyes. "I just wish he hadn't escaped."

"Me, too," I said.

I bent over and reached down to tickle her little baby on the chin. Which is just when he decided to spit up.

"Oh, here, use this washcloth I keep in my purse," she said.

I took that moment to swear off the little ones for the rest of my life. You try to tickle them, and they barf all over you.

As I dried my finger, she said, "Everything was going so good, too. He was finally going to get the promotion Mr. Kenny promised him before the fire."

"Promotion?"

"Yeah. Lou figured out a way to mix the paint faster and so Mr. Kenny was going to put him in charge of production. But then he went and got in all the financial trouble, and then he had the fire on top of it."

I handed her back her washcloth. "You know a man named Davey Hovis?"

"Sure. He was her boyfriend. Suzie's, I mean. Till she and Lou started— Well, you know what they started doin'."

"Hovis ever bother you or Lou?"

"Lou must've told you, huh?"

"Told me?"

"About Hovis pouring gasoline on the floor out in our garage. I happened to be taking out the garbage that night and I saw him. Then I made Lou tell me what was goin' on. He told me about Suzie, then. Told me he thought it was all over." The vivid brown eyes burned with painful recollection. "I kept waitin' for him to tell me it was all a joke, you know, about him and Suzie and all. But it wasn't a joke, was it?"

"No, I guess it wasn't."

"And he kept right on seein' her."

"I'm sorry, Ida."

"But I don't want him to be killed. That's what I'm afraid of, with Sykes and all."

"If you hear from him, let me know right away, all right?"

"I sure will, Cody. I sure will."

She started pushing the stroller down the walk again.

"So you're starting to favor this Hovis character, huh?" Judge Whitney said.

I'd told her about my conversation with Ida Pentecost.

"I sure am."

"So am I."

We were in her office; the beautiful Pamela had gone home for the day. The judge had broken out the brandy, which we were drinking from fancy glass snifters.

"What was his motive?" she said.

"Jealousy."

"And if he killed Suzie and blamed Lou—"

"—he'd get double the satisfaction."

"You may be onto something, McCain, you know that?"

Her phone rang. She picked up and said, "Eleanor Whitney." There was just a smidgen of arrogance in the way she said it. Sort of like, "God speaking, may I help you?"

She listened.

Didn't say a single word.

Then hung up.

"Trouble, McCain. Sykes and his posse've got Lou Pentecost cornered in the old livery stable, and they say that he won't give himself up."

I was up and at the door in moments. "I'll give you a call soon as I know anything."

The ragtop got me there in five minutes. There were two crowds, the first being the onlookers, who ringed the posse, and the second being the posse, who ringed the old two-story barnlike livery stable. These days, the sole blacksmith worked only part time, and by appointment.

I grabbed Sykes's arm. "I'm going in there."

"He'll shoot you."

"I'd bet he's unarmed."

"He says he's armed."

"Saying and being are two different things. He was drunk last night and can't remember things too well. He's scared."

Sykes said, "It's your life."

I worked my way through the posse.

Kenny put a hand on my shoulder and said, "Tell him to give himself up. Tell him I'll pay his legal bills. He's a valuable employee."

"I'll tell him that, Mr. Kenny. I appreciate it."

Davey Hovis didn't look happy about Mr. Kenny's words at all. He just hugged his shotgun, obviously eager for a chance to use it.

The whole thing took twenty minutes and, frankly, most of it was pretty boring so I'll spare you the details.

The upshot was that once I got inside the livery, I stood in the center of the floor and looked up at the shadowy loft where Lou was hiding.

I called his name out a few hundred times, and finally he squeaked, "Get out of here, Cody."

"I want to help you."

"You can't help me, Cody. Sykes has already got me convicted and ready for the noose."

"If you didn't do it, Cody, I'll be able to prove that. I really will."

"You got a lot more faith in our justice system than I do."

And that's pretty much how it went until I said, "Your little one upchucked on my hand this afternoon."

"My little one?" he said from the shadows above me, where he was hiding.

And I could tell I'd said the right thing, the way warmth and pride replaced the fear and anger in his voice.

"You should've seen her," I said.

Then I told him about this sweet little frilly pink dress she was wearing.

"I can't seem to remember that one," he said.

"Well, she was wearing it."

"Ida look good, too?"

"Ida looked great."

"I'm scared, Cody."

"I know you are, Lou."

"I want to give myself up, but I can't quite seem to do it."

"I'm coming up."

"Please don't do that, Cody."

"I'm walking over to that ladder and I'm coming

up and the only way you can stop me is to shoot me and I don't think you'd do that, Lou. I really don't think you would."

Behind me, I could hear the crowd murmur. It doesn't hurt your ego any to have your fellow townspeople thinking that you're one brave guy.

Lou didn't have a gun, at least I was pretty sure he didn't, so I was going up, and then I'd bring him down, and I'd probably get my picture in the paper and everything.

To the crowd, this was just like watching a movie.

Well, as you might expect, I went up the ladder and Lou didn't have a gun and after letting him cry a little, I took him gently by the arm and led him over to the ladder and watched him climb down.

I don't know if I exactly figured on applause from the crowd, but at least I expected *some* recognition of how brave it seemed I'd been.

But as I climbed down, I realized that everything had grown very still. When I got to the floor, I saw in fact that the entire crowd, including Sykes and his posse, had gone somewhere else.

What the hell was going on?

I grabbed Lou by the arm and started yanking him along behind me.

The crowd had its back to us and was ringing Sykes's own squad car.

And in the back seat of that car, his hands bound together with handcuffs, was Mr. Kenny from the paint factory.

"What the hell's going on?" Lou said. "How come Sykes is arresting Mr. Kenny?"

And then I saw her, Judge Whitney, standing off

to the side of the squad car, a tiny smirk on her face, while Sykes glowered at her.

Lou had it right: what the hell *was* going on here?

In the morning, after parking my ragtop in an empty courthouse slot and leaving behind the strains of the Del-Vikings' "Come Go with Me," I walked up the steps to Judge Whitney's office and went inside.

Pamela, looking ever lovely, said, "She tell you yet?"

"Tell me what?"

"How she figured out Kenny was the murderer."

I nodded.

"Yeah, she did."

"God, how?"

"She just kept thinking about all the new furniture and stuff that Suzie kept buying, wondering where Suzie could ever get that kind of money. So the judge looked at all the people involved, and decided that Mr. Kenny was the only one who had a lot of money. Then she tried to figure out why Kenny would *give* Suzie all that money."

"And then," said Judge Whitney, coming out of her chambers, "I realized that there was only one reason he'd possibly be so generous—she had something on him. Turns out, she worked late many nights, and she saw Kenny set fire to his own building. He was broke and the only way he could get any money was insurance. So she blackmailed him, and he finally couldn't tolerate it anymore, and he killed her, hoping that Sykes would think Lou Pentecost did it."

"But didn't the fire inspector know that the fire was arson?" Pamela said.

"Lord, Pamela, you're forgetting the last name of the fire inspector," Judge Whitney said.

"That's right," Pamela laughed. "Mike Sykes—Cliff's cousin."

"And just as dumb as everybody else in the Sykes clan," the judge said smugly. Then she smiled. "That makes five, McCain."

"Five?" Pamela said.

"Five times she's humiliated Sykes," I said.

The judge said, "Hold my calls, Pamela. I want to sit in my office and gloat for a while."

Then she was gone.

"Those Tony Curtis movies are still on at the drive-in tonight," I said.

"Oh, McCain, aren't you ever going to give up?"

"Not in the foreseeable future."

She made a clucking sound. "Poor, poor McCain."

Then she started doing some furious typing, just as if I wasn't there at all.

TANTALIZING MYSTERY ANTHOLOGIES

HARLEQUIN

Heartfelt or thrilling, passionate or uplifting—Harlequin is more than just happily-ever-after.

With twelve different series to choose from and new books available every month, you are sure to find stories that will move you, uplift you, inspire and delight you.

SIGN UP FOR THE HARLEQUIN NEWSLETTER

Be the first to hear about great new reads and exciting offers!

Harlequin.com/newsletters